MORE

THAN

ENOUGH

Naleighna Kai
Vee Denise Kai
Kevin Kai

Infinity Publishing
Lansing, Illinois

ISBN   0-9702699-0-0
LCCN   00-134202

Edited by Chandra Sparks Taylor
Cover design by Loren Jordan
Cover photographs by Pete Stenberg
Interior book design by Sandra A. Spears
Cover models: Julie A. McKelphin, J. Spears, Aisha K. Lusk

ACKNOWLEDGMENTS

Naleighna Kai

I would like to thank the Creator for allowing me the opportunity to express myself in print. To my spiritual mother, Sandy, thank you for your inspiration, encouragement and the occasional "get off your butt and finish." To my soul mate for love and consideration. To my son for his patience, and my brother, Donny, for his belief and support. To Sesvalah for her direction and guidance. To the people who read this work and are touched by it in some way.

Vee Denise Kai

All praises to the Creator for allowing me to share my gift with everyone. To SAS for accepting me into her heart as one of her own. To my soul mate for unconditional love and understanding. To my mother and sister for their encouragement and for believing in me. To Sesvalah for all your words of wisdom.

Kevin Kai

All love to the Creator for allowing the world to see how a wicked mind can also be an intelligent mind. To my father, the man who gave me my wickedness and intelligence, I love you and I miss you. To my mother, who guided my mind to reach great lengths and to cut out the b.s. I love you! To my daughter, the reason why all positive changes have been made. I live for you. Thank you for making me responsible and defining my priorities. I love you, Baby Girl! To my "dangerous ones," thank you for putting our wicked minds together. I love you.

Naleighna, Vee Denise and Kevin would also like to thank: Chandra Sparks Taylor for her expertise and advice; also for the invaluable input of Sesvalah, Yosha, Lady Avalon e'lan, Renee Cobb-Dishman, Yvonne Tolbert, Aisha K. Lusk, Julie A. McKelphin, J. Spears, Delores Y. Cortez, Sherese Patten, Carla Nelson, Loren Jordan, Pete Stenberg, our sponsors and all the "train ladies" and coworkers that took the time to read this work and give us their honest opinions.

Love, While You Can

Embrace them, Love them
Be it man, woman or child
Love them, Cherish them
They're only here for a little while

Love who you love
And do this while you can
Let them return that love to you
Be it woman, child or man

Love the sweetness in their spirits
Love through the pain within their souls
Love with enough force and power
To help make them become whole

When the spirit inside you
Knows the deepest reaches of hell
Love yourself and love others
Experience a taste of heaven, as well

Enjoy love without guilt
Receive love without pain
Love each one unconditionally
Even when you don't receive the same

Hold them, love them
Be it woman, man or child
Embrace them, love them
You're only here for a little while

Naleighna Kai

DEDICATION

NALEIGHNA KAI
To my loved ones, my thoughts are with you...
My grandmother, Dearest
My brother, Ricky
My aunts Mabel and Ruth

VEE DENISE KAI
To my cousin Jacqueline Jacobs

KEVIN KAI
To Ronald William Thorne

"Do you want the truth or the version that will let us remain friends?"

Lori

"I didn't realize it then, but this trip wasn't purely a sexual experience...it was also a learning experience."

Ray

"Are you ready for me? I guess by now you shouldn't be shocked by anything we say—or do."

Diane

All who enter, keep an open mind....
Do you dare?

*H*er kiss is a first-class ticket to heaven. I would make love to her right here in the middle of the airport– that is, if we wouldn't be arrested. I've been in love with this woman for seven months and this is the first time I've ever seen her. I place my hands on her waist and pull her close. I feel her hands touch my face as her arms surround my neck as we kiss again. I move my hands to explore her back and the rest of her curves. I feel that familiar stirring in my loins. It normally happens every time I hear her voice, but her touch is just as powerful.

She's letting her hands, lips and body do all her talking right now and I don't want to let her go. She's every bit as sensuous as I imagined. I don't want to stop, but I have to. There's another woman that I'm waiting to see for the first time too. My second love is the patient one, and she's preparing the room for our arrival. The one I'm holding right now couldn't take the anticipation of waiting to see me any longer than she had to.

I thought eight days would be more than enough time for me to fully experience and appreciate them. Suddenly, I'm beginning to think I was very wrong.

It feels good to be here in Chicago and in her arms....

RAY

As the limousine glides easily through the traffic, and we approach downtown Chicago. I find that the real scenery is right here in the car. I reach for Lori and take another kiss. I could do this all day. She then rests her head on my shoulder. My dick is saying "Hello? Can I get a witness? Can you hear me now? Do we have to wait? Are you feeling me? I can't believe I'm behaving myself. I normally wouldn't know the meaning of the word *behave*." This woman is luscious! I've had my patience tried before, but this has to be the worst. If I've waited seven months to have her, then I can wait at least until after dinner—no matter how much my dick protests.

Lori rests her hands right in my groin area and I moan. "Don't start woman, it's hard enough as it is."

She laughs as she pulls her hand away and says, "Just doing a sound check, that's all. Seems that everything's in working order."

"You don't know how much I'd like to show you it's in working order," I say seriously. She looks at me and laughs.

"Ray? How about another kiss?" she asks.

"Hell no, that's what woke him up in the first place."

She tilts her lips upward and laughs again as I lean in for a kiss anyway.

* * *

Actually, what started our relationship was her voice. I remember the first time I called her, and I heard that voice. I was floored! I especially remember the day I called her from my hotel in Chicago…I never knew that a woman could take a man to the place she took me.

LORI

I "met" Ray on the "Zone" playing spades. After a couple of days he found me interesting enough to contact me outside of the card room to chat. And I found him interesting enough to respond. I found more than enough time to "chat" with him because my boss was away on business for three weeks. One day Ray mentioned that he was coming to Chicago for a sales presentation so I sent him a message with my phone number. Not even thirty seconds later the phone rang. I answered the phone, heard a sharp intake of breath, and then the sexiest male voice I ever heard said to me, "You have a beautiful voice, Ms. Morris." We talked for hours that day and I found Ray to be "real," intelligent, comical and just as wicked as I was.

I received an e-mail message from Ray on the second day of his visit to Chicago letting me know he was bored and could use some excitement. I decided to give him something more and sent him a message to call me. When I picked up the phone, I began speaking in my sexiest voice and took his imagination someplace he couldn't believe...

"Ray, we're just waking up and I'm lying next to you in that spoon position. Your body feels so good next to mine. Imagine having your face buried in my hair and your hand resting on my buttocks. Ray, can you feel my buttocks pressed up against you? I'd like to have a *loooooooong* conversation with your dick. Let me see if your dick feels like talking. I don't think that part of you would mind waking up. Are you with me, Ray? Can you feel me? I move my buttocks slightly back and forth on your dick until I feel it stirring. Oh yes, it's hard now and I'm listening to what it has to say. It says it wants to feel what it's like inside of me, Ray. You can put it in there. There's nothing between you and me. No boxers, no sheets, no gowns and no resistance. I'm all yours. All I have to do is spread myself and you can come right in. And I want you to come right in. Can you feel the heat, Ray? Don't hold back, honey. Give it to me just the way I like it."

From there I took him all the way until he had an orgasm.

As he regained consciousness, his voice slurred...

"Woman, how the hell did you do that? Lori, I have to go. I'll call you back. I can't believe this! I have to go take a shower now. Woman, do you know what you just did to me? Baby, I've got to go. I don't believe this. I'll call you back...."

I received an e-mail message from Ray a few minutes after he hung up: *I had to write this e-mail because one of my coworkers came into the room as I was going to the shower. I have on dark-colored boxers and the wet spots you created are showing. Lori, I can't believe you did that to me! No one has ever done anything like that to me before. Damn! I can't believe this! If you're this powerful over the phone, you must be three times as powerful in person. I have wet spots on the sheets and my boxers are in an uproar! I'm going to get in the shower now. See what you did! Lori, with this sexual mental trance I'm in, I really don't think I could handle meeting you in person right now. I will call you later.*

Ray was totally amazed at my ability to do this to him. What he didn't realize is that when he reached his orgasm, it also brought me pleasure too. One thing was for sure, he wasn't bored anymore. The next day he called me and tried his hand at letting his creative juices flow. I wasn't ready for what he had to say. When he was done, Ray had me cumming so hard that I had to stand up at my desk to let it flow.

Ray started by asking, "Lori, is there anyone near you right now?"

"No, everyone's at lunch," I answered.

He said, "Close your eyes for me, baby."

I did, and he lowered his voice and said, "Lean back in the chair and spread your thighs for me, and let me make love to you....I'm on my knees and I'm resting between your thighs. I reach under your skirt to pull off your panties. I hold your buttocks in my hands and I feel the softness. Do you like that, Lori? I reach up to open your blouse and place my hands under your bra. Your breasts are so beautiful and your nipples are *soooooooo* hard. I lean in to take one into my mouth and taste it. Are you with me, Lori? I run my tongue over the other, and place both of them in my hands with the nipples close together. Can I suck them for a while? You don't mind, do you, Lori? Spread your thighs a little wider for me, baby. As I wrap my arms around your waist, I kiss your breasts, your shoulders, your lips. You taste so good! I'm getting really hard now. Would you like to touch it, Lori? Reach down and touch me, Lori. Feel how hard I am for you. Can you feel the blood pulsing through the veins? It's ready to experience what heaven is like. It is heaven between your thighs, isn't it, Lori? I move your buttocks to the edge of the chair and I'm ready to enter your heat, your wetness.... Hold me close, Lori...."

This became a routine. It eventually led to us writing stories to each other.

Ray called me about an hour after he got out of the shower following our first interlude. He had a lot on his mind....

"Lori, even though you haven't said anything about dealing with me. I didn't think of you on that level because I do have someone. But I have to do this! Lori, all I ask is for the opportunity for me to be on that list you've been telling me about. I've never met a woman with your thinking, with such an open mind and a wicked imagination. I'm not trying to hurt you in any form or fashion, which is why I want to make sure you know about her. Right now, things are pretty rough but I can't make that promise of leaving her because that might not be the case. Even though I've tried to change things, it doesn't seem to be working, but I'm still not ready to leave right now," Ray said sincerely.

"Ray, you're more than welcome to follow the requirements for being on The List. But know this: until you are single and unattached, being on The List is all that's available to you."

"I understand your point, Lori, but I still want to be the only one you are considering for your man. What do I have to do? How can I show you that I'm serious? How can it work if I live here in New York?"

I told him, "Yes, it can work even though there is some distance between us. First, you have to understand what we need."

"*We?* What do you mean 'we'?" he asked.

I cleared my throat and said, "I apologize. Further clarification may be needed. When I say 'we,' I mean me *and* my friend Diane. We need a man that can be a balance to both of us."

After I said that, Ray remained silent so long that I finally kept going. "It has to be a man with flexibility, adaptability, aggression, compassion, humor, intelligence and a certain level of wickedness. It takes a man who is willing to do the work, and it takes understanding what we're trying to achieve."

RAY

I listened as Lori told me about the requirements, list and plan that she and Diane had created, and it totally blew my mind....

Chapter 1

THE POTENTIALS, THE LIST AND
THE REQUIREMENTS

LORI

Weeks before, when Ray asked if I was in a relationship and he first found out about my List of Requirements, and my short List of Potentials, he jokingly asked when he would be allowed on The List. I told him he would have to wait until I ran the course with the ones already on it. Diane and I were working our way down from a list of men who had the potential to be our mate. I told him honestly that there was one who was a strong factor, but his chances were dwindling due to neglect. He was someone we were involved with before we created The List. Diane and I hadn't made love with him for months, and we were giving our bodies and minds time to adjust before ending the relationship.

Omarr was a thirty-year-old East Indian man with a sexual appetite that was just like ours. Unfortunately, mentally, emotionally and spiritually he didn't cut it. Omarr had decided that his sexual performance was so spectacular that we wouldn't be able to do without him. He had since found out that he was wrong. By the time he got the message and started being more appreciative and attentive, it was much too late. With the creation of The List, Diane and I moved in a different direction. Omarr's lack of dedication along with his arrogance moved him from "the one" to nonexistent. We eventually realized that he was a zero–just a placeholder until a real number came along.

Diane and I narrowed The List down to a few men that had met our requirements. When we met Ray, Potentials #1 and #2 were still in the running.

Potential #1

Cameron was a twenty-nine-year-old black architect from Memphis who was very attracted to me, but scared as hell of me. He was fascinated by me because I was different from the type of women that he usually dated. My honesty and wickedness kind of took him off guard. Cameron was intelligent and had a humble and peaceful nature. Unfortunately, he was not open-minded or sexually adventurous. He hadn't even been introduced to the concept of the trio; he was having a hard enough time just dealing with me. Cameron's fear eventually moved him from potential to improbable.

Potential #2

Jim Kwan was a twenty-eight-year-old Asian male from Arizona who had never experienced being with a black woman. Jim was a chemical engineer at a Japanese firm, and he was a total workaholic. I spent most of my time encouraging him to remember to take some time for himself. Jim worked sometimes sixteen to eighteen hours a day and was so serious that he never took time to relax and have fun. Jim had a lot of qualities from The List, but didn't have a sense of self-preservation. Jim was another person that would have been overpowered by the thought of maintaining two women at one time. His inability to enjoy life moved him from potential to impossible.

Potential #3

Raymond Hearne was a twenty-five-year-old black male from New York who was very much interested in eliminating all of the above. About a month after he met me, he was introduced to Diane, and from then on we all talked on a regular basis. Diane and I encouraged him to read *Speak It Into Existence* by Sesvalah, as well as *Mind of My Mind*, *Patternmaster*, *Clay's Ark* and *Wild Seed* by Octavia Butler. Surprisingly he enjoyed them as much as we did. These books were chosen so that through our discussions of them we would be able to explore Ray's level of understanding and get an insight of his views about certain issues. He was determined to be the only one on The List, and that determination was something we admired.

The List

Diane and I compared the pros and cons of our previous relationships. We wanted to improve on them, so we could experience a little better in the next one. We decided to create a list of what we wanted to experience from the relationship rather than the usual set of qualifications.

We wanted a relationship with a man who was trustworthy, honest, compassionate, loving, spiritual, respectful, and who had a wicked sense of humor. He needed to have a peaceful nature but also a sense of self-preservation and survival.

List of Requirements

Must be intelligent and mature
Must be able to maintain a healthy relationship with women
Must be discreet
Must have an open mind and be flexible
Must have aspirations or goals to become self-employed,

if he has not already done so

Must be sexually adept, explorative and creative

Must read *Speak It Into Existence* by Sesvalah and the
      following books by Octavia Butler: *Mind of My*
      Mind, Wild Seed, Patternmaster and *Clay's Ark*

Must not have a heart or asthma condition, and must be in
      decent physical condition

Must provide proof that he does not have any sexually
      transmitted diseases

Must be a nonsmoker

Must be male

RAY

Before hearing the plan, I initially thought *This is going to be easy*. Most men have dealt with two women at one time. Until the plan was thoroughly explained to me and I realized that *fucking* two women at once is one thing, but *maintaining* the emotional, spiritual and sexual support system of two women in the same household is something else.

I understood The List to mean that Lori and Diane wanted someone that was close to them or just like them in most ways. I gathered that from how they each explained what hasn't seemed to work in the past, and ended by telling me of their own individual needs. It is good to have that in perspective because for some people their needs are hard to identify. It took me a long while before I understood exactly what I wanted. I can thank Lori and Diane for that. (Don't ask me to explain that comment right now—read the book.) I would have to know both women thoroughly, and in some ways it would help all of us achieve a certain level of balance and growth. I would have my own system in place that would be an outlet for expressing my thoughts, achieving my goals and fulfilling my desires. Not a lot of men would consider it from that perspective.

These women are powerful. I couldn't have a conversation with them and walk away without something to think about. I know men who would love to be in Omarr's old position. A man would have the opportunity to sex two women at the same time. All most men would see is the sex aspect. A lot of men wouldn't see the picture that The List and The Plan paints of the relationship. It's not just a sexual encounter, and it was unlike any relationship that I had ever experienced. I respected Lori and Diane for how they carried themselves and for their minds. These woman have balls! One thing they taught me was that my idea of the perfect woman starts from the mind; it wasn't all in the physical. Both women had interesting minds, interesting views on life, plans mapped out to achieve their goals and strong sex drives. Most men fear that. I could say that in the beginning, I was a little intimidated, but eventually I was so amazed by them that I became determined to have them in my life.

Chapter 2

RAYMOND K. HEARNE

I think getting to work is more interesting than actually being there. New York is more fast-paced and a lot less friendly than other places. People are very cautious and trust levels run low. The trains are always packed and people get angry very quickly. A train ride isn't normal unless there's an argument or someone is trying to sell you something you don't need. But this beats the alternative—driving—because rush hour here is ridiculous. Highways are always packed with people sitting in one place and blaring their horns–and no one is moving. Traffic in the city is real dangerous. Cabs will cut off cars and damn near run over pedestrians to get to a person hailing a cab. That is, if the person is the right color. New York is also a tourist attraction and some tourists hold the attitude that they are better than the "natives." Within the first hour of their stay here, tourists will find out just how much better the natives actually are.

The Golden Rule does apply here, but it's been changed a little: "Do unto others before they can figure out what the hell happened." They say that there's a sucker born every minute and you can rest assured that the "suckers" are not from New York. People who move here find that you either work with the system, work around the system or know someone who can work the system. New York can toughen a person up real fast, because if you don't toughen up, you won't make it here.

The news always tells us that racism is still an issue here. Favoritism is also a big factor and the majority of corporations hire on a who-you-know basis. Even though I was very qualified for the job I have now, a college friend had to put in a good word for me. I made sure that his trust in me was well-placed.

On the flip side, you can make some decent money in New York. There are a lot of opportunities if you find them and show that you want them. Anyone can walk down a block and see three of the same type of businesses competing with one another and each one doing well.

I grew up in the projects and led what would pass for a normal New York upbringing. I was very scholastic and was considered the "outsider" so I had very few friends. Overall, I'd say I fared pretty well in my high school years, but during that time I put my mom through a lot of unnecessary pain and it would have been worse if my father hadn't been there to put his foot in my ass. I'm grateful for it now because I couldn't begin to explain why I did the things I did back then. Like everyone around me, I spent my share of time on the streets. While I didn't get heavy into the drug thing, I also didn't separate myself from family members who did. I don't feel guilty about it now—it's life in New York. Having a gun placed directly to my forehead and hearing that click, which meant the gun was jammed, made me change my lifestyle and take a different approach to life altogether.

I am into music and at one time ventured into the music world with an aspiring R&B group called Wicked Ones. I wrote most of the material and put together the ideas for the instrumental arrangements for the songs. The group found later that we just weren't ready and we parted with no hard feelings. My creative talent laid dormant for years until Lori and Diane came along and awakened the desire for me to express myself through words again.

To sum up my life: I generally try to live by the original Golden Rule as my father and mother taught me. "Do unto others as you would have them do unto you." It seems I've got the "do unto others" part down pat, but "do unto you" is something that everyone else seems to have learned from a different school. Don't get me wrong, I've done my share of dirt, too—even though it's not something that comes naturally to me. I will stand up for myself when necessary, but I don't like to lose my temper. I find that I can let a lot of things go before that happens. I don't seem to get respected for that. People think that because I handle things the way that I do, that I'm an easy target for misuse. They are very much mistaken.

I love my six-year-old daughter, Janese, and take good care of her. I work at a job that isn't stressful but requires more attention to detail than anything else. I don't smoke, but I do like to drink occasionally, and can party with the best of them when the mood strikes. When I was younger, I did my stint of being a short-term player and after giving pain and getting it back threefold, I am now a man that does not play with the emotions of a woman. I like long-term relationships and stay loyal until loyalty is no longer appreciated or desired. Things are as they should be: I have good health, a job, a girlfriend and I handle my responsibilities the way I'm supposed to. I should be happy but I feel that something is still missing from my life.

I've only had two serious relationships: Angel and Shawna. Since Angel's untimely death, I have the sole responsibility of raising Janese. I made arrangements with Angel's parents for them to keep Janese on weekdays so they could spend more time with her. Now I've been informed by their lawyer that they want full custody of Janese. Angel was their only child, and I can understand that they want to hold on to her memory, but I am capable of taking care of Janese myself. Angel's parents hired one of the the top lawyers and unfortunately everything seems to be in their favor right now, but I'm still fighting.

My current girlfriend, Shawna, is a handful. In the beginning she was so sweet and loving. That lasted all of three months, and I haven't seen the woman I first met since then. She's been in a very rotten mood lately. To be honest, she's always in a rotten mood. It's like walking on eggshells. Shawna has been confined to the house because of her injuries—only a few are physical; the rest are mental. She doesn't want anyone to see her less-than-perfect face right now. Shawna was in a fight.

Alright, let me tell the truth: It was a straight-up brawl. We were at a club and Shawna went to greet a friend when another woman came up to me and asked me to dance. Shawna immediately came back and confronted the woman. The woman apologized and that would have ended it. Unfortunately, Shawna called the woman a bitch as she walked away. Them's fightin' words in New York (and probably everywhere else). The woman turned around and asked Shawna what she said and Shawna had the nerve (or the stupidity) to repeat it. It was on!

The woman slapped Shawna so hard I felt it. Shawna pulled back her fist and it was time to rumble. I learned a long time ago never to get involved with domestic disputes or woman-to-woman combat. It can be dangerous to one's own health. This was no time to make an exception. Shawna and the woman cleared a twenty-five-foot area and by the time they were done, both women needed a trip to the emergency room. As much as Shawna loves her looks, maybe next time she won't be so quick to let her mouth overload her ass. Maybe but I wouldn't place any bets on it.

I'm taking care of the household. Actually, I'm biding my time until she heals and gets back on her feet before I make a move to leave. Not that I'm being a perfect gentleman about this, but Shawna deserves at least this much from me. She has been with me during a low period in my life, and I'm grateful for that. Truthfully, I'm also benefiting financially by staying, but the arguments are more frequent. Shawna has never really been a "mother" to Janese anyway. If I didn't know any better I'd think that Shawna is a little jealous of Janese. When my daughter is home I keep her near me most of the time so she doesn't have to interact with Shawna. I thought they would have developed a better relationship, but it hasn't happened and probably never will.

When things were good between Shawna and me, they were really good. When we disagreed, she would get volatile. I've lived in New York all my life and thought I'd heard everything, but there are times when Shawna comes up with some names that I must have missed. I love her, but I know the reasons we continue to stay together are the wrong ones. I'm still not ready to uproot my daughter at this time or to take on the responsibility of handling the expenses of a move and apartment alone. I've always known that eventually I would have to do it, but my finances right now say otherwise. One thing I can say, is that Shawna was there for me, in her own way, and without her, I would have handled my father's passing a lot worse than I did.

My father and mother loved each other deeply, and remained together until his passing. At the request of my mother, I was in my father's room when he took his last breath. I really didn't need to see that because I was very close to my father. He was a strong and positive presence in my life. I watched him go through years of triumph over his illness only to see him give up when the doctors said the word *chemotherapy*. He was so strong until then. I watched him leave this life in installments and he seemed to take a little of me with him. When he died, I wasn't a pleasant person to be around, but eventually I came to terms with his death and my life moved on from there.

I didn't realize what was missing in my life until I met Lori and Diane. These women were not about bullshit! They were blunt to the point of distraction and were so alike mentally that talking with one was like talking to the other. They were so open, and they weren't judgmental. They were about their program and knew what they wanted and went after it with a passion. They seemed to know what was important with them and to them. It was very obvious to me that these women had a tight, long-lasting friendship.

I noticed Lori on the Zone when she came to the Spades Room where some of my friends were playing cards. What impressed me was how quick she was when responding to other people's sarcastic remarks to her. Lori always had something to say and she said it in such a tactful way that the person knew they needed to leave her alone. I actually thought Lori was Caucasian at first because of the way she worded her sentences. She was a little offended when I asked her. She said, "I'm a sister. Can't you tell?" Nope, I couldn't.

Hearing her voice over the phone was a total shock. She had the sexiest voice a man could ever want to hear. Lori could alter the depth and range to assist in whatever she was trying to achieve. I knew automatically when she was trying to make love to me. Her already sexy voice would get a tad bit lower and even sexier. Her voice could relax me or it could give me an instant hard-on. The first time Lori "took" me she was also playing spades. She used an awful lot of concentration to play the game the way she does and make me cum at the same time. I was thoroughly impressed. Diane's voice sounded similar and at times it was hard to tell them apart.

As time moved on, Lori and I both stopped playing spades altogether and started talking more to each other. I couldn't explain why but I looked forward to talking with her every day. When I didn't, I felt like the day wasn't complete. Talking with Lori was so encouraging, and we covered a variety of subjects. As we began to learn more about each other, there came a time when I decided I wanted this woman. There were obstacles: one of them was the man that she and Diane had been involved with earlier that year.

At first Omarr would call, and Lori would interrupt our conversations and ask me to call her back or tell me that she would call me later. Over time, those interruptions became less and less. He would be on the phone for a few minutes and then Lori would come back to me. The happiest day of my life was when she told me that Omarr was no longer a factor. His time was up, and it had been several months since they had physically been together. She had been giving him the opportunity to come correct. And he wasn't doing too well at keeping ties with both women. He could handle them sexually, but he was lacking sorely in the communications realm. His mistake was my good fortune!

As things progressed and I started to see how special Lori and Diane were, even though it made no sense to me at the time, I wanted them to consider me to replace Omarr.

The second obstacle was my current relationship. I mentioned at one point that maybe it was possible to maintain a relationship with all three women being in my life, especially given the distance between us. Lori and Diane would not go full force with the relationship until I was single and would not change that requirement. I never really saw Shawna as an obstacle. Lori and Diane never asked me to end my relationship with Shawna. I knew it was only a matter of time.

I was so unsure of things at first, but I got a clearer look at what I should expect from a relationship. Eventually I wanted that relationship to only be with Lori and Diane. I don't normally share information about my current relationship with women who I want to be involved with, but at times things became so frustrating that I had to talk to someone. I could talk to Lori and Diane about anything.

I was glad to find out that the other men on The List became non-contenders. I didn't feel sorry for them, but Omarr was another story. He had a real good thing and lost it. He was feeling every bit of it, too, judging by the frequency of his calls once Lori told him that they could only be friends. Omarr would call sometimes eight times a day, but by then it was too late. Lori and Diane had allowed him the opportunity to make things up, and he failed. Diane told me Omarr went to India for what was supposed to be one week and ended up being there for seven. She and Diane had been very worried about him. There were no calls or cards and with the war going on over there, they thought he was dead. When Omarr returned to the States, he acted as if nothing out of the ordinary had happened.

Black women do not take kindly to being neglected. He pressured them for things to go back to normal. When he got frustrated by his inability to get a response from them, he started making demands and they cut themselves off from him physically for three months. He wasn't able to have sex with them no matter how much he pressed for it. After the three-month-period Diane and Lori started reassessing their needs and decided that Omarr was not going to meet their requirements. They started weaning themselves slowly away from the idea of letting him back into their lives. The more they pulled back, the more he would try to push his way in. Eventually Lori had to resort to the "we've found someone else" tactic. Lori said she never wanted to do it this way. A relationship ends because it ends and not because of someone else. Omarr was not trying to understand that friendship was all that was available between them. He still kept trying to walk through a closed door. As a last attempt, he even brought up the subject of marriage and proposed to them but they weren't hearing it and moved on.

Praise the Lord and pass the ammunition!

I started what I would always refer to as the "Lori and Diane Male Training Program" and began reading the books they recommended. I always joked about being in training although Lori and Diane didn't find it as funny as I did. They didn't want it to seem as if I were being treated like a boy. Diane said that the way I said *training* made it seem degrading. It made it seem as if they were the knowledgeable ones and that wasn't how it was or what they wanted me to feel. I wasn't embarrassed because I recognized that there was a reason for me to read the books. Our discussions of them were intense. I have to admit that the books were quite interesting and opened me to new ideas and new ways of looking at life. But it was when I starting throwing some of the information back at them that I caught their full attention. I became more than a consideration. I was hoping to become the only one they were considering. I respected that they weren't the type of women to just jump in the sack with a man. Omarr waited five months before there was any sexual activity between them. When I reached the top of The List, we set a date to meet about six months later. That way, we had time to get to know one another. They were patient like that. If I were the type of man I used to be, I would have hopped on a plane to Chicago immediately.

It took some time to get used to the fact that Diane and Lori did not compare notes about their conversations with me. Whatever I told Lori stayed with her, and whatever I talked about with Diane stayed with Diane. I have to say that I tested this out many times in the beginning. One thing I learned and admired quickly was that they were women of their word. If they said it, they meant it. I didn't always meet up with people like them and it truly took some getting used to.

The true test of Lori's self-confidence was when she finally sent me a picture of herself. I told her that I received her picture and then we went on to other subjects. About a half-hour into our conversation I said smartly, "By the way, you're cute. I know you were curious about what I thought."

"I wouldn't ask you about it, because your opinion doesn't really count," she said confidently. "I love and approve of myself and anyone else's opinion really doesn't matter. This is who I am. This is who I chose to be and I'm alright with it. And I'm not 'cute.' I'm unbelievably outstanding!"

She chuckled at her observation and then said, "And even if you felt that I wasn't good-looking, you wouldn't say that to me because you have more tact than that."

That kept me silent for a long time. I was really being a smart-ass knowing how vain most women can be. I wasn't sure if I felt that way about myself. She told me then that she received my picture from three other sources a day before I sent it to her.

Really? Now I was wondering what she thought. She didn't say a word about it. I couldn't help but ask, "And what were the responses to my picture?"

I'm not going to tell you that, that's between me and those people. Ray, people who are not close to you shouldn't have an impact on your life that way."

No matter how much I tried to persuade her, she wouldn't tell me. I had to admire Lori for the fact that she could keep a confidence, even that of people she's never met, but I was also a little disturbed. What did those people say to her? I always have been the curious type. I asked Lori if she was just being kind when she told me that I was handsome.

"Honey, I would never lie to you. If I felt differently, I would not have said 'you're damn unpleasant to look at.' I would have said 'my computer isn't working right and the picture didn't come in too clear.'" We both laughed at her unique brand of humor.

The first time Lori and I sent on-the-spot poetry to each other, my head hurt like crazy. She was tapping into a part of my brain that had been asleep for years. Little did I know that I was doing the same for her too. One day Lori and I disagreed on a subject and all of our responses to each other were in rhyme. I was too thrilled because Lori was just as creative as I am. Our disagreement was about the performance of oral sex. I found that Lori liked giving it and didn't enjoy geting it. I love the taste of black women; you can't get it from anywhere but the source. If I trust a woman enough to make love to her, I want to be able to do all the things that can bring her pleasure. My father once said, "if it's not clean enough to eat, then it's not clean enough to fuck." Wise man, my father was.

After much prying and pressuring, Lori explained why she didn't like it. I found that Lori confused the intense pleasure she got from oral with giving a man a certain level of power over her. I would have to work on her belief system because if we get to that point, I want to be able to go full speed ahead. After I won that argument, I had to ask Lori to hold on for a moment because I needed to get some aspirin. This poetry process went on for a few days before my body and mind adjusted to it.

The more I talked with Diane the more I understood her too. I had a lot of conversations about New York with her. She had some points of reference because she had lived here once. We discussed plans to start our own business, and Diane sent me the forty-day prosperity plan to work on. She also started me on a separate set of affirmative statements. Every morning I would look into the mirror and say, "I am willing to change" and "I deserve everything good that comes to me." It wasn't long before I started seeing positive changes in myself. I realized that these women were in my life for a reason.

You couldn't bullshit these women. You had to come correct. I found that Diane could "hear" what I didn't say to her. These women actually listened to me, and they could pick up when something was wrong with me. If they would ask me something, and I would say that I wasn't ready to discuss it, they let it go. Eventually I felt the need to share things with them, and they didn't have to ask. They were unlike me in that way because I happen to be more curious. I would ask, change the subject and ask again. I could keep changing my way of asking until Lori would wear down. Unfortunately, this would not work on Diane—she was a totally different type of woman. This is what I loved about them. Diane eventually gave Lori some tips on the "art of evading Ray," and it made my job a lot harder.

People have always been interesting to me and how they exist is something I want to know. The way these women existed and lived is something I could learn a lot from.

Diane taught me that sometimes with change comes struggle. I thought I was willing to change, but struggle was something I had never really experienced before. Those words *I am willing to change* carry a whole lot of power with them. I was about to learn firsthand that when the shit hits the fan, you don't want to be standing downwind. Upwind isn't all that great either.

Chapter 3

Loriana Denise Morris

I grew up on the south side of Chicago. My family moved from the Robert Taylor Homes projects when I was four and our new neighbors greeted us in the driveway with shotguns. It didn't shock us when they, along with the rest of their pale-skinned brothers and sisters, decided to make a mass exodus. We weren't too unhappy about it, but I was upset that they took Dunkin' Donuts with them. As if black people didn't eat doughnuts.

I was raised by two women who have been friends since I was two years old. My mother, Rose, was the breadwinner and disciplinarian. Her best friend, Paula, was the homemaker. Paula raised me and her son, Harold, along with my brother, Donny, and my sister, Cara. To this day, it is Paula that I consider my true mother. I had a different father from my brother and sister, but we never used the word *half* in our house.

I loved school. We had less work than the students do now, but we seemed to learn a hell of a lot more. I also remember those fun games of kickball in the driveway, hula-hooping, Mr. Freeze, jacks, Red Light/Green Light and the all-time favorite, double dutch.

My brother was heavily into music and those basement parties you might remember were always at our house. Stepping or bobbin' was the dance style in Chicago, and my brother would step with me since I was the only child at those parties. Boy, those were the days!

I remember in the winter Paula would bundle us up real tight and then slap three layers of Vaseline on us. We got really hot and by the time we got to school the Vaseline had turned to baby oil. It was a major meltdown! I see a whole lot of people these days are still familiar with the Vaseline program, even in summer.

I also remember one the few fights I had in grammar school. Big T was the most feared kid because she whipped the girls *and* the boys. My time came for the most stupid reason—jealousy. Big T didn't like the idea of her brother liking me, especially since she was close to his previous girlfriend. I was supposed to meet her at 3:15 P.M.—the traditional fight time in Chicago back then. I understood where the term shittin' kittens came from. Every day I made a beeline for one of the seven exits the school had. That is, until Big T had her friends to stake them out, then I started riding home with teachers. I got tired of running and came out of the front door one day and shocked everybody. One thing about people I grew up with is they don't instigate, and they won't help either side, because all they want is to see a really good fight. Big T swung at me and I bent down and she missed. When I came up, I got her down by divine intervention, and I went down with her so I could keep swinging. *I didn't want that girl to get up!* The teachers pulled us apart and I gained a new respect from people that day. They knew I would fight instead of running. Fortunately, I didn't have another one all through grammar or high school.

Actually, my real fights were at home with my natural mother, Rose. Paula tried as much as possible to protect me from my mother's anger, but she wasn't always successful.

Recently, while playing spades with Diane, my brother and mother, we got on the subject of beatings. I told my mother that I thought she used my beatings as a form of sexual release. I imitated her using a bullwhip, which she did have back then, and made a lashing motion. I then imitated an orgasm. My brother fell out of his chair laughing as Diane put her cards on the table and held her sides as she walked away. My mother laughed so hard tears were streaming down her face. I looked at her and realized I had been angry about those beatings for years. I had finally forgiven her for my own peace of mind. I was glad we both could laugh about it now.

Diane and I beat them so bad in cards that night, my mother angrily said, "Take your child and go home."

I responded, "But mom, you're at *my* house." We all busted up laughing again.

High school was a wonderful experience. I went to Chicago Vocational High School (called C.V.S. by Chicagoans), with a student population of 5,000. My class started with 1,400 freshmen and ended with 753 graduating seniors (go figure). There was always something happening with so many clubs, games and talent shows. You can't go anywhere in Chicago without seeing a fellow Cavalier. I remember my English teacher, Ms. Richardson who made us *e-nun-ci-ate* and *pro-nun-ci-ate* our words. She also had us study and recite the Bible as literature in her classes. Until then, I never knew there were so many books left out of the King James Version of the Bible. I have her to thank for my good research skills.

I didn't get to do as much as I would have liked to in high school. All my extra time was spent in church. We were Baptist and my mother had this funny idea that keeping me in church five days a week, with three services on Sunday, would somehow keep me a virgin. She'd be really hurt to know that some of the best sex I ever had was right downstairs in the choir room. The first time was while the choir was singing "Love Lifted Me." I totally agreed. I found church to be a rather *uplifting* experience (if you know what I mean).

Paula became real frustrated with the conditions at home and moved out one day. Things were really bad, and I ran away to stay with my father. I ended up right back home, but I paid for my travels. My father had a dick where his brain was supposed to be. I didn't go back home fast enough to escape untouched and I've carried the pains of this mistake into my relationships. I never have trusted men completely and I seem to only attract the ones who could reinforce what I felt about myself. I didn't like my size or my body after having my son and I didn't feel that I was worthy of love. Every relationship I had served to further push my ability to love others deep inside. It also meant that I didn't learn to love myself either.

Paula returned home to be with me and though she could feel that something had happened, I was too ashamed to tell her. I didn't trust another living soul with part of this secret until I met Diane. I finally told Paula when I was twenty-six. The day after I told Paula, my father ended up in the hospital with blood poisoning. I was his only living relative and I had to go back and forth to the hospital and sign forms for treatments that would keep him alive.

At one point he became totally paralyzed and couldn't even blink his eyes. When a hospital representative called and told me that they were going to have to remove the skin around his penis because it was turning blue, Paula finally said "Lori, he's waiting for you to forgive him for what he did so he can leave here. Tell him you forgive him, so he can go."

I was quiet for a moment while I thought things over. "But I don't forgive him. I can't even understand why I keep seeing about his hospital treatments."

"It's because you're human, baby," she said, her words barely a whisper, "You're not doing it for him. You're doing it for yourself. You don't owe him anything more. Just tell him that you forgive him, even though you know in your heart you don't right now. There will come a day and time when you will, but three months of this is enough, Lori. You don't have to keep putting yourself through this anymore."

I went to my father's bedside and said the words "Daddy, I forgive you for what you did to me." I left the hospital and when I got home, the nurses called to say he had passed. I'm glad I waited to tell Paula. In addition to being ashamed, I knew that if I told her, she would have killed him and spent a majority of her life in jail. I loved her too much to lose her again.

When I was seventeen, I stopped going to church altogether. I didn't set foot in another church until years later, and then I changed from Baptist to Apostolic for one day. I was in a place called the "tarry room" for six hours trying to receive the "gift" of tongues. That was supposed to be the proof that I was saved. After six hours of saying "Thank you, Jesus" over and over, I was through gambling. I folded and went home. The next Sunday, I joined the Nation of Islam and stayed with it for four years.

I went to college for computer programming and at seventeen I was actually the baby in my class—all the other students were mature adults with jobs and families. I would type their papers because I had more time on my hands, and it didn't hurt that I could type seventy words per minute.

I became pregnant during my second year and decided to drop out. When I told my classmates of my plans to leave college that year, they ganged up on me. In addition to their studies, I became their responsibility. I wasn't poor or destitute, but I am truly grateful to them for what they did. They assigned classmates to teams that handled different details. Two people called in the morning— one to make sure I got up in time and to remind me to take my vitamins; another one made sure I ate before I came to school. When I arrived at school a second breakfast would be waiting for me. Two more classmates encouraged me to eat a healthy lunch and if I stayed late to test my programs, someone would stay with me, buy dinner and take me home. Someone else bought bus and train passes every month. One of the women went with me on my doctor's visits. All I had to do was show up. I had never received such attention and care from total strangers—people from all ethnic backgrounds. They didn't even know me and yet they made it their business to make sure that I finished and received my associate's degree in business.

I had my son, Brandon, two days before graduation. The hospital waiting room was filled with all of the computer programming angels from my class. They waited the entire twenty-six hours of my labor and after I saw Brandon, the hospital staff set up a place for all of them to get their first. My classmates stopped in after the graduation ceremony to bring my diploma. That experience taught me a great deal about people and how a little kindness can truly change your life.

I stayed home the first two years of Brandon's life to raise him. The experience was one that had me laughing at times and worried whether I could really be a good mother to him. I was nineteen and I didn't plan to have Brandon, but I can't say that having him was a mistake. I love my son, and I've done the most growing in my life during my time as his mother. Brandon didn't experience the terrible twos when he was supposed to. He's going through them during puberty and his antics have me ready to beat the cow-walking bullshit out of him.

Brandon's father was ten years older than me, had an excellent job and was supposed to be more responsible. He wasn't. Go figure. Brandon decided to force his father, Cortez, to come into his life by showing up on his doorstep one day. Cortez made him wait outside in the cold for two hours before he even opened the door. Brandon hadn't taken the hint all the other times his father stood him up, and he sure wasn't taking the hint that day. Brandon was twelve when Cortez tried his hand at being a father. For three months, he made my life, and Brandon's, a living hell. Finally, the principal of the school Cortez chose to send Brandon to, called me and suggested that I take back over my son's life because his father's way of handling things was unfair to Brandon. It was obvious to the principal that Cortez didn't care. Brandon finally decided he didn't need the headache—or his father.

I bought my first house at nineteen so that I could raise my son in a more peaceful environment. Actually, I "homesteaded" or "squatted" it by taking over one that was in foreclosure. I changed the locks, turned the utilities and telephone on in my name and made some improvements. The company that owned the home sold it to me because I was maintaining the property. I wasn't working when I started the process but after all was said and done, I had a job with the City of Chicago and a home that was all my own. I wouldn't have those kind of balls to do that for myself. I had to do it for my son, and it was the first of many successful risks that I took.

Making a long story short, I had my share of sexual relationships from the Permanent Student (Brandon's father became one trying to avoid paying child support), the Professional, the Intellectual, the Back Door Man and the East Indian Man. None of those relationships amounted to much. I didn't truly learn to love until someone showed me that I could be loved.

Chapter 4

DIANE MARIE FOSTON

I was born in Houston, Texas, and grew up in what, at that time, was an upper-middle-class town called the Fifth Ward. I had two sisters and one brother and as a family, we got along well. I was a real tomboy and wore jeans most of the time. I wouldn't wear a dress unless it was to church or a party. Hell, I looked good in jeans then, and I still look like a can of kick-ass in them today.

At Isaac Elementary School and Lamar Fleming High School, my siblings and cousins seemed to follow one another through grades back to back. The teachers really hated to see us coming. All of us were basically good students, but we seemed to have bad attitudes when it came to authority figures.

Some people are destined to be entrepreneurs. All throughout my childhood I took advantage of opportunities when I could find them. I'll share a few with you:

I was the oldest child and my brother was born a year after me, so we were really close. I remember when I was about eight years old, and my dad would go fishing with his friends from work. Four coolers of fish always ended up at our house, and my brother and I had to clean them. We got real tired of that shit! One day we decided to canvas the area and find out who would be interested in buying some. My dad had to leave for a business trip early that day. He wasn't even five blocks away before we were taking orders. All the orders were bagged and filled by 8:00 P.M. We counted the money as we walked home and found that we had collected one hundred seventy-five dollars.

That next morning my dad came home, and as soon as he stepped through the door, the phone started ringing. My dad answered the phone and a few minutes later he called us inside. My brother and I came into the living room and my dad asked, "How's the fish business?" What could we say? I started stuttering, and the phone rang again and he answered. It was Ms. G from across the street placing an order for some fish. *Damn!* My brother moved behind me and pushed me forward as he spilled the beans…"Dad, we made one hundred seventy-five dollars, and we have it in the room and…" My dad didn't want to hear it and told us to go get the money. I wanted to slap my brother upside the head. My dad counted the money and gave us fifty dollars each. He smiled at us and said, "Don't sell all of the fish. Save some for the house." Unfortunately for us, he didn't go fishing nearly as much as we wanted him to.

My dad worked for a bread company, which means eventually my brother and I went into the bread business too.

I was nine years old when we started. It began when a lady came over one day and asked if we could spare some bread. She didn't know my dad worked for the bread company. I told her, "We can't really give you ours, but we could do something else." My brother and I knew what the regular prices were, so we decided to sell the bread for half the cost. We told her the price, she gave us the money and all of us came out of the deal with a smile. The next thing we knew, it wasn't just the next-door neighbor, it was people who lived within a ten-block radius. We kept sales down to a reasonable limit and Dad was really too tired to notice what was going on. That was alright with us!

Dad managed to always have a decent supply because ever so often a company or store didn't want its delivery. That meant there were leftovers and my dad would ask for them. He would bring home whatever was available, so we never knew what the supply would be. It was everything from Texas-style bread, mini-loaves, raisin bread, rolls, honey buns, cupcakes, pies and Twinkies. We would call people and ask them if they needed the "special of the day." We would take orders, and deliver them up until 5:00 P.M., which was a "safe" time to beat my dad home. My uncle had just bought us bicycles, making deliveries a lot easier.

To avoid the problem we had with the fish business, it was "don't call us, we'll call you." One morning my brother and I were on our way to school. We turned around to look back at the house just in time to see the bread business go down in buns—ours. Unfortunately, if people couldn't reach you by phone, they had this bad habit of sending their children. Jamie's appointment was much earlier but he was late that day. We wanted to be at school on time and not waiting got us in big trouble. Jamie was knocking on the front door and Dad had just gone to sleep. *Damn!* My dad came to the door in his underwear, and he was highly pissed. We were close enough to hear Dad say, "They're not here, what do you want?" Jamie said "I came to pick up our order."

We were hauling ass through the trail in the backyard, when we heard my dad yell, "Diane and Chuck, come here, right now!" We would have gotten away with it, but it was just our luck that the order we had sold the previous day was for Dad's company picnic. When Jamie said he wanted cupcakes, Dad went looking for his packages and there wasn't a slice of bread or a cupcake in sight. He asked us where they were and of course we couldn't tell a lie. He yelled at us, "Y'all just can't keep selling everything 'round here. From now on unless I give you permission to sell it, whatever I bring in this house *stays* in this house." We were finished in the bread business.

Needless to say we didn't make it to school that day because we got our asses whipped. My brother wanted me to go first, so Dad could wear himself out on me. After that my brother said, "I'm not listening to you anymore." That was really funny because every time I came up with a new idea he was right there. He knew it was going to make us some money.

Another time I figured I could make money because everyone liked my marbles. They were special to me because they came from my grandparents. At ten, I was the marbles champion and I began to collect them too.

My grandmother sent two sets of marbles by way of my dad. Actually, one package was for me and the other was for my cousin. My dad gave both packages to me. That day while shooting marbles, my friends decided that they liked what I had. If they had something I wanted, I traded a marble for it, but I expected them to have some cash too. Especially since my marbles were much more valuable (you know, *sentimental value* and all). Nothing wrong with trading, but cash was always better to me.

The next morning, Dad realized that he had given me both packages of marbles by mistake. My dad asked me, "Dee, where are those marbles I gave you yesterday?

I realized that something was up. I averted my eyes

and asked, "What marbles are you talking about, Dad?"

"Come here, right now!" he said angrily. "You know which ones I'm talking about!"

As I started to explain, he didn't even let me finish. "You sold them," he said.

I sighed and shut my eyes. "Yes, Dad, I thought both packages were mine and I sold all the extras."

He looked at me in disbelief. "You sold fifty marbles in less than a day?"

I nodded and then he asked, "Where's the money?"

I had sold the marbles for two dollars each, plus whatever each person had to trade. I mean, I thought it was a good business practice. Dad showed me exactly what that was. He collected the money and didn't even give me a cut. Oh, well. At least I kept my trade items. I learned an early childhood entrepreneurial lesson: Going into business for one's self is always subject to parental control.

Fighting didn't come easy to me, but I learned that sometimes it had to be done. The person who taught me was a girl named Theresa Johnson. Theresa was a beautiful, five-foot-eight, two-hundred-pound girl with flawless dark skin. The students called her Midnight. A group of us were walking behind her, saying degrading remarks. Someone said something really funny and most of the kids laughed under their breath. Unfortunately, I laughed out loud. Theresa looked over at me, rolled her eyes and said, "I'll see you after school."

Here I am a little-bitty person, and this amazon wanted to break off a piece of my ass. I wanted to go home right then, but my cousins wouldn't let me. They said, "if you run now, you'll be running forever." Personally, I thought running forever was a good idea right then. My cousins were laughing at the time, but I didn't find it so funny. I came out of school, and Theresa was waiting for me. She walked up and hit me so hard I saw stars with my name on them. I fell on the ground and she got on top of me and I couldn't get a punch in at all. It wasn't a fight, it was a slaughter! My cousins were hollering for me to bite. I bit Theresa's leg, her arm—anything I could reach. Once she got off me, I started kicking everywhere and finally managed to get free. My jaw was swollen, lip was busted and I was in bad shape—but I was still fighting. One thing about it, girlfriend can tell you, I was not giving up. I was making my presence known. Sometimes in life that's what you have to do. You have to take a stand. Or in my case, *the ground*.

The next thing I knew, everybody was running. That is, except me and Theresa. The principal grabbed Theresa as someone helped me up off the ground. I didn't know where the hell I was. All I knew was I got my ass kicked. I'm glad that I stayed to fight. If I didn't fight that day, I would have been running all throughout school. I didn't have to run from anything or anyone again until I left my husband. Then it was a matter of life or death.

I was the oldest of four children and sometimes it felt like the weight of the world was on my shoulders. My brother had already left home to live in Marshall, Texas. My life consisted mostly of watching out for my sisters and school. I wanted to go to movies, have friends over or maybe have a boyfriend. It just seemed like I didn't have any fun, so I became rebellious. My parents would think I was at school when I was actually over at my cousins' house. But whenever I showed up for school, I had my homework. Thank God for my cousins—the bookworms, the ones who went to class every day.

During this time I really felt the need to be heard, and it wasn't happening. The more I tried to get my parents' attention, the more it seemed that they weren't listening. I didn't realize that my parents were going through something too. They just didn't seem to understand that I was older and that I wanted the freedom to go places and do things. They were holding such a tight rein on me because I was the oldest girl. I was supposed to be setting the example for my sisters. They didn't realize that I had my own mind and I wasn't going to do anything that I didn't want to do. I would ask my father if I could do something and he would say, "Ask your mother." Then my mom would say, "Only if it's alright with your dad." No one was really saying anything and I got fed up with that, so I stopped asking and started doing whatever I wanted to. I don't think that they trusted me enough to make the right decisions, so I proceeded to make the wrong ones. I started smoking cigarettes and then went one step higher to marijuana and beer. I just wanted to have a life of my own outside of caring for my sisters. But my parents didn't understand that, and it eventually drove me to run away.

My brother and I had kept in close contact so I caught the bus and went to visit him in Marshall one day. I liked Marshall and decided to stay there with him. This was my first time leaving home and I managed to find work where I could. I was the type of person who always had money to do whatever it was I wanted for recreation. There was this middle-aged lady, named Ms. Faith, that lived across the way from us. She showed me how to play cards for money. I would sit at table games with adults and the pot would be seventy-five dollars and up. Most of the time I would win and give half the money to Ms. Faith. It's called "greasing the palm" or "blessing the house." Either way it was how things went down back then.

The wife of the family that my brother was staying

with was really nice but her husband was an asshole. Actually, he was a whole ass. A few weeks after I moved in, he would find ways to pass by and touch me on the butt or rub his hand in my hair. I would always tell him that I didn't like him touching me and that he should keep his hands to himself. My brother was never too far away, and I thought he would keep me safe.

One night we went to a party, and my brother went somewhere to get more booze. While I was standing on the porch alone, I was hit in the back of my head. When I came to, I found myself on the ground with my clothes torn, and I was bleeding from my lips. I was sore all over, and I couldn't move but I saw the man we lived with pulling away and zipping his pants. I could hear my brother talking as he was coming up the stairs. I started calling his name, and he heard me. He stopped what he was doing and found me under the porch. He picked me up and asked me what had happened. I told him that I couldn't remember everything clearly, but I did know that I had been raped by that asshole we lived with.

When I was taken to the hospital, my mom and dad were called, and they came down to see about me. The doctor asked me what had happened but I didn't have to say; he already knew based on my injuries. When my parents got there, the doctor told them that I had an infection. My brother and I had pleaded with him so hard that he didn't tell my parents the truth. The doctor made me promise in return to go home and be with my parents. My mom and dad took me home where I recovered. I didn't tell another soul about what happened until I met Lori years later.

I found out that God doesn't like ugly, and isn't too keen on pretty either. I went back to Marshall to pick up my things. While I was there, the man who raped me had a heart attack. I watched his pain and discomfort, and it was quite ugly. As he pleaded for help, I struggled with my desire to do the right thing. I never called anyone for help because I was too busy remembering that this motherfucker had raped me. I couldn't bring myself to pick up the phone and call the paramedics, and when my brother walked in, he didn't call them either. My heart just pumped purple piss for him. I was comforted by the fact that he wouldn't harm anyone else.

His wife wasn't sorry about what happened either. The man was verbally and physically abusive to her and the children. With the insurance money, there was plenty of green-and-white Kleenex to wipe her tears. I'm almost positive there weren't many tears. The wife called me after she settled somewhere else. She told me good-bye and thank you. I knew exactly what she meant. As time went on, I began to heal, but I never forgot what had happened. My brother and I never spoke of that incident to each other again. It was something I thought we would both take to our graves.

While back at home and trying to get my life together, I found school to be much tougher for me now. Although I went every day, I was only going through the motions. Whenever I felt the need to be free, I hung out with my friends.

I finally forgave my parents for not understanding my need to be a teenager. They did the best they could, and they loved me and I loved them. At that point there were just so many things going on with me mentally and physically, I could never blame them even though I wasn't too happy at the way things turned out. As I grew older, there were certain things I felt I still couldn't discuss with them. They still thought of me as a child even after all that had happened. I decided to return to school and knuckle down and take it seriously. At least, what I thought was seriously anyway. I graduated and decided to join the military.

Sergeant Dishman decided to keep a few of us in a special little boot camp so we could see exactly what being in the military was going to be like. The one thing I did learn was that I was a natural with a gun. Every time I used it, I shot right between the eyes or in the heart. That's the way to do it. You don't want to miss if it's a matter of life or death. The interesting part was the miles of running, pushups and sit-ups and other things that are now against my personal religion. After a week of this, I knew the military was not for me. I had expressed this to Sergeant Dishman and I was glad for hell week, which could have ended up being a hellish four years.

I happened to go with a friend named Carrie to a gentleman's house to pick up a package. We knocked on the door and Carrie introduced me to Melvin. He kept looking at me and sizing me up. He was wondering why I was hanging with Carrie because he knew what business she was in. I didn't know it then, but I would stay with this man for thirteen years in marriage. In the end, circumstances led to a point that while he was attending the Million Man March in Washington, DC, I was on a sole woman's mission to find freedom, protection and peace of mind in Chicago.

Chapter 5

THE PLAN

RAY

   Lori took the time to explain things thoroughly and gave me some background information on what she and Diane were looking for.

LORI

   "You already know that the type of relationship we're talking about is different from the traditional relationship. What we're trying to do is not for everyone, but it can work for those who make a conscious effort to make it happen. In today's society, women outnumber men. If there are more women available for every desirable man, and one man marries one woman, what do the other women do? Do they just wait around for their turn or go without? Hell no! They'll be giving up sex out of both panty legs! If a woman is being satisfied by her current mate/husband in all areas except one, does she kick him to the curb and start over? Not if she's smart. She'll keep him and get what's missing from somewhere else. Sometimes it's hard to find everything we want in one package. Women will have their needs met somehow and somtimes it's at the possible expense and pain of someone else. We decided that our way of having our needs met meant that there would be one man for the both of us. In this way, all that we've accomplished together as friends stays intact.

"The way we see it, if everyone is honest about what they want and expect, then everyone involved will benefit. Some women are already involved in a relationship that bears a resemblance to the one we're talking about— we'll call it a trio—where three individuals agree to have a relationship and to make it work for them. It doesn't matter if it's one woman and two men, or one man and two women. It's not a religious or cultural thing, it's an alternative for both women and men.

"A prime example of another type of trio: My sister Cara has been in a trio for more than ten years. Her mates Timothy and Lynn are legally married. Their trio works well for them, and theirs isn't the only one in the country—there are a lot of silent trios at work."

Lori went on to explain. "In the beginning, I tried hard to dislike Lynn. My thoughts were that Lynn was making my sister unhappy by keeping Timothy from Cara, when it was so obvious to me that Timothy and Cara loved each other. But as time went on, I understood this concept from all three sides. I've learned a lot from Lynn and love her like a sister. I was there in the beginning when all three of them sat down to talk this out. There was a lot of heated discussion, and Lynn said that there was no reason for her to accept this. Timothy and Lynn had been married for fifteen years and had a child together. Lynn felt that if Timothy wanted to be with Cara then they could divorce, and she could go her own way. She loved Timothy, but why did she have to put up with this?

"Timothy loved his wife, but he loved my sister

and her children, too. The women were both strong-willed, intelligent and financially independent. He felt he was able to maintain both women physically, spiritually and emotionally. He was persistent and refused to give up on either one of them. Cara loved Timothy and wanted to be with him as well. She didn't want to take him from Lynn, but if Lynn wasn't willing to comply with his request, then Cara would possibly have him all to herself anyway. But in that way, Lynn and Timothy would not receive what they needed from each other.

"In the beginning, it was Lynn who had the problem with the relationship because the way it began was more like an unfaithful situation that ended up being an ultimatum. No woman would respond well to that. Later, it was Cara who had a problem. As second wife, it irritated her that she could not have as much of Timothy's time as Lynn did. There were a few times when Cara was upset and threatened to leave the relationship but Timothy was always able to persuade her to stay. Each woman gave him something special and in turn they received what they needed from him.

"Lynn was a nurturing, loving, caring and compassionate woman. Cara was a feisty, aggressive, hot-blooded and passionate woman. Timothy spent his time bringing out the fire in one woman and calming the other. Lynn gained something else from the relationship as well. I think she started off tolerating Cara and just biding her time, but it's been more than ten years and the three of them are still together. To this day Cara and Lynn are both good friends as well as wives to the same man. They all take vacations together with the children and sometimes Timothy takes a vacation with each woman individually. Both women have used some of their time to help him start a successful business that enables him to financially maintain both women.

"Personally, I think the trio works better for my

sister than for Lynn. Cara had three previous marriages and they didn't end too well. Not that Cara wasn't willing to make the marriages work, circumstances didn't allow for them to. One thing for sure is that Cara didn't take no shit. The last two husbands found that out in good measure.

"Cara's first husband was a little on the weak side and she didn't appreciate the fact that she could run right over him. When the second one started being physically abusive, she picked up the nearest weapon, defended herself and then left him.

"The last one was verbally abusive and was always putting Cara in embarrassing and humiliating situations. One day he planned this big celebration for his family and friends. He never asked Cara if she wanted to do it, he just expected her to. With all the problems between them, Cara was already at her breaking point. She was a gracious host through most of the event. She waited until all of the people had arrived and then the sheriff came to give him the divorce papers. The sheriff waited patiently as she gathered her things. The family celebration instantly turned into a shouting match between her husband and his family with them demanding an explanation of what he had done to her that she would go to this level to get away from him.

"I believe that Timothy is a perfect blend of all the things Cara needs. He's a strong, aggressive, resourceful, but calm individual, with calm being the key factor. I also believe Cara's relationship with Timothy has lasted longer than any other relationship she's been in because she has so much time to herself that they haven't gotten on each other's nerves. Truth be told, if Cara were to spend all of her time with Timothy, and he came home to her every night or lived with her, the relationship wouldn't have lasted half the time that it has. There are some women like Cara who would have a better relationship if the man weren't always around. Certain women require more breathing room than others, and some don't want to be bound in a relationship by marriage. In this way, Cara could walk away from the relationship whenever she wants.

"On the other hand, there are women who, like Lynn, prefer to have their men with them most of the time. Women like Lynn have a lot more to weigh when considering the trio option. Her decision would mostly have to be about her need for balance and her love for the man. Lynn's love for Timothy outweighed her hurt and pain and she made the decision to stay in the relationship, not because she didn't have a choice, but based on what she needed. He gives her what she needed for herself and that would be enough until she decides to move on. And at some time it will probably reach that point, and when she leaves the trio it will be right for her.

"Timothy divides his time, as needed, between both households and now manages to keep both women happy. It took years to achieve, causing Lynn, and eventually Cara, some unnecessary pain.

"I'm not saying that every man can or should do this. There are some men and women who can be happy with one mate and that's all they need. There are some men and women who cannot see themselves in a position to share but would rather end the marriage or relationship and be alone or wait until the next mate becomes available. That's each person's choice and it's alright if it works for them.

"The relationship that we're talking about takes a man who is willing to give a lot more of himself to complement more than one woman. This man would have to know what he wants and be honest with all of the women in his life and with himself.

"The trio concept would have to be modified to fit our situation. The man must be able to maintain two separate relationships with women who already live in the *same* household. Any man that comes to us will have to understand this and not try to come between us. The man will have to respect both women, fulfill the needs of both women and maintain his balance without creating a competitive environment. Women are not supposed to be adversaries. Diane and I wanted to make sure that our bond was strong and tight before bringing a man into the relationship. It takes time for people to bond and blend, and throwing women together in that way can set up feelings of inadequacy in one woman and an unhealthy aggressiveness in the other. It's much harder for a man to introduce two women to each other and expect them to get along immediately. If Cara and Lynn had not become friends over the years, Timothy would still be having a rough time today. Because each woman would have pulled him in different directions and he would not have been able to keep up with their demands. No one would be happy and one, or both, of the women would probably end the relationship with him altogether.

"Diane and I felt by developing the relationship where the women search for a mate, it would make the blending process much smoother. We made the requirements in such a way that we could place higher value on what each person contributed to the relationship rather than unrealistic expectations. At one time a man's value was on what he did: bring you flowers, pay the bills, treat you nice, fix things around the house, etc. Now value is placed on what he doesn't do: doesn't beat you, doesn't do drugs, doesn't sell drugs, etc. Things should never have gotten to the point where we expect less from a man because of things he doesn't do. Now men expect less from and give even less of, themselves. Some women aren't happy, and believe it or not, even if they're screwing everything in bras and panties, some men aren't happy either.

"The best thing any of us has to give is our minds,

our bodies and our hearts. Everything else is secondary. For women it's been that way since creation. We give the comfort, protection and nurturing only a woman can give a man, and we have the responsibility of bearing children. That is truly a gift. For men it's the comfort, strength and sense of being secure and protected that they provide women. Now, it seems that some of us have placed no value on our bodies. Using them in a way, worthy of nothing more than a simple fuck. Women and men are worth more than their sexual parts. It's just time we started acting like it and appreciate one another for who we are. We took the time to figure out what we really want, and we want more out of relationships than we've been getting.

"In the past, the men Diane and I were dating were able to handle us sexually but not in the other areas we needed. We've done our thinking and we know what we want to experience in a relationship. That's why we created The List. We need a man with emotional, spiritual, mental and sexual balance already within himself. It takes a man who is willing to do the work. You need to decide if you really want to be on that list. Are you ready to take the steps of getting to know us individually and as a team?"

I knew Ray was listening intently because he didn't interrupt me at any point. He was very quiet for several minutes and then asked the question that I hoped he would.

"Lori, can I think things over for a little while?"

"Sure, Ray. Take as long as you need."

The first time I really considered Ray a potential was the day he called to tell me that he had picked up all five books and was reading the second one. He started using the information from the books in his conversations. I found it to be quite humorous. He was persistent, and Diane and I started "feeling out" his character through several intense conversations. During a seven-month period, Ray got to know a lot more about us, and he opened himself to us. We learned a great deal about one another—and about ourselves.

RAY

I took a few days to think things over. I had more questions and I wanted to really understand where Diane and Lori were coming from. I wondered why they didn't want two men—one for each of them. When I asked, they told me that the possibility of finding one man with the qualities they needed was slim. Finding two would be virtually impossible. They wanted a man they could share, who was able to fulfill both of their needs and had the maturity to handle the relationship. It also meant that one man would not break up what they had already established—the house, finances, and the flow of their lives. One man would add to it. Two men could create confusion because each man would pull Lori and Diane in separate directions, and they didn't want that. One man sharing their mutual goals would work well.

That also meant that both women shared the responsibility of taking care of one man's needs. It would mean that each person would have more time to develop as individuals during the process.

Everyone is in a relationship for different reasons. It's not often that the same "reasons" end up in a relationship together. Diane and Lori's requirements weren't lightweight, and most men wouldn't take the time to search themselves or develop the ability to handle things. To some people it's just about the sex, the ego, the thrill, the misuse or the abuse. Lori and Diane had defined their needs and took out the common things. They weren't looking for money, abuse, misuse, deceit or anything like that. I wasn't looking for those things either.

Chapter 6

SHAWNA MONIQUE WILLIAMS

*T*he words *built like a brick shithouse* were invented to describe me. I look in the mirror and I like what I see. A five-seven carmel-colored beauty. My Mexican heritage shows through my cheekbones and in my hair, but my African heritage shows in the structure of my body, the curve of my breasts and in my hips. Unfortunately these stitches and scars that I have, detract from the perfection right now. That bitch had that ass-kicking coming. I only wish she had received more on her end and a lot less on mine.

Before the fight, I actually had a job I could deal with. All I had to do was smile and look good for the customers. Ray actually thinks that all of those bonuses came from hard work. If he only knew how hard it was getting my boss to give up plenty while I gave up nothing. Promises, promises.

Men are only good for two things: money and worship. Money has always been the key, but worship doesn't hurt either. If I'm with a man, he must be useful to me. It's just like asking for my hand in marriage: He can expect my hand to be out all the time. I know my art very well. Sex isn't really all that important to me. I love pleasure, but no one fucks me better than me.

Men always tell me how beautiful I am, and I let them know up front that being with me is a privilege. They always ask about my childhood. I mean, of course I had a mother and father–isn't that how everyone gets here? My parents don't bother me, and I return the favor—unless, of course I need a little cash if I'm in between men, but I try not to let that happen. What's my past got to do with anything? Why should I tell my boyfriends that I made it through school with the help of a little sex and blackmail? There was too much going on in school to actually go to class. Who wanted to do all that work anyway? Just the promise of some of this sweet pussy was enough to get a man to move mountains. And those mountains moved an *F* to a *B* any time I wanted. The teachers actually thought I would marry their old asses after I graduated. Not!

None of my boyfriends knows my past. They don't deserve to. All they need to concern themselves with is what I'm doing for them while I'm with them. It does help that I now choose my men from a young crop. A woman has to know how to keep her boyfriends in line. I'm twenty-seven (actually thirty but no one has proof), and the young ones have all the energy with none of the intelligence.

Although Ray was nosier than most of the men I've been with, he knows that when he asks about my past, it makes me angry, and I shut off the sex, cooking (yes, I will do this when I feel like it), conversation—everything. I just stay in our room and keep quiet until he comes apologizing. He's always the one that's wrong in an argument and that's an art too. As long as he's the one making up with me, then things are as they should be. It took several times to get Ray to stop asking about my past, but he deals with it because I will not tell him what he wants to know. It's my business. He on the other hand, shares mostly everything with me, and I know more about him than he can realize. The boy has nerve enough to have a conscious. If I didn't know any better I'd say Ray wasn't born in New York.

Come to think of it, something's up. Maybe Ray hasn't been sharing everything because he's been acting very strange lately. He's so quiet, and I win our arguments too easily. He bought some new studio equipment, he's writing again and reading all the time. He used to come home and just spend time with his daughter, helping with her homework, reading to her or playing video games with her. He still does that and when she's in bed he's up writing. What's going on? He stopped doing his music a long time ago. I made sure of that. I didn't want his attention on anything but me. Tonight I'm going to find out what's going on with him.

Sex hasn't really mattered to me as long as he kept me happy buying me things. But I can't remember the last time that Ray gave me some. I mean, he does have a way with his lips and tongue. I think I do miss that. That's the one thing I can't do for myself. He's into cuddling and shit like that. I can do without it. It's normally after his little brat is in bed that he asks for sex. I make sure that he has to ask me for it outright. No gestures, signals or catchphrases. He has to ask, and it makes *him* aware that I'm doing him a favor.

He'd better straighten up and fly right because I've never wanted for a man. If I didn't have these stitches and severe back pains to boot, I'd be out and about, collecting and rejecting. Maybe have two or three men on the hook by now. Let me be real: Ray does serve his purpose, especially since he's paying all the bills right now. He won't be going anywhere because he's got a good thing here. All of his friends tell him that every time they see me with him or when they come here.

He used to go out on some Fridays with his friend

Chris. Come to think of it, when was the last time he did that? Chris. Oh, sweet, sweet Chris. He's so cute and good God, what a salary! It would hurt Ray to no end if he knew that Chris calls here when he's not home. Chris always asks for Ray, but I already know that Chris knows that Ray's not here. He's not fooling me. He's trying to work his way in, and if Ray doesn't start acting normal again, I'm gonna let him. You can never have plan B (and C) in place too early.

My reflection in the mirror is always something I can appreciate. Damn these scars! They're destroying my flow! Moving around has been hard, but therapy has helped some. What didn't help was that my nurse decided she couldn't take care of me anymore. She wanted a relationship with me instead. Imagine that! If she had come to me before informing the agency, I might have given her the promise of something as long as she kept using her hands on me. She had such a wonderful touch. Now the agency has set me up with this hard-nose bitch named Gretchen with the sensitivity of an alligator. Damn, why do people have to complicate things?

Why can't Ray act normal? I've got a plan going here! My girlfriends always tell me that I was lucky to get him. It wasn't luck, it was careful planning. Angel used to look so smug with Ray on her arm at the club. Little did Angel know that she would be on the outside looking in within a matter of weeks. The way he dressed said money, and he treated her nice, so I wanted him. I had to work hard on Ray. He doesn't let a relationship go easily–even a bad one. A man with a conscious! Who'd have thunk it? He was so ripe for me. I was right there to pick his tired ass up when his father died. I can be the "caring, compassionate woman" when necessary. But it will cost somebody in the end, and it has cost Ray plenty. Trust me.

Angel was beautiful, but I had a lot more going for me, and she made taking Ray easy. Then that bitch had to go and get herself killed. By her fiancé no less! I even had to take in his little "Nubian princess" as he calls her. She's more like a little nugget—looks just like him. Good thing she didn't get any of her mother's coloring; it would not have helped. I didn't know she would be part of the package. I would definitely have passed him by. I had already overlooked his meager salary and I only allow one flaw per man. It helped that he was willing to spend most of his money on me—until his daughter came into the picture and his priorities changed.

Before the fight, I didn't realize how little Ray makes. His money was fine as long as I had my own money coming in too. You can only trust men so much. It's always good to have Plan B: Keep yours and spend theirs. Ray is so busy paying the bills right now that he doesn't buy me things like he used to. Hell he should do both. I guess I should be grateful because most men wouldn't even pay the bills. But I know my power, and his conscious, and I can get him to do anything. I just wish his paycheck could do everything. Maybe if I withhold the sex a little longer, he'll start shifting his funds to get the things I want to keep me happy.

Ray's mind really seems to be somewhere else. He's been so quiet and to himself. Alright, maybe I need to quit playing and give him a little bit to bring him back to where his mind should be. Sex can do that to a man. If I didn't know any better Ray seems almost...happy about something. Did he get a promotion and not tell me about it? He would have told me, so that couldn't be it. Has some other woman caught his attention? That couldn't possibly be it. I'm the best that he's ever had. I'm not going to lose him to anyone–at least not until I'm ready to let him go and have his replacement in order.

What's with those books he's always reading? I really don't want to, but I'll ask him to give me one so I can see what he's putting into his head. I have more time on my hands, so maybe I'll finish it faster than he can. Always have to stay one step of ahead of motherfuckers like him. Think they're so damn smart.

I still look the same so I couldn't be losing my touch. I take good care of this body and pay a great deal of attention to this gorgeous face. My measurements—38-24-36—are enough to turn heads, even with these stitches on my face. Maybe I'll have Ray take me out tonight so his friends can remind him once again about this good thing that he has. Jealousy always keeps a man on his toes.

Chapter 7

COMMON GROUND

RAY

*T*his particular day has been an absolute bitch! I knew Lori was in the middle of a project and didn't want to disturb her with what was going on with me. I knew I could call Diane and talk to her right now because she was at home today. I had every intention of making small talk before I launched into what was going on with me.

When she picks up the phone, my thoughts come rushing right out of me "Diane, what if I came to Chicago right now just because I need to regroup?"

I must have caught her off-guard because it was a few seconds before she said, "Ray, what's going on?"

She sounded really concerned and I felt comfortable enough to just let her have it. "I guess it's just one of those days that the problems are built up in my head and need to be released."

Diane must have heard the tension in my voice. "If you were to visit us at any time, it would be as a friend, Ray. There will never be any pressure for intimacy." Then there was a slight pause. "That is, as long as you could stand to see us walk around in the nude, and it wouldn't bother you," she said and laughed.

I had to laugh at that one. Diane could always take

me there. I had a good comeback for her. "I think I can
control myself as the both of you walk around in the nude.
Does that mean I can't talk dirty to you? I mean provoking
the two of you would be fun. Don't you agree?"

Diane took the conversation back to the reason
for my call. "Not if you're coming to get a handle on your
life. Making love with us before you're ready would cloud
your issues. When we add sex to this relationship, you
should know that it's what you want. If you're coming to
think about things—your life, your goals, the direction
you should take—we'll be available to talk with you but
we want you to have a clear head. No pun intended."

Then she laughed again, letting me know that she
was about to be wicked. "And, no, you couldn't talk dirty
to us. You would have to behave yourself too," Diane
said. "Unfortunately, if seeing you in person disturbs my
sexual balance to a point that I need release, I'll just have
to pull out one of my toys and take care of personal
business. You could understand that, couldn't you?"

I howled with laughter, and my thoughts began to
lighten. It took a few minutes before I answered. "Yes, I
understand, but you don't have to do that. Personally, I'd
prefer it if neither one of you used your equipment at all.
I'd like to have you both just for me."

It was a few moments before Diane said again,
"Ray, tell me what's wrong."

She didn't need to ask me twice. "Diane, I have a
lot on my mind today. I've tried to fight these feelings but
I can't. I'm not happy here anymore, and I'm not happy
with my job or finances. I'm not happy within my home or
with the way my daughter is being raised. I don't know if
this frustration comes because I'm carrying a household
by myself or if it's simply that I don't love Shawna the
way that I used to. I'm tired of being unappreciated for
my efforts. I'm tired of feeling like an unwanted person in

what is supposed to be my home. I'm tired of going all out to make sure other people are happy and not getting the same treatment in return. I searched my feelings to see if you and Lori are the cause. Surprisingly, you're not. I am so close to saying 'fuck it,' and leaving this place and everything behind me."

DIANE

I listened as Ray poured out his heart to me. He didn't use a lot of words to express how he felt, but he said a mouthful. The force and power of his anger took me back a little. I finally managed to say, "Gee, Ray, tell me how you really feel about it!"

When I heard him let out a deep breath and laugh, I knew that he was ready to listen to what I had to say.

"Ray, you have to look at things clearly. Don't get frustrated with things because of the promise of better situation here with us. The relationship would work whether you're here or in New York. There is no pressure for you to leave New York to be here. You should ask yourself why you are feeling the way that you are. What has changed in your relationship? Your finances are the way that they've always been, and so is your relationship. *You have changed.* You might not have been happy, but were comfortable in what you had. When you changed your way of looking at things and started defining your needs and desires, your 'normal' situation wasn't so comfortable anymore, was it? Why do you want to make a physical change in your living space now? Why did you change?"

"I want peace, Diane," Ray said sincerely.

"You want peace?" I continued speaking in my most soothing tones. "That's something that most people *think* they want. Ray, are you sure you want that? Especially if it means a change in things that you've grown used to? Or if it means changing how you are as a person, or changing the way you look at life or how you handle things. Are you willing to change? You need to really think about that."

Ray was still listening so I continued with the best advice I could give—my experience with change.

"When I first started seeking a change in the way my life was going, it wasn't easy. I went through hell to get here, Ray. In some ways, I'm still affected by it. I had to abandon thirteen years of marriage, my home, my job, my business and a great deal of my personal belongings. I was afraid, and I had good reason to be. I had to go through it in order to come out with what I swore up and down that I wanted: peace. It was a simple thing to say, but achieving it took some serious work.

"Ray, ever since I came to Chicago I've seen my life change as my spirit has changed. I'm calmer and more peaceful, and I'm not just talking about from the change in my environment. This has come from inside me, and I can focus on it. When you focus on your spirit and its development, you can bring about a change in your current situation and surroundings. I also see that I can physically manifest my desires and needs and it doesn't have to come from my paycheck. That's just seed money for my expenses. Everything I need comes to me a lot quicker. But when I do something that my spirit says is wrong— the saying 'what goes around comes around' happens a lot faster because I'm more spiritually aware. The more you listen to that inner voice, the stronger it becomes; the less you do, then it goes away. Listen to that voice, Ray. It will help you make a decision that's best for you."

Ray took a deep breath and then said, "Diane, that voice has been saying that I should have left Shawna's place months ago. I just can't see it happening right now with my finances and all. It has to come at a better time for me and Janese."

I was quiet for a moment and then I gave him some

food for thought. "Then you need to think about that before you start saying, "I am willing to change, or I want peace. Because words have power, and when you say that you want something, it can happen whether you're ready or not. As far as finances go, no one is truly happy until they're working for themselves. I know what you would really like to do is use your creative talents in your own business. Right? Why don't you start from that end. Think of your job as your expense fund. Your employers get what they need from you and you, get what you, need from your employers. Bottom line: It's a learning ground to develop yourself, not spend your entire life in the service of others."

"Diane, I've always enjoyed being in the communications field and want to go as far as possible. But I can't see myself working at my current position until I'm sixty-five. Believe it or not, I've always wanted to be surrounded by music. I thought about owning a record store at one time. I used to write songs and have had a couple of them used by a major record label," Ray explained. "I stopped all of that when I moved in with Shawna, but lately I think I'm ready now more than ever. I've expanded my music preferences and I have some recording equipment in her home. A few years ago, some friends and I tried our hand at the music business, but we really weren't ready, and it turned out to be a disaster. I wrote some of the material then and I have a lot more of it ready to surface. I'm reluctant to try this again, but I will. It's just with everything that's going on right now I don't know where to start."

I took some time and let all that Ray had said to me sink in. I was able to come up with some ideas. "Let's start with the first thing on your list. Don't just think about owning a record store, write out what your store would entail. Draw up floor plans, include a recording studio in those plans so that that space could serve a dual purpose.

See the end result and then work your way back to your business plan. If you need help with that, I'm here for you. You have to believe in yourself and that you can achieve what you want. You must stop looking for everything to come from where you think it should. Once you define what you want and need, it will come to you. Have faith."

Ray was still with me, so I decided to let him know that he wasn't the only one with aspirations for being successful. "The whole reason that Lori and I are starting our own businesses is because we want to do things that provide people with fun, laughter, music and dance. We're thinking of moving to Memphis to open a nightclub and a day spa. Lori is more interested in providing relaxation and comfort, and nurturing and reawakening of the senses. She's thinking of a day spa. Her mother's care center will provide a place for the children to be entertained while their parents are experiencing what our other business has to offer. The care center will not be an in-home type, but an actual play center with sleeping areas. This way all bases are covered and people won't have an excuse not to have fun and all of our businesses will be successful."

Ray's enthusiasm came to the surface as he agreed. "Now that I can get with!"

I further explained, "If you didn't seem to get to where you wanted to be last time—don't have a pity party, get off your ass and do it again. Does the fact that you're scared mean you won't try it? I hope not. I hope it means you're going to do this anyway. I understand that you're cautious, but don't let being cautious cause you not to progress the way you should. If you don't succeed this time, Lori and I won't see you any differently than we do now. We'll be right there to give you that kick in the ass you'll need so you will try it as many times as you want to.

"Do you know how many ventures we've undertaken? Whatever event that would spring to mind, we've tried it. Some were extremely successful, while others just barely broke even. But it was all an experience. I needed those experiences to prepare me for what I'm going to do now. Don't you think that the possibility of moving to a place where we hardly know anyone is frightening to us too? But as frightening as it is, we're going to do it if we have to. We want that new house, the businesses and time to enjoy what we have. We already know that our businesses will prosper in an untapped market down south or if we decide to stay right here in Chicago.

"While you're here, we can take you to the studio that Lori goes to so you can get an idea of other equipment you may need." A thought suddenly hit me and I asked, "Ray, do you also play an instrument?"

"No I don't," Ray answered "I play keys until I find a note that sounds good. You don't have to schedule any time while I'm there. I'll be there to spend time with the both of you. I do thank you for your words and your confidence in me. I guess I should say thank you for everything. I'm just not used to things happening without having some sort of control over them."

"Ray, control is something we never really have. We can direct, but not control. Let me tell you a story: After I had been here the first few months, the landlord decided to go up on the rent something miserable. Lori said 'We need to buy a house. Let's pack.' She had just lost her job because the company moved out of state and she didn't move with it. I didn't question her or say 'Girl, are you crazy? You don't have a job, and you want to buy what?' I packed my stuff and we prepared to go. We contacted a real estate person and we started looking for houses. The next week Lori got a job at a major phone company and during that week we found a house we liked. We didn't ask, but Lori's mom gave us the money we needed to take the house off the market. We closed three months from the date that Lori first said 'We need to buy a house.' That's faith, not control. The control of everything is in the Creator's hands. But we can ask for anything and then get off our asses to do the work so things can develop.

"We didn't look at the normal obstacles and say, 'we'll have to wait.' We said what we wanted to happen, we packed and we acted like we already had the house. When we moved in, we learned another lesson. Lori had a severe allergic reaction to the cats the previous owners had. We needed to gut the house and remodel it. We didn't have the funds and since we already had a new loan for the mortgage, we thought another one was out of the question. A flood came through the house two weeks after we moved in and destroyed quite a bit of our things. Even though we couldn't see it, I said that there was a blessing in it for us somehow. With all the flood agency grants and loans at extremely low rates, we were able to repair and remodel the house ourselves, and buy items we hadn't been able to afford when we moved in. The house started to feel like ours. From her one statement, the job, the real estate person, the mortgage company, her mother, the house, the flood and the grants and loan, all fell in line to achieve what it was we wanted. We were willing to leave the control of things to the Creator. I love and understand this principle. Now that we recognize how to use it, we're going to expand on what we want in every area of our lives."

"That's inspiring, Diane," Ray said. "I needed to hear that. You know, I'm really enjoying the books you recommended to me. I'm already done with *Mind of My Mind* and *Clay's Ark,* I'm in the middle of *Patternmaster* right now. I read a little of *Speak It Into Existence* on a daily basis."

I couldn't conceal how elated I was to hear that. With all due respect, Ray had done more than any other man on The List. The only problem was that he was still in a relationship—although it was on the rocks, it still existed. The person who will be with us had to be unattached, so right now the only thing that can be between us is friendship. It mas really funny to me that Ray's whole approach to us was as if he had every intention of being with us, so we joked constantly about his future "trip" to Chicago. While Ray was serious, Lori and I could only hope. I turned my thoughts back to the conversation.

I said, "Ray, I'm really glad that you like the books. They're well-written and make me think about myself and the people around me. These books are the concept of powerful people working together. They're about being flexible and adapting and overcoming adverse conditions."

Ray paused for a second or two and then voiced his opinion. "Well I guess if you want to see it that way. I see them as being about change and control. The misuse and abuse of power and the consequences of it."

"Diane, what do our discussions on the books tell you about me?" he asked suddenly.

I knew he was going to ask this one day, so I was prepared to answer him. "You've only been given a certain part of The List. Your responses to our questions help us to gauge if you think along the same lines as we do. They also help us to measure your integrity and sincerity."

Then Ray asked a question I wasn't prepared for. "I have to know, Diane. How am I doing on your scale?"

I couldn't help it, I took the coward's way out and answered a question with a question. "Ray, we're still speaking to you, aren't we?" We both laughed and then I continued to explain "If we gave you the entire list, you would know how to respond to our questions. In this way it comes naturally from you because of your understanding of the situations the stories present. We've actually found out the core feelings of some of our friends because they've read the books too. A lot of people claim to be open-minded, but their responses to some of our questions let us know differently."

When Ray spoke again, the tension had left his voice and I knew he would be alright. "I can feel the passion the both of you have for those books. I read them because after seeing them in the bookstore, they did catch my interest. A lot of people have referred books to me but that doesn't mean I read them. Now, if the books had been some mushy love stories, I might not have been able to read them."

Diane asked, "What's wrong with love stories? Those books are love stories of sorts—love of self and then love of others. Those books are special to me. The messages in them are so important. I'm glad Lori turned me on to them. I love the way the stories unfold and they are so realistic. Octavia and Sesvalah's books are not for everyone. It takes an open mind and a mind that can grasp deep concepts. The lessons that you learn from them is something that should last the rest of your life. That's my gift to you," I said.

Ray was silent for a few minutes, and I could feel that he was gearing up to express another deep thought. "The more I look at it, it seems I'm getting more out of this relationship than both of you," he said.

I was right, it was a deep thought. I said, "Ray, you can't look at things that way. If you give us what we need, how can it be considered less than what we give to you? There is no comparison for that since it is all based on each individual's growth and needs. You must be comfortable with the concept that we all work together to balance one another. Also know that Lori and I would never do anything that will put ourselves in a desperate position, so what we give to you, we give from the heart. What you give to us should be from the heart."

Ray sighed and before he opened his mouth, I knew we were still in deep water. "Speaking of giving," Ray said, "Diane, I must tell you that I don't make nearly as much money as either of you."

I thought to myself *here we go*. It took a lot for him to admit that. "Ray, you don't think we know that already? Right now most black women make more than our men. If this were just about the money, then it would have been the main requirement. We would seek out a man strictly for financial purposes. Some women do that, you know. Materialistically we have everything we want. If we don't, then we make arrangements to get it. That's how it works for us. We're beyond just money issues and want you to feel comfortable on that score. If you don't get over this now, you'll always feel uneasy about it and we don't want that. Just bring yourself to this relationship. That's the only thing we're truly giving is ourselves," I said.

Ray was silent—again. He wasn't through wading in deep waters. "If you don't need me in financial terms, then, are you sure it isn't really just sexual?" Ray asked in a low voice.

I decided to give him an answer with my spicy sense of humor. "You mean, just the dick? Ray, we've got three of those in a box under the bed right now. I mean, although they don't pulsate and cum like a man would, they're a damn good substitute—veins and all."

Ray couldn't help himself. He dropped the phone and laughed like hell! After he recovered, he came back with a question. "Wait a minute. Why are there three of them when there are only two of you?"

I told him bluntly, "It's always nice to have backup." He let out a second peal of laughter. When it died down, I explained further: "Ray, we only expect your consideration, your care, your honesty and eventually your heart and your ass, but that's another story for another time. For now, we have to be sure that who you are is going to be enough for us. We're not trying to change you in any way."

I felt it necessary to give him a deeper explanation of what Lori and I wanted in a man. "That's why we're using the books and discussions on the variety of issues presented in them to find out the difference between who you think you are and who you actually are. We want to know the person that resides inside of the body of the man. We have to learn more about your spirit, attitude, drive and presence; as well as the way and manner in which you handle yourself. We have to know if you're comfortable with who you are. What makes you a man is not just the ability to get a hard-on or maintain one. It's not all in that part and how you use it. It's how you handle things, the way you view things, your presence and your drive. We want to know the man who will be with us will be perfect for us as he is."

Ray finally said, "I guess I'm trapped in the New York way of thinking and get touchy about these issues. It's hard for me because I'm used to doing things in a relationship a certain way. I've always thought that doing those things made me a man. I like to buy my women things and in some way provide for them. I can already see from your lifestyle that I would have a hard way to go based on what I make now. How can I do the things that I'm used to doing when both of you already have more than I can provide? What if I buy you something? It would be so small in comparison to what you can do for yourselves. I would probably have this problem with just one of you, and here I am thinking of getting involved with two mature, intelligent and independent women. *What the hell am I getting myself into?*"

I chuckled a little inside. The reality is that Ray always talks with success on his mind and for the first time Ray actually sounded afraid. I notice how he's working his way through the things that he sees as obstacles to having a relationship with us. "Ray, whatever you do for us, we want it to be from your heart and not from a sense of obligation. What about giving us time, care and attention? I'm not saying that this means not to give anything by the way of finances, but when a man can't give as much financially, there are so many other ways to contribute to the relationship," I said. "People tend to forget that and miss out on perfectly decent relationships because they eliminate potential mates for financial reasons or because they don't meet certain physical criteria. Then they get the person they chose for those reasons and find that they're still missing some very important values."

Ray said, "I've known women to accept a man with the intention of changing him to fit their needs, when a man can only change himself and most women don't realize that. I think if people would accept others for who they are, relationships and friendships would last a lot longer. But I've also thought that a man should stick things out in a relationship even when the going gets rough. Relationships are not always picture-perfect. Sometimes trying to get into a better one is hard to do. It seems like I'm jumping from the frying pan into the fire."

I knew Ray was speaking a little on his current situation and what was going on with us, so I was very careful in how I answered. "Ray, I'm not saying that people should stay in uncomfortable situations. What I'm saying is that a lot of those situations would not arise if people would get to know one another like we're doing right now. We're really good friends, Ray. A lot of intimate relationships don't start out like that. Some people start off being good friends and forget to maintain their friendship."

"Diane, I'm glad you are the way you are," Ray

said. "I have to get used to it. It's so different from what I normally experience in my relationships. I didn't understand that at first but a lot of things are coming to me."

RAY

After I ended the conversation with Diane, I realized that I've done the most growing in my life in the months that I've known Lori and Diane. Everything—from the books to our conversations—has helped me. I can't remember a time before now where I learned new things and found some humor in them too. I don't have to hold my tongue; I can speak my mind. If something is bothering me, I can talk it over with them. I don't lose their respect because I make my thoughts or feelings known. I look forward to talking with both of them every day. They take my mind in totally different directions.

Chapter 8

OUT IN THE COLD

RAY

*A*fter he called about twelve times today, I decided to go out with my best friend, Chris. He's always late, so here I am sitting on the sofa watching television, waiting for him to get dressed, after he bugged the hell out of me. An advertisement for a local black bookstore comes on when it hits me: I left something in the book I'm reading at home that I didn't want Shawna to see. I normally carry a book everywhere and leave the rest of them at work. How could I have been so careless? I yelled to Chris. "We have to go by my house first."

"Why?" he yelled back.

"Because I forgot something," I replied.

He let out an exasperated sigh. "What?"

"I left my book in my briefcase," I answered.

"Damn! We have to go all the way back to your house to get a book? What's up with that?" Chris asked.

I really hated to tell him everything so I just said, "Chris, it's important. I didn't mean to leave it there."

"Alright, Ray, whatever you say." I can tell that he isn't too thrilled with it. But this is damage control.

CHRIS

As I'm in the bedroom dressing, I begin thinking,*What's in that damn book that has Ray tripping?* Must be about a woman. I wonder if Shawna knows. Shawna. That is one gorgeous piece of ass! I can't believe Ray beat me to her that night. I normally get to the fine ones before he can make a move. Shawna was on Ray like he was the only man on the planet. I really didn't appreciate it. Maybe she's seen the error of her ways.

I decide it's in my best interest to make a phone call. When she answers I say,"What's up, Shawna?"

"Hey, Chris, Ray's on his his way to your house right now."

"No, Shawna, he left a book in his briefcase and we're coming back to pick it up."

"Are you serious?" she said in total disbelief.

"Yes," I said. "It must be something awfully important for him to do that. What's with that book?" I asked innocently.

"I don't know. He won't talk to me when he's reading. He's so quiet lately that I think he's hiding something. I can't get him interested in anything." Shawna said. "His head is always in a damn book, or he's spending time with his daughter. Oh, Chris, I'm so lonely. He doesn't even take care of my needs anymore. I'm getting really *frustrated* by it. I wish *someone* would take care of me."

The way she said *needs* really woke up the dog in me (as if it wasn't already awake). "Is that right?" I said. "Hmm. I'm very sorry to hear that. I understand what you're going through. If you need to talk, you can call me anytime," I said sympathetically.

"I'll keep it mind. So, it seems Ray doesn't talk with you about the books either?" Shawna said.

"No, and this is the first time I've been able to get him to go out in weeks." The devil in me couldn't help saying, "Shawna, maybe you should see what's inside that book."

"You know, Chris, I think I may just do that."

"Hurry up. We're on our way over there," I whispered before hanging up.

RAY

We arrived at my house, and I told Chris that I'd be right back. I walked into the house and saw my bags and my daughter's things packed and sitting at the door. My aunt Mary always had a saying: "Something in the milk ain't clean." I think I'm about to find out exactly what that means. I walk into the bedroom and find Shawna waiting for me.

"What the hell is this?" Shawna asked.

She was holding one of my books, *Wild Seed*. That wouldn't have been so bad, if notes from Lori hadn't been inside. Lori's picture fell out, and her perfume was all in the book.

"Who is she?" Shawna demanded.

"She's a friend, Shawna. She doesn't live here and we've never met," I explained.

"How did you meet her, and why is she sending you these notes and books?" she asked.

"On the Internet," I replied calmly.

"On the fucking Internet? Now you're ordering women through pussy-vision or some shit like that? And she's the best thing you could come up with?" Shawna screamed.

I was still trying to keep my cool as I said, "We play spades together along with some other people."

"So why is she sending you all this stuff?" she asked.

I was careful in my response. "She thought that I would be interested in the books because I like to read this type of material. I bought the books, but she sent me the notes about them." Every question seemed to dig me deeper into hot territory.

"Then what's with the perfume?" Shawna asked.

"The notes are about points in the book and I guess they carry her personal scent."

"So she knows enough about you to know what you like, and you've given her your work address. Do you love her?" Shawna demanded.

"Shawna, you're not listening to me. I've never even met Lori. I've only talked with her over the phone."

"Oh, so you have her phone number too?" Shawna was livid!

Damn! I couldn't say anything right.

"I can't believe you'd be attracted to a woman who looks like that."

I didn't say anything to her because the truth was that Shawna would never understand why I was interested in Lori. My interest was not purely physical, but Shawna was right, I was attracted to Lori. Very attracted. But I could not explain that. Life was already about to be hell on wheels, and I didn't need to put Shawna any further in the driver's seat.

I opened the window and made a signal to Chris that I would not be going out tonight. Then the argument became even worse and at one point Shawna let me know that she needed her space. I didn't understand it. I made it very clear to her that Lori was just a friend and that I'd never seen her and that she doesn't live in New York. Talking was a wasted effort. For the umpteenth time this week, I wished that Shawna and I could communicate like I did with Lori and Diane. I could express myself without shouting, being insulted or cursed out.

Shawna never really listens to me. I believe part of

her frustration is that, just like me, she knew the relationship was over, but she wanted to hold on at the same time. This was evident when after she told me to leave, she asked where I would go. I told her that she didn't have to worry about it. She then told me that she didn't want it to be like that. She wanted to know where I was. Shawna wanted her space and she wanted to keep me on a leash too?

Here's the killer: I stayed up until 3:00 A.M. arguing with Shawna about her reasoning. I wasn't trying to get her to change her mind. No amount of talk was going to do that. I just could not leave that night. My daughter was sleeping in the next room—I made sure before I went out that she was tucked in. I woke up at 6:15 A.M. and the last thing Shawna said before I left home for the day was, "If you want to be with someone else then you better just go."

When I reached for my daughter's things she said, "Oh, it's like that huh? You do have someone else." I told her that I wasn't going to argue with her about it anymore, seeing as she already had my bags packed along with my daughter's. I made preparations for me and Janese to stay with my aunt Sandra who lived close to Janese's school. I left Shawna's house that day, and the week proved to be very interesting.

I could only carry Janese's things with me that morning when I moved in with my aunt. The plan was that I would retrieve my things from Shawna's later. Even though my mom would have welcomed me, I didn't want to move in with her even temporarily. My mom had moved into her own apartment a couple of weeks before, and I didn't want to descend on her like the plague.

I can't believe things went down like this. Here it is, I've been hanging in there trying to help Shawna even through all the bullshit she put me through, and she throws me out like this. I can't believe this shit! I mean damn, I'm not really involved with Lori—yet. Thank God Shawna didn't know about Diane too! She probably wouldn't have taken the time to pack.

I can't believe Shawna would be this cold. I should have seen it coming though. I went over our conversation last night. She needed her space? In the three years that we were living together, what happened to it being my space too? I put a lot of time and effort into the relationship even when things were really bad, I stuck with it. I was always hoping things would get better. How could I have been so careless. I'm so angry I could well, you know—shit a brick.

SHAWNA

I'll just give him a few days and he'll be begging me to come back. I know he couldn't be seeing anyone else. Lori couldn't hold a candle to me. I just want things to get back to normal. Maybe packing his daughter's clothes was overdoing it a little. I know how he feels about his little nugget. I'm glad I'm not having one of those. Stretch marks, breast-feeding, uuugh! Pregnancy would destroy this glorious figure!

Oh, well. He'll get over what I did. At least I made my point, and soon he'll be back in line. I've got to pull the reins in on this boy and show him that I'm still the one in control here. Maybe I'll call him on Friday to give him a little make-up nookie. Let him know what he's missing. How dare he even think about being with another woman—even on the phone. He would think of leaving me for someone that looks like that? She doesn't have a figure like mine. He could at least get someone that looks something like me. Now that I might understand. Lori. What an insult! How could he even consider her in the first place?

RAY

I check in on my daughter and find her snuggled up with her favorite bear. It was one of the toys her mother bought her. She doesn't go anywhere without it. That's when the realization of things came to me: It was time for me to get my act together and find my own place. It would be a struggle for a while, but I can't have Janese sleeping in different places every week.

I guess Shawna got tired of waiting for me to contact her. While I was in the middle of my apartment search, she called and said she wanted me to come home so we could give things another try. I already knew that I could never go back, but I also couldn't let Shawna know what my plans were until I had everything squared away. As much as I had loved her, we had been growing apart and holding on at the same time. Being physically separated from Shawna gave me the opportunity to think about what I wanted for my life and to make plans for the future. I told her that I was looking into some things and would talk to her again soon.

One thing's for sure, Diane was totally right when she said that a man should always have his own place. Even if he moves in with a woman, he should just sublet his place. That way he is never left out in the cold.

Women with children have first pick of the apartments in New York. I guess the concern is that it's better to have them indoors and let the men fend for themselves. I knew that it would be hard to find an apartment for me and Janese. But I finally found one that was perfect, and it took some tall talking and the rest of my savings for the landlady, Ms. Sparks, to accept me on such short notice. I promised her that the condition that I saw the apartment in was one I could work with. I would clean and paint it myself. I thought I was on the right track and could work my way up from there. A week after I moved in, Shawna decided to teach me a lesson that no man should ever have to learn.

Chapter 9

BRANDON MORRIS: FROM THE MOUTHS OF BABES

RAY

I had the opportunity to speak with Lori's son, Brandon, about four months after I started talking to Diane. He was very mature for his age, and I learned a lot more about Lori and Diane through his eyes. He was always fair about his opinion of a situation, even when explaining that something was his fault.

Lori doesn't keep things from Brandon that could affect him, so he knew about the three of us and about her sister's trio. I asked Brandon how he felt about the relationship between Diane, Lori and myself. He said, "As long as what makes you happy doesn't make them sad, I'm alright with it. It will be good to have someone on my side for a change. I'm outnumbered here!"

I laughed at him as I told him, "Well I have a daughter, too, and then we'll *both* be outnumbered."

He asked me how old Janese was, and I told him she was six.

He said, "Well she doesn't count, she's not of voting age." Neither was he for that matter, but I got his point.

Brandon loved talking about Lori and Diane, and his views of them were a little along the same lines that I felt. He was very intuitive when it came to them.

"My mom and Diane play all types of games, and

they're real competitive," Brandon once told me. "One night Mom was playing Monopoly with me and my cousins. She was beating us so bad that my cousins were slipping in extra money with their rent payments so that they would become bankrupt. I didn't take the hint and stuck it out. Mom was clowning! It was so embarrassing. She would let me slide on some of my rent just to keep me in the game. I would pray to land on one of the corners—Free Parking, Go, Jail, and especially Go to Jail because I could stay there for three rolls. Mom didn't make it pretty at all. For a minute, I think she forgot I was her child."

Brandon had me laughing—hard. I liked Monopoly myself, and it is a cut-throat game. I'll try to give Lori a run for her money.

I asked Brandon about Lori and Diane's type of discipline. "At one time when I got in trouble I had to write a certain number of lines, such as I *will not forget to clean my room.* Years ago, Mom used to whip my butt. Now she only puts me on punishment. When I'm on punishment, Diane pulls out the cards and teaches me something new. She taught me how to play blackjack, poker, gin rummy and pitty-pat. If Mom isn't too tired when she comes home, she'll join in. Sometimes I hope Mom can't play. Mom is so lucky. She comes in and starts beating the both of us. I always stand a chance to win if I'm playing with Diane."

"Brandon, that doesn't sound like punishment."

"It is if you can't do the things you want to do or go to the places that you normally go to," he replied.

"Mom says punishment should be about improving myself. I also have to read a book, write a report and then type it before I get off punishment. That's her method of improvement."

I had to laugh at Lori's ingenious way of turning a

punishment into something that benefits Brandon too. By now Brandon is up to typing fifty-five words per minute and has read the works of Octavia Butler, C.S. Lewis, Anne McCaffrey and Sesvalah. I took the time to discuss with him the books that we've both read and found that he's way ahead of children his age.

Eventually we touched on the subject of Brandon's father. "My dad just doesn't care. He doesn't see me as his son. He sees me as money out of his pocket. I was with him last year for a little while and it was real clear that he didn't want to spend time with me. He lied on me to my mom when he was the one who forgot to pick me up from school one day. I was so angry I was still up at three o'clock the next morning when Diane was getting ready to go to work. Diane held me and stayed with me until I finally went to sleep. I didn't go to school that day, and Diane stayed at home to be with me.

"One day after visiting my dad, I asked Mom if I was a mistake. She looked at me and said 'I wanted to have you, and you were determined to be here.' She smiled at me and then told me all the good things that have happened to her since I've been born, and all the risks that she's taken. She said I gave her a strength she never knew was inside her. She hugged me and told me, 'Thank you for coming. Thank you for chosing me as your mother.' I knew that she meant it. I love my mom. I love Diane too. I haven't wanted to see my dad since that day."

Brandon told me that Lori also takes karate lessons and most times Brandon is her instructor. He has to teach classes in order to get a higher belt. "Her first week, she said she was 'through gambling.' She told me that whoever invented the phrase 'the bigger they are the harder they fall' was lying. She found out in class that the bigger they are, the harder they seem to hit. I told Mom, 'Don't quit, you can do it. You wouldn't let me give up so easy.' That got her attention and she's still in class to this day. She doesn't compete in tournaments or anything like that, but she's still there. It's nice to know that parents can listen too.

"My mom and Diane can do anything. I've seen them say they want something and then go after it like gangbusters! I tried that approach with my dad because I thought I wanted him to know me, and act like my dad. When he came, I was sorry I had asked him. My mom always says be careful what you ask for and how you ask for it. My dad taught me what that really meant. My mom can just let things go. I can't. One day my dad's going to need me for something, and I won't be there for him. Why should I?"

I could tell that Brandon's interaction with his dad left him with a pretty bad feeling. I did let him know that he could call me whenever he needed to talk.

Brandon felt that both women were superhuman and it was obvious that he loved them. He wasn't the only one. I told him that I couldn't take the place of his father, but I would like to be his friend. He surprised me and said, "Being my friend is good. I can never have too many of those."

Chapter 10

NOBODY KNOWS THE TROUBLE I'VE SEEN

RAY

I went to Shawna's and found that my recording equipment had been damaged and all of my clothes were destroyed. I left before I could do something that would land my ass in jail.

When I got to my new apartment, there was no gas or electricity, and my phone was acting funny. What the hell was going on? I found out later that Shawna called the electric company and told them that there was some rewiring being done in my new apartment and asked to have the electric service shut off. She had also called the gas company and said there was a leak, and since no one was home so they could check it, and the landlady and super had been mysteriously called away by a crank caller, everything was shut off.

Shawna had the cable turned off and my phone calls had been remotely forwarded to her home line. All my phone calls were going to her house! She also discontinued my mail-forwarding request, so I couldn't get my mail either. Damn, she kicked me out and now she wants to give me grief because I've decided to get a place of my own? I learned the hard way that hell hath no fury like a woman scorned. I didn't know it then, but I was going to find out: Shawna wasn't through clowning yet.

I had been working steadily on a sales presentation to land a new account in Memphis. I prepared my team and everything was set to go. I'm really looking forward to pulling in this account. It would mean a promotion and a raise, and I truly need both at this time. On the way to the airport I blocked out all of my problems and focused on the task at hand. Janese was in good hands because my aunt Sandra loved having Janese with her. It worked out great because I didn't want Janese around Angel's parents. They were making some pretty ugly remarks about me in front of her. They didn't know that Janese starts telling me about her day from the moment I pick her up. She would question me about things they said, and I spent my time unnecessarily explaining myself and my actions to Janese. She loved her grandparents but I'm uncomfortable with her being with them right now.

I'm standing in this long line at the airport for early check-in and when it's finally my turn, I get the shock of the century: My reservation has been cancelled. That was impossible! I made these arrangements months ago. The reservationist checked again. The ticket in my hand was worthless because someone cancelled it two days ago. Unfortunately with my company, I have to pay for any expenses first and I'm reimbursed later. I tried to make other arrangements so I could leave with my team but all the seats on the flight were booked. I would have to take the next flight out. When I prepared to do that, I was in for shock number two: my credit card had been maxed out. That was also impossible because I always kept the card available for business and emergencies.

I let my team know that someone had screwed up my reservation and that I would miss the flight and would join them later. A little voice rang inside my head, and I followed the instructions. I went to the nearest pay phone and found out that getting to Memphis would be only half the battle. My hotel and car reservations had been cancelled too. Someone was really fucking with me today! It didn't take me long to figure out who that someone was: Shawna.

After a few more phone calls I discovered that not only had she cancelled my trip and maxed out all of my credit cards, she had also wiped out my checking and savings. Checks were bouncing all over the place— including the ones I used to pay for utilities and rent. Man, that's messed up!

I could lose my job and apartment over this bullshit! She's fucking with my life here! All because she's pissed off and flexing her revenge muscle right now. I'd really like to put my foot up her ass! As a rule, I don't hit women, but Shawna is making me understand why some people lose control. I really need to stay away from her right now.

Not to mention, that now I don't have finances for my vacation in April. Damn! I've been planning this trip for months, and with the new apartment, replacing my things, buying new furniture. I won't be able to go to Chicago. How can I tell Lori and Diane that I'm not coming? They'll think I've been bullshitting all along. Maybe they'll think that I had no intention of coming in the first place. I can't tell them about this. This is really fucked up! Why didn't I move out sooner? Why didn't I take Shawna off my accounts sooner? I was so focused on getting things in order that I didn't remember to. Wait a minute! How did she get my new address and phone number anyway? No one knows it but my mom, my aunt and Chris.

LORI

I haven't heard from Ray in a while, so I decide to call to check on him and when I did a woman answered....

"I'm sorry, I must have dialed the wrong number,"

I said. I was ready to hang up and dial again when the woman asked me, "Are you looking for Ray Hearne?"

"Yes, I am," I said hesitantly. "Is he available at this time?"

No, he's not here but I'm expecting him real soon, and I'll make sure he gets your message," she said.

"No message, I'm a friend and I can try again later," I replied.

"That's your choice but I'll be right here to take your call. You wouldn't happen to be that bitch he met on the Internet."

I was silent before I spoke. Now I knew who I was dealing with. How could this be? Ray has his own apartment now. Or does he? "I don't know about being a bitch, but yes we did meet there. What's it to you?" *Smart ass,* I thought to myself.

"Thank you for sending us those books. They were very enlightening. Ray shares everything with me, so I know just what you've been up to," she said smartly.

This woman was getting on my nerves, but I wanted to see how far she would take this. "Really? I find that strange that he would share any information with you. Ray's not like that at all," I calmly replied.

"How would you know?" she asked. "You're not here, are you?"

"No, but it doesn't take being there to know what's happening, especially when someone keeps you informed." I said confidently.

"Then why I am answering his phone? Did he tell you that we're still together?" Shawna bragged.

It was at this point I decided to be a real bitch. Actually she struck a nerve. I was wondering the same thing. Ray would just have to forgive me. "No. He told me that he was just using you for sex, which is very bad judgment on his part because he can do so much better. Have a good day," I said before slamming down the phone.

Shawna

The bitch! She hung up on me. *That bitch!* Who the fuck does she think she is? That motherfucker, already has a woman calling him and we haven't broken up yet! The nerve of that boy! Her voice. Damn, what I wouldn't give to have a voice like that! What is it about her? I've got to get my hands on Ray again. I can't lose him like this. Not to her.

I pick up the phone to dial Ray's cell number.

"Yes?"

"Hi, Ray, this is Shawna and…"

"Look, Shawna, I don't know what kind of game you're playing," Ray warned. "First you turn off my gas, then my electricity and cable. Now my family is telling me you're answering my phone. I don't know how the hell you did that, and you made sure to do it on the weekend, so I can't get it reversed until Monday. I'm going to straighten this shit out and set things where you can never do this again."

Ray sounded pissed as hell. I lowered my voice and tried to sound very sexy. "Ray, why don't you come over so we can talk about it?"

"There's nothing to talk about, Shawna. I've got people from my family and job stressing me because you've called them and made it seem like I'm the one that hurt you, and that's not how it went down."

"Ray, I didn't say anything like that,"   I said innocently.

"Bullshit!" Ray said angrily. "Then how would anyone else know? I haven't told anyone what's been going on, but I know you would if it's to your advantage. What are you trying to accomplish, Shawna? Not only is it no one else's business, but none of what you've done so far is going to change things between us. You've maxed out all of my credit cards and most of the shit you bought is nonrefundable. You've jeopardized my job, my apartment

and my ability to provide financially for my daughter. I've never done anything to hurt you, so I can't understand why you're doing this."

Now I was getting pissed at Ray. Let me remind him of a few things. "You've been dealing with another woman," I accused.

"Talking with a woman and playing cards with her is not 'dealing' with her. I was still in your home—still in our relationship—when you decided you wanted your space," Ray said angrily.

"Ray, I didn't want you to move out permanently,"

"What did you expect me to do—*be homeless*?" he demanded.

"No. I expected you to move in with your mom to give you some time to think about things. I mean, how can you pay the bills at two places, Ray?" I reasoned.

Ray let out a deep breath and said, "That's actually what it comes down to, isn't it, Shawna. Money. I never saw it until recently. You've never once said in any of our conversations that you love me and want me back for me. You want the convenience of me living with you under *your* terms. Have you ever really loved me, Shawna?" Ray asked.

"Of course I love you, Ray," I said quickly, silently adding *in my own way*.

"I don't think so, because it seems that the only person you love is yourself. I did think about things, and I knew that having my own place was best. I wasn't ending the relationship then, but after what you've done, you've made it all too clear that space isn't the only thing you need. No matter how pissed off I could get, I would never do this to you Shawna. Never!"

"Ray, I only wanted you to give me a little space for a while. I wasn't saying that I wanted you to move out completely. It's all your fault. When I said it was alright for you to come home, you said you didn't want to. I wanted things back the way they used to be, and you said you were looking into some things. Well I know what those things are...I see that you already have someone lined up to take my place," I accused.

"What are you talking about?" Ray asked.

"The woman with the sexy voice, Ray? Who is she? She said she would call you back, and I told her that we would be too busy fucking to take her call," I lied.

"What? Damn! Bye, Shawna."

"Wait! Ray, we need to talk. What is it about that damn woman? She's not even your type. You never deal with women that size. She doesn't look anything like me. What's she have that I don't?" I was truly puzzled. I knew he was hanging up with me to call her.

"A heart, Shawna. Lori has a heart and she has the presence of mind to be a friend," Ray told me. "There's nothing for us to talk about. We're not living together anymore and after recent events, we can't have a relationship either. I had some thoughts in the beginning that we might still see each other even though I had my own place. You've made that impossible, Shawna, and it's time for both of us to move on. I'm angry as hell about what you've done, but I understand why you're doing the things that you're doing. If my money is tied up in trying to recover, I wouldn't have an apartment, and I'd be so financially stressed that I would be crawling back to you. Well I have news for you, Shawna, there's more to a life than just money. I find that peace of mind is number one in my book these days.

"You're a beautiful woman, Shawna. I have to give you that, but there's nothing inside you. No life, no spirit and no love. At one time I was right there with you, but I want more than what my life has been, Shawna. Much more. I thought I loved you, but what I really loved was what I thought you were—a compassionate, caring woman. I've only seen that side once every blue moon, and I've always hoped that I would see more of it. I didn't realize that it wasn't your true nature. I've seen the real you, and it's been an eye-opener.

I could feel I was losing him. "Ray, just come over and we can talk about things. I'm really sorry for the things I've done," I said.

"That's the first time I've ever heard the words *I'm sorry* fall from your lips," Ray said. " I didn't know you could say them. I'm sorry, too, Shawna, but I can't give in to you this time. I have to find real love where it really is. When I give love, it has to be to a woman that can appreciate it. When I give my time, it has to mean something," Ray said.

"And Lori is that woman?" I asked.

"Lori is that type of woman but she's only half of it, Shawna. There are more women out there with her qualities. I just never took the time to look. I've basically been using the wrong criteria to pick a woman," he said. "Overall, I have to do what's best for my daughter and myself."

Ray was cutting me deep and maybe I deserved it. But I was holding on to one more piece of information. I was close to tears because he's never spoken to me like this before. I couldn't seem to reach him and it was hurting me, and I wanted him to hurt to. "Speaking of your daughter, Ray…" I began.

"Yes?" he asked impatiently.

"You missed your court date, and the court entered some kind of judgment against you in her grandparents' favor. Have a nice life, Ray…you and that fat bitch." I hung up the phone.

Ray

I think at this point I'm as low as I can go. Every time I say things can't get any worse—they do. So I need to stop saying that shit. I've heard this happens to people but I never thought it would happen to me. I always thought that since I never try to hurt anyone, that I shouldn't experience things like this. Life is unfair and sometimes it's not in your favor. I think of Lori and Diane and wonder if they would handle things the same way. How well do I know the women I'm eventually going to be involved with?

The only way to find out is to see how their last relationships were handled.

Chapter 11

LET ME LOOK INSIDE YOUR SOUL

RAY

    I took the time to ask Diane and Lori the next day...what were your previous relationships like?

LORI

    "You already know about Brandon's father and Omarr. There was also The Professional Lover who wanted me to take care of him. He lied about so many things in the beginning. His lovemaking was so good that at first I overlooked even the obvious lies. He was perfectly alright with me going to work every day while he stayed at home to watch TV. He watched me bring home the bacon, fry the bacon and I watched him eat the bacon. The Professional lasted two months before I realized that I couldn't take the bullshit anymore. Since I was basically taking care of him, and in his mind the method of payment was in his sexual services...I decided to collect. *Big time!*

    "Whenever I thought about it, no matter what time of day or night, I would give him the signal that I wanted some lovin'. At first he kept up with the demand, but after three weeks of making love, every day from the time I got home until it was time for me to get up for work—I was wearing his ass out! I would always make sure that I stayed aroused and ready for the process. It got to a point where he became too tired to do anything and would sleep all day. Fine by me!

"I could always get him hard, so when I came home I would roll him over, get on top and ride him. That wasn't so bad within itself, but I added my special touch: I would sing the chorus to "Love Lifted Me" during my entire performance. He probably thought I was losing my mind! It got to a point that all I would have to do was hum the first bars and his dick would assume the position.

"He became so frustrated that he finally called my mother and asked her to plead on his behalf. His ego wouldn't let him ask me himself. He knew Paula and I had a strong bond, and he felt comfortable enough to say to her, 'Please talk with your daughter and tell her that she doesn't need sex all the time. And ask her to stop singing that damn song!'

"My mother and I had a good laugh over it when I explained what I was doing. She said I was definitely her child. After two months of this, I came home one day, and The Professional was gone. He left his clothes and everything else he brought with him and things I had bought for him. I didn't have to get ugly about it. All I had to do was 'love' him to death. Love truly lifted me!

"The Back Door Man waited four years to have sex with me. He first approached me just before I joined the Nation of Islam and by the time he became serious, I was making a commitment to become a member. Joining the Nation would mean a change in eating habits, no sex before marriage, as well as other things. The day before I totally committed, I ate my last order of Leon's hot links and had some wicked sex with an old church partner. The Back Door Man would have to wait.

"When I left the Nation, he still wanted to be with me and was the first man I allowed to have sex with me.

He became a continuous booty-call. I made the first call to let him know that I was not in the Nation anymore. From then on, The Back Door Man was the one to call if he wanted some 'pokins.'

"We never got emotionally involved, it was just about the sex. I would rather have had a complete 'relaxer' than the 'touch-up' he gave me, but we both were afraid to move things to another level. There were a few times when he actually showed some compassion. The night my father passed was one of them. He called and when I answered the phone, he hesitated and then asked me what was wrong. I didn't think he could tell the difference in my voice, but he could. Even though I told him that night wasn't going to be a good time for a visit, he showed up anyway and just held me. It was one of the very few nights that we were in each other's presence and did not have sex. Sometimes he would come over and he was so troubled all he wanted to do was talk or just hold me or be held. Other times he showed up with dinner and movies. This began to happen more and more over a period of time.

"I always wondered why we didn't talk about changing the relationship because it was definitely going in a different direction. I didn't realize it then, but one of the obstacles was that I didn't fit his friends' physical description of the type of woman he should be with. In his way he loved me, he just wasn't strong enough to stand up to his friends or family's view of who he should be with. There were a lot of things he didn't voice his opinion on and doing so would have made his life better. I wasn't totally happy with the arrangement the way it was, but as his calls became more frequent, I believed that he would eventually admit how much I meant to him. I was very much mistaken.

"The calls came twice a day and some of those

calls were 'I just wanted to check up on you and see how you were doing.' It was a total surprise when he came over one day and told me 'Black men don't really like fat women, from now on you'll have to pay me for sex.' It cut deep, but I realized by accepting less from him and myself, it made it seem that I needed the sex so bad that I had been willing to pay for it with my self-esteem and dignity. So why not with cash too? I was really hurt, and I wanted him to hurt too.

"As I rode him that same night, I put a vaginal grip on his dick so tough, he ended up in the hospital with a permanent hard-on and a matching muscle cramp. A nurse gave him a shot of relaxant in his dick in order to bring it down and take away the pain. It was a small form of revenge and he didn't even remember to get his payment. I wonder why? I didn't hear from The Back Door Man until two months later when he called to apologize. He asked if we could talk about our relationship. He also said he was very wrong in what he said to me and how he had treated me all along. 'I love you and I want you to be my woman' were words I wanted to hear for so long. Unfortunately, by the time he said them it was too late. I had become totally turned off by him, and the thought of sex with anyone made me ill. I was hurt so deep that I didn't allow another man to be with me until six years later.

"The Intellectual had multiple personalities and all of them were persistent in their pursuit of me. He changed between the minister, the scholar, the whore and the user. He was charismatic, Afrocentric, well-educated and a bullshit artist all in one package. His lectures were plenty powerful and made a woman feel good about being a sister. He is the only man that I've loved, who I didn't give any loving to. Something about him made me hold back. I was still reeling from the effects of The Back Door Man, so sex wasn't all that important to me at that time anyway. The Intellectual told me once that if he made love to me, I would never leave him. When he kept pressuring me, I finally told him in the only way he would understand that I wouldn't fuck him with someone else's pussy. I found out later that that was the safest choice I could have made. This man had women in every town he ever lectured in. One thing they all had in common was that he only sought to use each one.

"Diane had even given some of them nicknames— Poly and Ester, Silk and Satin, etc. He would play one woman against the other, trying to get them to outdo each other in their plays for his affection. Each woman was useful to him for one reason or another—money, sex or a specific skill that was to his benefit. Some of them were sisters or had been best friends for years until he came into the picture. After he was done playing with them, a good majority had a parting of the ways. He enjoyed every minute of it.

"I made sure our relationship never became sexual, but I did transcribe his lectures. I liked his message because it was very uplifting. It was knowing him on a personal level that didn't inspire me to listen to anything he said. The best thing this man ever did for me was to put me in touch with the woman who handled his tapes and videos. This woman and I developed a friendship that has lasted to this day."

DIANE

"I used to hang out with a girl named Carrie. Even though I knew she was a 'paid companion,' it didn't bother me because what she did with her life was her business. She was always there for me. Basically, she was sort of like a big sister. She tried to keep me out of trouble, which was virtually impossible. (At least by normal standards.)

"One day we went to Melvin's house to get a little 'smoke,' and Melvin asked how old I was and what I was doing hanging with Carrie. I told him, 'My age is not your concern and why I'm hanging with her is not your business. I'm not here to talk about my personal life or my friendship with Carrie.' So he said, 'Feisty, aren't we?' I said, 'Call me whatever you want, but you're dipping your stick somewhere it shouldn't be stirring.'

"As time went on, Carrie and I continued to go to his home for our little packages. One day, out of the clear blue sky, he asked me if I would go out on a date. I was in total shock. *Me?* Go on a date with *him*? He was twenty-eight, and I was eighteen. For that reason I said no, and he didn't force the issue. Carrie and I would go out to clubs all the time and one night we saw Melvin. I was talking to a guy and evidently it was someone Melvin knew and didn't care for. He immediately came over to the table and asked if he could have a moment of my time. When we found an empty corner he asked, 'Why are you hanging out with that guy? Don't you know that he's a pimp?'

"I told him, 'I know what he is now, but we were friends when we were in school. What he does with his life is his business.'

"Can't you tell he's recruiting?" Melvin asked.

"He's been trying to recruit me for a while," I replied, "but it's not happening. The bottom line is, if I'm going to sell a piece of my body, I don't want anyone getting a percentage. I want the whole enchilada." Melvin looked at me, and I could tell he was in shock.

"He said, 'Girl, you're something else!'

"He asked me to come over to his table and have a drink with him. I did and as we talked, he asked me, 'What do you plan to do with your life?'

"I said, 'Well at this point. I really don't know. I was trying to find out who I am and to be perfectly honest,

I'm not in that much of a hurry. I just want to have some fun for now.' He looked at me and laughed as he said 'man, I tell you, you youngsters.'

"I said defensively, 'Youngsters?' I'm grown!"

"Well that's yet to be determined," he replied smartly.

"I answered, 'And that's your opinion, and opinions are like assholes—everybody has one.' Melvin looked at me in total surprise and said, 'I can't believe you. Where do you come up with these sayings?' I told him, 'My grandmother was a very wise person and that saying is definitely true. Opinions are like assholes, don't you have an asshole?' I couldn't help adding, 'Or do you just plan on being one?'

"He said, 'Alright, alright, I hear you talking.' We both laughed.

"Eventually Melvin and I started seeing each other, and I found that he was a decent person. He worked for the railroad and also sold weed on the side, but eventually his side business stopped. We had been seeing each other for about six months when he asked me to marry him. Of course, I thought he was just playing. After months of asking me, I found that he was for real, so I said yes. My friend Carrie couldn't resist telling someone in the neighborhood. Unfortunately, the only person she told was a woman named Lynn. It was Lynn who told everyone else, and the information got to my dad before I could tell him.

"When I went home to introduce Melvin, my dad was livid! He still didn't believe it and wanted to see the marriage license. We had to wait about a week for it to come back and then we went back to my dad. He was not too thrilled with Melvin. Dad quickly let Melvin know, 'This may be her decision, and while I don't like it, one thing I can say is that if you hurt my daughter, the planet is not going to be big enough for the both of us.'

"I moved in with Melvin and while married life was not perfect, I stuck with it. As time went on, I created a separate life for myself within the marriage, and it was a good thing I did. There came a time when my mother needed my help, and I didn't want to go to my husband for assistance.

"My parents seemed to drift farther apart. Melvin and I had been married five years when my mom called one day and said that she and my dad were separating. Of course, I had felt that it was coming, but my mom was still understandably hurt. She really wanted to try to stick things out, but it was useless. She needed to find an apartment and of course I was going to do everything within my power to make sure she had one. (Even if that power was a little unconventional.) I found an apartment that she liked, and I told my mom not to worry about things because she would have it. She asked how I was I going to come up with that kind of money. I told her, 'I'll get it, but you can't ask me any questions as to how I get it. If you can live with it, then this can work.' She really didn't have a choice and neither did I. I did whatever it took in order to get that money as long as I didn't hurt anyone and I didn't get hurt.

"Once she moved into the apartment then we had another problem. The previous renters hadn't paid their gas bill so the meter had been taken. There was an empty apartment about two or three doors down, so I pulled out my trusty tools and later that night my mother had gas. It was a temporary measure until I could get the money to have the gas turned on.

"Over the weekend you could imagine that I was a very busy person. I heard there was a card game at Mr. Jake's place, so Carrie and I dressed up, and went to watch who was playing. I had about one hundred bucks to enter the game. I made some folks angry that night because they couldn't believe the luck I was having. I was kicking ass and taking names, and I was getting excellent cards, and people thought that I was cheating. Those weren't the kind of people you did that with. I said 'If you think that I'm cheating then we should have a house dealer.' They had someone join the game strictly to deal the cards. So that meant that none of the players would deal. This was fine with me, because I already knew luck was in my favor because I was on a mission. I went in thinking and knowing that I was going to come away with money. The card game went on until four in the morning. People started falling out of the game left and right because they ran out of money. The game finally moved down to two people: me and Monty.

"Monty was a very cool and suave old man. He was just playing the game that night because he was bored, and he didn't want to get into anything too heavy. It was just him and me now, the cards were falling hot, so before my luck changed I risked everything that I had earned, which was about $800. The old man said 'For a short person, you've got a lot of balls.' I didn't say anything to that, because it wasn't balls—it was the small prayer I had said to the card God before I got there. He asked, 'Are you sure you're willing to risk it all on one game?'

"I told him, 'Even though it's hot in the kitchen, I still have some cooking to do.' He said, 'Okay, if that's the way you want to do it.' The table was surrounded by people who wanted to see how this game would play out. The house dealt the cards, and I picked up my hand and I couldn't believe it. I only needed one card! After several plays, Monty pulled from the top of the deck, discarded the card on the table. I knew then that the Creator listens to everyone's prayers! I looked at the card for a few moments before I said, 'I need that card.' I picked up the card, and

I spread my hand out and said, 'Hey, here's the winner.' People in the room started clapping and Monty was in shock, but he extended his hand as he said, 'You lucky rascal.'

"I walked away from there with enough to turn on the gas, buy groceries and put some money in my mom's pocket too.

"Melvin worked nights so I was able to go out and have fun. I never cheated on him because it was something that I never thought of doing. As far as gambling went, he really didn't know I was doing those kind of things. He believed that the reason that I always had money was because I saved what he gave me. Little did he know.

"Things were alright between us until I decided to go back to school. Melvin wasn't too happy about it, and we had several heated arguments over it. I finally told him that this was my life and either I attended business school or we could call it quits. When I got married I hadn't set my own goals, but I did have my own mind. I told him that there were some subjects I wanted to brush up on so I could get a job. He totally flipped out! He asked me, 'What do you need a job for?'

"I was getting tired of staying at home and was tired of my *unconventional* employment. I wanted my own money and getting an education and a job were the ways I wanted to do it. Eventually, he seemed to get over it. I picked up some business courses and completed the hours to get my certificate. I landed a job and that's when things really got stressed between Melvin and me.

"I found a job working nights in a hospital. Melvin wasn't too happy about the fact that I was working, but I told him it was something that I wanted to do. For about three months we argued about it, until one day, I just got tired of arguing. I told him, either this is the way it was or it wasn't. He said, 'Well I'm not going to have it.' I looked at the place, which was spotless before I left for work and found a bunch of people in my house along with beer cans, bottles, ashes and cigarette butts. I walked into the kitchen and found dishes everywhere. The food I cooked for our dinner was all gone. *And he's not going to have it?*

"I started packing my bags and then he got all huffy, grabbed me by my arm and slapped me and then pushed me down. I said, 'Oh, no, we're not having any of this shit!' We could argue forever, but when he put his hands on me, it was on! I went to the bedroom and while he was trying to figure out why I was going there, his brother tried to head me off. He was too late. I reached underneath the mattress and came out with a gun. I said, 'I'm tired, and I don't need to hear this shit every day or have anyone roughhousing me.' I came out of the bedroom with the gun and said, 'Everybody get the fuck out of my house right now.' My brother-in-law was trying to grab my hand, and people were standing in a daze trying to figure out what the hell was going on. My husband and I needed to reach an understanding. The people weren't moving, and I was done explaining. That's when I pointed the gun toward the ceiling and discharged. Twice.

"When the shots rang in the air, let me tell you, people started running out of that house in every direction, about forty going north. Melvin held his hands high above his head as he said, 'Come on, Diane. Now, you know we can talk about this. We don't need this.'

"I said, 'What I need is peace and quiet, and for my husband to support me when I'm trying to do something right. You don't want me to work, but you're laid off and there's no money coming in. How the hell are we supposed to pay the damn bills? I don't need to hear no shit about not working. I need to hear your plans about trying to find some work, especially since you don't want me to!'

"I could understand that he was upset about the loss of a good job but after several months he didn't need to be in the house feeling sorry for himself or trying to control me. He was a hardworking man. Instead of bitching at me, he needed to get off his ass and find a job. I told him I was not going to be coming home every day to find folks all over my house making it dirty and filthy. They ate up everything I cooked and didn't even save me a damn bite! I work and then come home to cook, clean up and hear him bitching too. That was not going to happen. Everyone in the house had to get their act together. I had Melvin's undivided attention for a change. Maybe the fact that I was still holding the gun had something to do with it.

"Melvin went to the phone and called my mom. He said, 'Your daughter has lost her mind!'

"My mom asked him what he had done to cause me to lose my mind.

"The look on his face told me what she had just said. I couldn't help it—I started laughing. Did he really think my mom wouldn't know me enough to figure things out? She asked him to put me on the phone. She said, 'Now, Diane, what are you doing over there? You know that you can't be shooting guns and stuff.'

"After I explained what happened. She said, 'If you need a break just come over here.' I spent a few days with Mom (along with my trusty .45 caliber friend). When I returned home I was in better spirits, and my friend found its way into the nearest river. By then Melvin had a job that he liked, and it was paying him a great deal of money. He was very happy at the job, and he was very good at it.

"I began having severe abdominal pains. First it was just nagging pains and then I went to the doctor, and he put me in the hospital for tests. He found out that it was my appendix. The next day when the hospital staff came to get me for surgery, I was unconscious. Melvin called my mom and dad and let them know that I was being taken to emergency surgery. My whole family came to the hospital and while they waited, they prayed. During the course of surgery, my heart stopped. My family, and even Melvin, was crying as the doctors let them know that they were doing everything within their power to make sure that I came through okay. The doctors later told me that I was the most stubborn person they ever saw. I didn't give up, and I was fighting to stay on this earth.

"All I can say is I thank the Creator for the tender hand of mercy and for pulling me through. I made a promise to myself that I was going to live life to the fullest. I can tell anyone that when you've had an experience like that, it makes you think twice about things. It makes you think about what's important to you. If you don't take care of self, and if you don't love self, no one else can do it for you.

"My recovery time wasn't long at all because I'm a quick healer. I never knew being at home could be so nerve-racking. I soon got bored with staying in the house all the time, and I was ready to get about and do things. Of course, by that time I was also getting fed up with Melvin. We were having arguments about petty stuff. When I started making trips away from the house, it was then that I found out that Melvin was also very jealous. If I wasn't home, he would call everywhere he thought I could be and ask if the neighbors or my friends knew where I was and what I was doing. I finally had to tell him, 'I'm not a child. I'm a grown woman and I'm also your wife, but I'm sick and tired of you calling all over the planet looking for me. You're going to have to get out of that. If you can't control your jealousy, then you and I don't need to be together.'

"He calmed down and things were fine until he came home one afternoon from work. It was one of those days that I was feeling horrible and didn't cook. Melvin got bent out of shape. 'Woman, how come you don't have anything on the stove? I'm hungry.'

"I told him, 'I'm not feeling well. If you're hungry today, you're going to have to cook it yourself.' He came over to me and said, 'Look, I want something to eat.'

"I replied calmly, 'Then find something in the refrigerator and cook it. I'm not cooking *anything* today.'

"He looked in the refrigerator and didn't see anything he wanted, so he went to the store. He came back and put the groceries on the table and went into the bedroom. I was sitting down watching television, minding my own business when he came back out. 'Woman, I told you I was hungry. I didn't buy those groceries just to be sitting over there on the table looking at you.'

"I said, 'Like, I told you, if you're hungry you'd better go in there and cook, because I'm not going to do anything today.' He came over to me, picked me up by my arm, pushed me into the kitchen and told me to cook something. I told him once again, 'I'm not cooking anything today.' He got really upset and when I went to sit down, he lost his mind and slapped me. Front and backhand.

"I was crying as I told him, 'If you raise your hand to hit me again, I'm not going to be responsible for what I do.' So he backed off and fixed his own dinner. After he was done, he laid across the bed and went to sleep. It was about 7:00 P.M.

"I waited until about 9:30 or 9:45 when I knew he was snoring and in a deep sleep. I took that nice, well-greased, cast-iron skillet that he used to fix dinner, opened the door to the bedroom, went in, and commenced to hitting him upside his head. He woke up fully startled and asked me, 'Are you losing your mind, woman?' I told him no as I kept right on hitting him. He jumped out of bed, and I was right behind him—still swinging. I told him, 'You son of a bitch, don't you ever hit me again.'

"He ran for the front door and I was right behind him—still swinging. Melvin had lost his mind earlier, and I was doing my best to help him keep it. He managed to get the door open and went through it, and I was right with him—still swinging. He ran from the house in his bare feet, butt-naked, dick swaying in the wind, and I was right behind him—still swinging. As he managed to pick up speed, me and my trusty cast-iron friend couldn't stay with him. He made it to a neighbor's house down the street. I'm sure he was a sight for sore eyes. If I hadn't been so pissed, I would have found it hilarious.

"Melvin called my dad, and Mevlin told his version of what happened. After listening, my dad told him he was lying because he wouldn't be outside wearing nothing but sweat and bare ass if he hadn't done something to me. Then my dad came over, and I told him the whole story. My dad called the neighbor's home where Melvin had made his 'special' appearance and asked for him to come over. My dad talked with both of us and told Melvin he was going to have to learn to keep his hands to himself. 'Don't call me anymore for this foolishness because next time I will take care of things.'

"My husband called his friends to come pick him up so I could have time to cool off. He called me a few days later to ask if he could come home. After making him wait for a few more days, I said yes. All marriages had their ups and downs, and I didn't think these fights were anything special. From that point on, Melvin was the one who did the cooking. He also started sleeping in something to cover his ass too. And that was the end of that.

"We moved to New York, and Melvin's personality totally changed. He became so wrapped up with others, and allowed himself to be used by people with poor intentions and he didn't even realize that our marriage had practically ended. After a couple of years of being in New York, I asked Melvin for a divorce, and he hit me so hard, I had pain in my lower back, and I was practically immobile for about four months. This was during the time I was taking classes at another business college, going to work nine to five as well as maintaining my own business. I had to let everything go while I recovered. Melvin said he would kill me before he let me have a divorce, and I believed him. One of his brothers had made the same threat and ended up killing his wife and himself while their children lay sleeping in their beds. The wife made the mistake of returning home after she was away for a few days to repeat her request. He went into the bedroom, came out with a pistol and shot her while she sat on the sofa and then used a shotgun on himself.

"Because Melvin let me know in no uncertain terms that there would be no divorce, I realized that I could never *ask* him for one again. I began to save every extra dollar I made. I started making plans to leave, but couldn't decide where I would go. If I went home, he would find me, or in anger hurt my family trying to get to me. I had to go somewhere that he didn't know very much about.

"I was tired of New York—apartment living, the bitter cold and the unfriendly environment. I had only met a handful of people that I could say that I liked talking to. I wanted a house, and I didn't want to hustle to make a living. I wanted my freedom from this man who didn't care anything about me. Melvin was comfortable with the way things were, and it didn't matter how I felt. I was convenient to him because he was illiterate, and I was his eyes and handled all of his personal business and affairs. I wasn't supposed to have any feelings. But I did. I started drinking to ease me into sleep every night.

"Some months later, I was introduced to Lori through one of the lecturers who was a part of my business. The lecturer asked me to send her some tapes so she could transcribe them. It was so easy to talk with Lori, and soon we were discussing the world. We talked on the phone for about a year before I went to visit her. I had a wonderful time in Chicago. Lori was very intuitive and eventually she asked me what was going on with me. I finally explained how I felt. She told me that her house was open to me and all I had to do was tell her how to help me.

"About thirteen months later, I packed as much as I could reasonably take with me to Chicago. Lori and I were on the phone at 3:30 A.M. talking about the trip. She said, 'I wish you could leave right now. Suppose he doesn't go to the Million Man March?'

"Melvin had already changed his plans twelve times, which meant I had cancelled and repurchased tickets just as many times. It was a costly process. I think Melvin knew something was up and was reluctant to go, but he didn't want to miss the event either. While Lori and I were talking, I got the signal that there was another call. It was my husband, and he told me that he was *still* in New York. I couldn't believe it! He hadn't left town because the police were keeping the buses from reaching his group in front of the Apollo Theatre. He told me if the buses didn't come within the next thirty minutes, he was coming home.

"Shock and fear ran through me, and I could barely stand.

"I hung up the phone and it rang again. I forgot Lori was on the other line. I said 'Lori, with your high-jinx ass! He's still in town!' I told her I had to leave right then because there was a good possibility that he would be coming home. There was no way I could unpack all my things in time for Melvin to get home, and I really didn't want to. There was no turning back now! I called a cab company and asked for someone to come right away. When the cab arrived I threw some of my bags out of the window. They were really heavy, and I couldn't carry them down the four flights of stairs. Someone was supposed to help me but, wasn't coming until the time I was originally supposed to leave. The cab driver got me to the airport in record time.

"I hid in the bathroom until twenty minutes before boarding time. I had never been so frightened in my life. If Melvin came home and found me gone, there was more than enough time for him to make it to the airport.

"When I tried to board the plane, there was an even bigger problem. I called Lori and let her know the people at the boarding gate wouldn't let me on the plane. Security had been beefed up due to a bomb threat. My ticket was in another woman's name so that my husband couldn't track me. I didn't have the money to buy a new ticket. I had sent all my funds to Chicago to secure a new apartment, and the rest had been used to pay all those cancellation fees. I would have to wait for the next flight out at 6:32 P.M.—*twelve hours later!*

" It seemed like an eternity waiting for Lori to get to the airport in Chicago. I called home and sure thing, my husband picked up the phone. Oh, shit! My heart dropped when the flight crew told me they couldn't hold the plane any longer. I learned later that Lori was in tears as she asked the people in line to please let her go ahead. She explained that there was a domestic emergency and that she had to get a friend on a flight leaving in three minutes. The people in Chicago were kind enough to let her go and the staff opened up the line early so Lori could buy the ticket. Normally, boarding closes five or ten minutes before a flight is scheduled to depart, but the New York crew held held the plane hoping they would get a call from Chicago. Lori paid for my ticket on her end as they were closing the doors to the plane on mine. I had never been so frightened in my life. People in general aren't too willing to get involved in domestic problems and there was no one in New York I knew could help me. I was going to be stuck here and my husband would have time to find me. The customer service people in Chicago called the boarding desk in New York. My flight was supposed to leave at 6:32 A.M. Lori paid for the ticket at 6:31 A.M. my time. The flight was closed. At the last minute, a sister from the New York boarding desk called to the crew on the plane and had them to open the doors. She, too, had been in similar circumstances at one point in her life. I hugged her and was escorted onto the plane. Talk about divine intervention! When I arrived at the airport in Chicago, for the first time in my life I fainted.

"When I finally came to, Lori, Brandon and I all hugged before we retrieved my luggage. I don't know how Lori did it, but she got to the airport in half the normal time. I learned later that Brandon forced himself to sleep when the needle hit 120 miles per hour because he couldn't take seeing all those cars going past him that fast.

"I didn't notice until we reached the car that not only were Lori and Brandon in pajamas, but Lori didn't have on any shoes."

Chapter 12

HOW MANY OF US HAVE THEM?

RAY

I still have to wait for Monday to get things straightened in my apartment. My aunt said that I should get out for a while and release some tension. She'll watch Janese for me. I wouldn't have asked her to do that, but I do appreciate the break. I'm at the nearest bar and call Chris to come join me. I haven't talked to him much lately. I've only told him that I needed some time to think and that I would call him soon. I did give him my new number and address and let him know that I was okay. This would be the first time he's seen me since my untimely departure from Shawna's.

Chris walked up to the bar and asked, "Man, what's been happening?"

"Shawna found Lori's picture and notes in one of the books I was reading and she straight tripped. She put us out," I told him.

"Who the hell is Lori? Have you been holding out on me, Ray?"

"No. She's a friend—a really good friend. I've been talking with her for the past few months, and I've learned a lot from her. She's the one who introduced me to some very interesting books," I answered.

"You're always reading one. What's up with that?" Chris asked.

"The stories are fascinating, and you can really understand where Octavia Butler and Sesvalah are coming from. Once I read the first one, I was hooked. I've learned more from Lori than from any other woman that I've been with. I have nothing to show for the three years that I've been with Shawna. No growth, no nothing. I mean, I know that we weren't married or anything, but I did love her, man. A few more weeks, and I would have been happy to give Shawna all the space she needed," I said.

"What happens in a few more weeks?" Chris asked.

"Her stitches come out, and her back would be well enough for her to return to work. Then if I left, the timing wouldn't have been bad for anyone. She could fend for herself, and I could have been prepared. She's not able to care for herself right now. So when she put me out, I knew she was trying to pull something. What pisses me off is that it's got my daughter in the crossfire," I said. "Chris, it was all I could do to keep my anger in check! If this is just a game, man, she's in for a rude awakening. Right now nothing is more important than my daughter. Shawna has gotten angry before and has threatened to kick me out, and there have been times when I've been so frustrated that I've threatened to leave, but we've never reached this point. She packed our things and had them sitting by the door like we were last week's laundry. For a while, Shawna really mattered to me. My daughter, Shawna, my mother and my job, they were all that mattered to me," I explained.

Chris immediately came to Shawna's defense, "Maybe she just wanted to give you time to think about things and when she cools off everything will be alright."

"No, man, not this time, Shawna went too far with this. After what's been going on, it's obvious that she's never really cared about me or Janese. I know she doesn't want to have kids, but she was at least nice to Janese. She was never really a mother figure; she was more like a friend to her. Having Shawna around did mean that there was a 'family' situation for Janese on a daily basis, and I thought that was important. I must remember from now on that if there is a woman in my life then it has to be a special type of woman. One who can care for a child and give her the type of love only a woman can.

"Shawna told me to get rid of Lori or we were through. Get rid of her, like she was a dog or something. I mean, aren't men allowed to have friends? You don't throw good people out of your life like that. I've been talking to Lori for months and that's all there is right now is talk. I need Lori's friendship. I don't have Shawna as a friend. I can't tell Shawna what I'm thinking about or what I really feel inside. She's just not that type of woman. She started in on me as soon as I told her that I wasn't going to move back in. The way things went down made me realize I couldn't have that happen to me again."

I want to tell Chris about Diane and the trip that was planned in April, but my instincts tell me not to. I always keep my personal business close to the chest. That's why Chris didn't know about Lori before now. This was the most information I've ever shared with him about my relationship with Shawna.

"Shawna has never looked through my things before. Why would she do it that night? It's amazing that she would find that picture on the same night I accidentally brought it home," I said.

Chris looked at me and said, "Yeah, that is something. Real fucked-up timing. You have to be more careful, Ray." Chris stood up and started moving away from me. "Hey, man, I gotta visit the john. I'll be right back," he said.

Chris has a hard time working his way through the crowd. The place is packed tonight. I might not see him for a whole hour. I sip my drink and think back over recent events. Chris left his cell phone on the counter and it rings. Shawna's number pops up on the display. *What the hell is she calling him for?* This is his new number. How did she get it? I couldn't have given it to her. I decide to answer and see what the deal is. The background is so noisy here that she can't tell that it's me answering.

"Hello," I say in a low voice.

"Chris, where are you? Why haven't you returned my calls?" Shawna demanded.

I was silent and then I heard her say, "Never mind. You were so right. There's a lot of shit going down with Ray. That ungrateful motherfucker had notes from some bitch named Lori! I wouldn't have known a thing if you hadn't phoned me. I really appreciate you caring enough to let me know what was going on," Shawna said. "Chris? *Chris?*"

I put down the phone on the counter, and it hits me full force: I don't have Chris for a friend anymore. How could he do this shit? I mean, granted, maybe I shouldn't have kept Lori's picture and all, but why would he direct Shawna to the place she would find it? I can hear Shawna's voice angrily calling Chris's name. I probably would forgive him eventually but I would never trust him again.

My best friend since grammar school. We've been through shit and shinola and this is what it comes down to? The thought hits me that Chris was always watching Shawna. I understand. He wants me out of the picture so he can get with Shawna. I wouldn't appreciate it, but if he wanted her, he didn't have to do it this way. I mean that's normally crossing friendship lines to sleep with another man's woman. But men have forgiven each other for a lot more. Men are always looking at her, so it's no big deal for me. Shawna is beautiful to look at. It's living with her that's been hell on the rest of me.

Shawna and I argued so much about bullshit, that it was the only way we seem to talk. So I kept my mouth shut, made sure Janese was taken care of and kept my head in the books and hoped that when Shawna's stitches came out, things would get a little better. I look around and see Chris walking back toward the counter. For a second time this month I could feel my blood pressure rising as I remembered what he said…"You have to be more careful, Ray." Yeah, more careful of who I trust as my friends. Chris takes his seat and looks in my direction.

"Hey man, what's going on?" he asks.

I want to see how this plays out. I point to the counter as I say, "You have a phone call…"

He picks up the phone and looks at the display, and I'm watching him the entire time. He was quick, but not quick enough. I saw the flicker of panic in his eyes, but he tries to play it off. "Hey, Shawna, what's up?"

Shawna is so angry, she's loud enough for me to hear her through all the noise around us.

"Are you crazy? How dare you keep me on hold like that! What's wrong with you? Have you been listening to me?" Shawna said angrily.

"Shawna, calm down. What are you talking about?" Chris asks.

"I've been talking to you for the last five minutes and you don't have the motherfucking decency to answer me?" Shawna yells.

"Shawna you're wrong, I just picked up the phone right now," Chris explains.

She pauses for a second or two before she asks, "Then who the hell have I been talking to for the last few minutes?"

Chris's eyes met mine, and he knew what I figured out a while ago: Our friendship was over. Not because he wanted Shawna, that I could understand. It was for the way he went about getting her. He didn't mind causing me and my daughter some grief to satisfy his needs. I could never trust him again after that. I walked away from the bar and toward the door. I felt Chris put his arm on my shoulder to stop me. I had been holding back my frustration for weeks. Unfortunately, while I wouldn't hit a woman, Chris was fair game. I pull my arm back and hit him so hard he took a few people down with him. "Sorry, people. He had it coming," I say to those nearby.

I step over him to walk outside. I needed some more time to cool off before I went home. As I walk away from the club, my cell phone rang. I check the display, and it was Shawna. *I didn't want to hear her bullshit explanation either!* She's accusing me of having an affair and here it is she's got Chris sniffing around like a dog in heat, ready to do her bidding. I wonder if they've been sleeping together. Chris isn't always too keen on wearing condoms. I've got to make a doctor's appointment to see if everything is alright with me. Damn, what a mess!

I try to hail a cab to my aunt's place and then I remember what I am and where I am—a brother in New York. Getting a cab will be virtually impossible. I start to walk toward the subway, and Chris comes up behind me and tries to talk with me.

"Chris, go somewhere, man, and leave me the hell alone," I say as I put some pep in my step.

"Man, it's not what you think," Chris says, trying to defend his actions.

I had to stop when he made that statement. "What do I think, Chris? That you've been fucking around with Shawna. Well the thought had crossed my mind. I mean how did she get your number, Chris? It's a new number, and I don't even have it yet."

"Yes, you do, you called me this evening, Ray," Chris answered with confidence.

"I called you at your home number, asshole. I called you there because I didn't have your new cell number," I said as I look him squarely in the eye.

He looks totally dumbfounded, so I continue. "I'm remembering the times that you told me how fine Shawna is, what a good catch she is. Well I guess you should know. You've been dipping in the mustard and now I can't catch up. She's angry with me for having a friend and here it is you've been dealing with her and want me out of the picture. I could forgive you if it were just my life you were messing with. *Maybe.* But we're talking about Janese too. She's involved in this mess. This whole selfish episode with you and Shawna can fuck with the custody of my daughter. The investigators are coming out to see my living area and to interview Shawna. She even withheld my mail, and I missed the notification of my court case and the date of the visit.

"Your timing stinks, Chris! All because you want to have total access, and Shawna doesn't look like she's putting up much of a fight either. Well go right ahead, man. You have my blessing because you two were made for each other!" I said angrily.

"I've never known you to take responsibility for anyone other than yourself. You don't even take care of your own children. You're living with your mom and think moving in with Shawna will be easy. Let's see you step in and pay the bills. Let's see you do what it takes to keep Shawna happy. Because let me tell you, it's going to take a lot. You think that because her place is all laid out and she's got everything, things will be easy. A lot of what you see in that place is what I've put into it. It's going to take more than I've ever seen you give to any woman. Enjoy yourself because you got what you wanted. She's all yours!"

"Man, we've never done anything," Chris lamely responded.

"Let's hope my doctor doesn't tell me differently," I said.

"Man, don't be like that," Chris said.

"Be like what? Cautious? I have to be, man, because I want to live. You're the one who tackles women who give up pussy out of both panty legs whether you have a condom or not. I don't get down like that. That's why I stay with one woman. I want my dick to last as long as I do. If the condom breaks, I don't have too much to fear. I can't be arrogant and think that nothing will happen to me just because the woman looks clean and seems to have it together. I tell you all the time about that shit, but you only listen to what you want to hear. That's fine when it's on you. But this is my life you're fucking with. I mean I do things with that woman that you wouldn't believe." The memory of it has me more than worried. I'm downright *scared*.

"Ray, I never had sex with her," Chris said. "I swear, man. We haven't gotten that far." Chris' eyes begged me to understand.

I understood him just fine. "But it sure hasn't kept you from trying. Has it, Chris?"

I arrive at my aunt's and find that she's resting, and so is Janese. I sit alone in the dark and try to think about things. Between the anger, the hurt and the uncertainty, my mind is so jumbled that I can't quiet my thoughts. I don't know what the hell to do.

I look in on Janese again, and I think that maybe I should place Janese in her grandparents' care. They can provide a more stable environment. Everything I do seems to fall back into my face.

Even my coworkers are tripping because they've basically seen me in the same outfits for the last two weeks. Shawna destroyed all of my clothes, except those, and with trying to secure the apartment and things for Janese, clothes for myself were last on the list. I actually had to wear a plaid shirt that someone gave me as a gift—that person didn't realize that I hate plaid—and overalls. Damn! I knew I hit bottom when my friend Eric—called me Farmer John and asked what I was growing that day. I'm not growing anything, but I sure have enough shit going on in my life to fertilize a few acres.

I haven't called Lori and Diane in days, and I know they think that I've forgotten about them. I always call them at least twice a day. I just haven't had the time. I want to talk about what's going on, but I can't let them know that all this is going down. They have their lives together, and it seems that every time I talk with them I'm presenting another negative aspect of my life. Come to think of it, I haven't received a call from them either. I'm always the one to make contact first. Is it like that with all women? Men have to keep making the effort? I'd better call just to let them know that I'm still alive.

"Lori?" I say when she picks up the phone.

"Hi, honey, how are you?" she asks.

"Kicking, but not too high. How are things on the Chicago front?"

"Not a whole lot going on. Diane and I wondered what was going on with you when you hadn't called us. It's not like you," she replied.

I was silent before I spoke. When I did, all of my

anger came to the surface. "Well you could call me sometime to check up on me, you know," I said angrily.

"Ray, I sent you an e-mail the other day, and you didn't respond. I also left you a voice mail, and you didn't call back. I try not to bother you because I know you get busy at times, and I don't want to disturb you. I normally wait for you to call first because then I know you're not too busy to talk," she said softly.

I was still angry as I said, "Did it ever cross your mind that's why I gave you two my cell phone number? Maybe I want to be disturbed by you sometimes? Maybe I would want to hear from you first for a change? I mean I'd think that you would like to stay on top of things knowing the services that you expect from me when I come there," I said. "There's a lot of things going on with me right now and it would be nice to know that you thought of me first for a change. I mean you always talk all this positive shit and not once did you dial my cell phone to reach me and see how I was doing. Positive thinking works fine for you because you and Diane have your lives together. Well I've been saying 'I deserve everything good that comes to me' and 'I am willing to change.' My change has come alright and none of it's been good."

Lori was silent during my entire tantrum. When she finally spoke I knew I had done some serious damage. The hurt in her voice was so evident.

"The services we expect from you?" she whispered. "The *services* we expect from you?" Her voice rose, "Ray, what the hell is wrong with you? I haven't done anything to you for you to use that tone with me. Or for you to say that to me. If you're spoiling for a fight, you won't get it from me. It's my birthday. My boss gave me the day off, and I'm at home enjoying myself. I've got better things to do with my time than listen to you talk about bullshit. I'm not for arguing or fighting with anyone about anything today. *Services?* We didn't order you from DicksRUs. If so, I'd asked for a large at medium charge because you're acting like a small order right now. You've misunderstood a lot of things, Ray, and I should let you go before you say something else, and I totally snap. Good night and good-bye." Lori broke the connection.

Damn! I've been so wrapped up in my problems that I totally forgot Lori's birthday. Why did I say those things to her? Where did those words come from? Lori and Diane aren't the ones who have been kicking me while I'm down.

DIANE

I watch as Lori puts down the phone. I walked in on the last sentence of the conversation. Her voice and facial expression let me know that something is very wrong.

She's silent, and the look on Lori's face has me worried. I put my hand on her shoulder and she turns to me and says, "I don't want to go through this process again, Diane. It hurts too much. We've put quite a few men up against The List—all good ones and not one single man can handle it. I'm beginning to believe that maybe we should split the requirements among two men—sex from one and love from the other."

I realize we're on a raw subject here and I have to tread smoothly. I don't want Lori to lose sight of our goal and start settling for less than what we want. "Lori, we don't want to deal with two men at one time," I said in my most comforting voice. "It would take a lot out of us and it won't serve our purpose. It's hard enough to keep up with the history of one dick, and for our health, taking on two men at the same time is not something we should do." Lori nodded absently, and I realize that she was barely listening to me. It was time for me to listen to her. I asked,

"What happened, Lori?"

She told me about her conversation with Ray and I felt my anger rise. I would definitely have to speak with him.

Lori was thoughtful for a moment, and her hurt and disappointment became obvious. She lowered her head as she said, "Diane, we've told Ray more about ourselves than any of the others. I believed that he could work because he was so willing. Now, I don't know what to think."

I rubbed her shoulders and tried to calm her, "We can't give up, Lori. What we want will take a while. We must be patient and not give up so quickly on Ray," I said. "Men have a harder time dealing with things when everything's caving in on them. It's especially hard when they feel they can't talk to anyone about it. Most men keep their feelings inside. Let's not kick him to the curb so easily."

"He's been able to talk to us about everything else. Why not this?" Lori countered. "Maybe we could understand what he's going through. What he said hurts, and I never wanted to go through that again." Lori lowered her eyes, and I knew Ray had opened an old wound. I wanted to kick his ass. What the hell was he thinking?

"I know, Lori," I said as I held her hand. "Sometimes when people are going through some things, they take it out on the people closest to them. It's not fair, but that's the way it happens. They feel that if we love them, we'll still be there for them no matter what. Sometimes people stick with a person and sometimes the hurt is so bad that they part.

"Ray is going through a lot right now, Lori. I can understand it because I've been where he is, and I know it's hard. I know he plucked a serious chord with you, but he didn't mean what he said to you. We have to learn now to hold true to our word and love him unconditionally. Not just when he's writing you poetry or stories or when he's calling you several times a day. Not just when he's making you feel good. Unconditional love means we can stick it out even when he shows his ass sometimes. But if we see a little too much ass, too many times, then that means we give that unconditional love at a distance, and move on. Don't give up, Lori. I really feel that he is the one. No matter how things look right now. It's going to be alright," I said reassuringly.

Lori laid her head on my lap and said, "Maybe the real problem is that in my mind and heart, I don't believe that I can have a harmonious, loving and peaceful relationship with a man. Maybe I still don't feel I can be truly loved by one. What we want is something that maybe Ray or any man can't give us," Lori says. "I want to know that everything will work out between all three of us. Maybe that's not something Ray's willing to do. It's been all or nothing for me. You hold your feelings in reserve, day by day. That's how you are. I feel that most times I've given my all toward this, and right now I'm more unsure about things than ever. It was so much fun in the beginning, the process of getting to know each other and working through some things. Now that it's getting down to the wire, things are getting kind of strange. Two months from now, Ray is supposed to meet us. I remember a time that my biggest fear was waiting for him in the airport and him not showing up. I didn't realize that there was something else to fear, that maybe what we want can't happen at all. Maybe what we're asking for is too much for any one man."

Ray

My cell phone rings, and I see that it's a Chicago number. Thank God! I can set things right. "Lori?" I said.

"No, it's Diane," she said coldly. What the hell just happened here? It's Lori's birthday, and she's in her room pissed off. She didn't tell you off like she should have. She basically told me what you said, but I need to hear it from you. What did you say to her?"

Diane's tone of voice was enough to chill boiling water. Evidently, I had just written my name on an ass-whippin'. So I gave her the news just the way she liked it—straight and to the point. "I didn't mean to upset her, Diane. A lot of shit's been going down here, and I took it out on her. I really didn't mean to."

I told Diane my version of the conversation, and how I felt when I didn't hear from them.

"Ray, I understand your position, and I'm sorry that you feel that we weren't there for you during this your rough patch. That's not it. We haven't heard from you in a while. You went from calling us several times a day to not calling at all. The only thing Lori was commenting on was the fact that not hearing from you wasn't normal. Nothing else. We've been through this once before with Omarr and are reluctant to go through it again," Diane says.

She took a deep breath before continuing. "What we mistook for inconsistency was actually your way of turning your thoughts and feelings inward and blocking everyone else out. It happens. When you gave us your phone number, it was because you wanted us to be able to contact you during your trip to Memphis. At least, that's what we understood it to mean. I'll admit, we were wrong. But basically we know that we have more time on our hands than you do. You only call us during the week because of your living situation, and we understand that. When you call us, it means that you're available to talk with us with no interruptions.

"You've always been the one to state that you bring nothing but problems to us. But Lori and I never see it that way. If I hadn't gone through what I have, then I wouldn't be the person that I am today. I would be a hypocrite to deny you that process," Diane said. "Believe me, the things you're going through will make you a stronger person. We wouldn't kick our friends to the curb because they have problems. All people have problems to a certain degree, including us. If we made it a habit of getting rid of people when they have them, we wouldn't have any friends—or family for that matter."

"Diane, is it possible that I can talk to Lori right now?" I asked.

"She's resting, Ray, and I don't think now would be a good time anyway. I think you should take some time before you talk with us again to make sure your head is clear. While I can take things with a grain of salt, with Lori it's a different story. You need to think before you speak, especially if you're angry," Diane said. "I know what's it's like for you because I've lived there, but Lori and I are not the same as the people you normally deal with. You can't treat us in the same manner. We show you respect, and we expect the same in return.

"Ray, take your time and do what you need to get things in order."

Are you ending our friendship, Diane?" I asked.

"I'm saying that you need some time to think things over and come to us correctly. Because if you ever have Lori in that state she's in right now, I will tell you about yourself in a way that you'll never forget." She gave me a mild warning, "And I *never* want to go there, but I will if if I have to. I hope you understand me. Good night, Ray."

The connection was broken…

RAY

I checked my voice mail and e-mail and found I had indeed missed Lori and Diane's messages. I sent roses and a card with an apology, and e-mailed Lori a few erotic stories to work back into her good graces. She responded each time with a short, simple "Thank you." I sent a message to Diane and she didn't respond at all. That let me know exactly where I stood. Damn! I've messed up with Lori and Diane—*big time!*

Chapter 13

BABY, GIVE ME ONE MORE CHANCE

SHAWNA

I thought Chris would at least call to console me. I've given him every sign that I am ready to be with him. After everything that has gone down, Chris won't even talk to me now. He hasn't returned any of my calls. Why did I even think about letting Chris in? I should have listened to Ray. The one fault Ray thought Chris had was that he was selfish and wouldn't take care of his children. Hell, if he won't take care of his little crumb-snatchers, how will he treat me? I should have thought about that before I went and messed things up with Ray. At least he always had his daughter in mind. At one time he had me on his mind too. I hate to admit that I've made a mistake but."

Ray and I did have some good times together. I've fucked up so bad! I've never seen him this mad, but I guess he has every reason to be. I could always get him to calm down with sex, but it's so hard to get him back when he stays away all the time. He wouldn't even come get the rest of his things.

Even though I've put him through a lot of shit, he hasn't once insulted me. He's definitely not the typical brother. He's always been a decent person. It's just that I didn't see it. I've got to get Ray over here and if we can talk face-to-face, I know I can get him to come back. I can be the woman that he needs me to be. I can be better to him than that Lori person. I still don't see what he sees in her.

I think I'll call him…

RAY

My phone rings and the display tells me who it is.

"Shawna, what do you want?" I ask, annoyed.

"Ray, I'm sorry. I don't know what got into me. I never really meant to hurt you that bad. I was so angry, and I wasn't thinking right. Please come over and let's talk about things. You still have some of your things here," Shawna says.

"No, you can keep those things, Shawna. There's no way that I'm coming there with the way I feel right now."

"I'm sorry, Ray, and you're right, I only did it because I wanted you to come home. You got your place just because I said I needed my space, but it was temporary—only until you got rid of that Lori person and started acting normal again. All you had to do was wait for a few days, and I would have let you come home," Shawna says defensively.

I let go and gave her a piece of my mind. "*Home,* Shawna? Was it ever really my home? Home is a place you feel is yours. Home is a place where you feel welcome. Home is a place that you run to when the rest of the world is through kicking your ass for the day. Home is a place where you can find peace, where you can think things out or talk things over. Home, Shawna? I don't think so. I think we've both been playing at this thing. Just existing together," I said.

Shawna interrupted, "It's just that everything was

okay until that bitch came into the picture and you started changing."

"Watch yourself, Shawna," I warned. "Lori is not a bitch."

"See, look at you defending her and everything," Shawna says, sounding hurt.

"No, Shawna, I won't let you call her that. Even after everything you've done, I wouldn't let anyone call you that either. Although I have every right to do so. Be honest, Shawna, it's not about Lori. Things weren't all that great between us to begin with. You were there for me when my father passed, but since then what have we accomplished? What have we done but live together, eat together and when you want to, we sleep together?" I ask her.

"Isn't that enough, Ray?" Shawna asked abruptly. "I can give you more sex if you want it. Don't you like being with me?"

"Shawna, listen to yourself, *you can give me more sex if I want it*. In other words you don't want it. What happened to you wanting me, too, Shawna? It seems the only person you've been wanting is Chris," I said accusingly.

"Ray, we never did anything," she protested. "He's never been here. I swear! We've never been together! I only want to be with you," she whined, and I could "see" the pout through the phone.

Shawna was not making sense to me. I had to set her straight. "It never seemed like you wanted to be with me. People who love each other want to share themselves with each other. It's really not about the sex for me anymore. How much do I really know about you, Shawna? How much of yourself have you given here?" I ask.

"Ray, I'll tell you what you want to know. Just come over, and we can work it out. I promise it can be the way you want it to be," Shawna pleads.

"That's the point, Shawna. I don't need to know it now. I wanted to know what was going on with you before today. How you grew up and what you've been through has a lot to do with how you handle things now. I needed to know it then so I could understand you better. It's too late. Knowing at this time won't help this relationship. Shawna, we are both used to each other, and I didn't expect any more from you than you were willing to give."

"Ray, you're talking so differently. You don't even sound like yourself."

I calm myself because getting angry was not going to solve anything. I lower my voice and said, "I've done some growing, and it's made me see myself and others more clearly.

"Shawna, I didn't get my own place to punish you for putting me out. I did it because I can't be put through that again. If I'm to take on the responsibility of raising my daughter, the first priority is her stability and my own."

"Ray, all you had to do was go to your mother's house for a little while," Shawna said. "Maybe letting Janese's grandparents have her would be the best thing. Then you'd have more time for yourself."

I can't believe the nerve of this woman! "You're missing this point, Shawna. When Janese came into the world, I couldn't just think of myself anymore. She should have me in her life. Grandparents shouldn't have to raise their grandchildren. They should be out enjoying life. I know how Angel would have wanted Janese raised, and unfortunately, I've allowed some things to slip. I shouldn't have to ask relatives to take us in. You and I should be able to talk things out without me or my daughter being displaced. I love you, Shawna, but I love my daughter, and she comes first. Things should never have gotten to the point that you felt it necessary to destroy my life."

"Ray, I'm sorry, and it won't happen again," Shawna said, sounding sincere for the first time. "I'll replace the things that I damaged, and I still have the money that I took from your accounts. Just tell your landlord that you made a mistake and you won't be keeping the apartment, and we can work things out. I'm sorry Ray, I'll show you how sorry I really am." It must have finally hit home how much pain she'd caused me.

"Shawna, you just sped up the process of something that should have happened months ago. We've both gone as far as we can go in this relationship. I'm sorry for the way things went down between us because I'm sure we could have handled them differently. Some man will come along and be exactly what you need. I'm just not that man anymore. I can't live the way we have been. We'll both pay for our mistakes. I just feel that I may take a longer time than you will," I explained.

"It's not just Lori, is it?" Shawna asked.

"No, Shawna," I said. "Lori has nothing to do with my decision not to come back to you."

"Then, it must be those books," she concluded.

"They are a part of my growth and that's something we all can stand to do," I said.

"Would you give me the names of those books, Ray?"

That was the last thing I ever expected from her, and I had to chuckle to myself. "I can do even better than that, I'll mail you a set."

"You really loved me, Ray, and I didn't see it when I should have. Ray, I know it won't change things but I really am sorry for what I did to you and Janese."

"I know, Shawna," I said compassionately, "I know you are."

Chapter 14

MAKING THINGS RIGHT

RAY

I called Lori and Diane, and for the first time had both women on the line…

"Lori, I know that I'm the last person that you want to hear from right now, but please hear me out. This call was hard, but I had to start making things right again. My first step was to be sure of what Janese wanted; the second step was to make sure that I still had you and Diane as my friends. From there, I think I can handle anything else," I said. "I was wrong and I'm sorry for what I said and the way I treated you. I should not have called you in the middle of so much going on. I should have waited for things to clear first or just sent a card or something. I never meant to hurt you or insult you. I wasn't thinking clearly when I spoke to you. I know I can't take back what I said, but I want you to know that I didn't mean those things. When you said the word *good-bye,* it really hit home for me."

I waited for Lori to say something, snap at me or just hang up. She was still on the line so I felt it was safe to continue. "There's just so much going on right now that I can't begin to tell you. The strange thing is that for the first time, the two people closest to me are people I felt I couldn't talk to. I thought that even the way I felt had to be kept inside because if I presented you with one more negative aspect of my life, you would give up on me. I know that I should have started by telling you that I was sorry for not calling and then giving you at least some explanation instead of attacking you the way I did. I always keep things to myself until I sort them all out. I've never had a situation like this and felt I could share it with those people close to me. Lori and Diane, you are both so important to me," I said.

"I realize that I don't deserve the chance to continue with our plans but even though I can give up on being your mate, I don't want to lose you as my friends. Right now besides my family, you and Diane are the only stable people in my life. I know I've only brought problems to this relationship and right now things are so messed up that I'm not making ends meet; it's more like the ends are meeting me. I have to know that you're still at least my friends. I'm going to need someone to talk to when all the smoke clears."

LORI

I listened and could tell he was sincere. I, too, had missed the opportunity to make things right by being stubborn. "Ray, I wouldn't give up on you just because you're going through so much right now. I wouldn't end our friendship because of that. I've been right where you are at one time or another in my life. I'm trying to understand that in a lot of ways, you are like Diane. She used to keep things inside until it hurt so bad that it turned to anger. When it turns to anger that's when the people you love hear about it. Even though I don't work that way, I understand that it works that way for you. When I feel down, I reach out for my safety net—the people closest to me—to keep from sinking. I think that's what you're doing by calling us right now.

"I'm sorry that you felt that we wouldn't be there for you when you're obviously going through so much. But you've known us long enough to realize that we're not that shallow. We're always here for you to talk with us. That's how our relationship started. I'm sorry for the way that I responded to you, too. I recognize that the flowers, cards and the stories you sent me were your way of apologizing and trying to put things back as normal as you could with me. Out of my stubbornness I rejected you and your attempts. No matter what your true intentions toward us were, from the beginning and even now, I was wrong for how I did things, and I apologize to you even if you don't feel that one is necessary.

"I had this same experience with my brother. I didn't forgive him because he didn't apologize in a manner that I thought he should. We never got the opportunity to make up because he passed a month later. It happened so quickly, and my family never saw it coming. He was so young, and I thought that young people didn't go out like that. I thought there would always be time, but it didn't happen that way. I felt so stupid and so guilty and that pain stayed with me a long time before I finally forgave myself. I thought I had learned that lesson. I know that if I can't learn to just let things be when a person makes an effort, then more painful experiences will come to me to help teach me about myself. I don't want to lose anyone else through separation of any kind for me to learn this.

"When you made the comment about the 'services we expect from you,' it really meant to me that you believe Diane and I only value you for your dick or techniques. And if that were the case, there was a whole lot of misunderstanding on your part. It made it seem just like that time when the guy I was seeing said I would have to pay for it. Like it is a professional service or something. I thought I had gotten away from that. If we wanted, there is still someone available to us for that purpose alone. We've already explained that we need something more than just sex. And, if you feel that it's all you're good for, then either you haven't been listening or you haven't been honest.

"When we didn't hear from you, it wasn't your services that were missed, it was *you* that we missed. We missed *you,* Ray. We missed you, your voice, your laughter and even your wicked sense of humor. I miss it even when it gets down and dirty, and the only way for me to fight back is to laugh. I approve of you the way that you are, and you are important to me too. What Diane and I need is you, and at times you don't have you to give. That's a hard one to take in, Ray."

RAY

"I love you both unconditionally, whether I'm with you or not. I enjoy having you in my life in this way. And if I can't give you that much then I shouldn't expect it to come back to me from any source. I only hope you hear my words and accept my apology and know that I really care for both of you."

"Lori, do you forgive me?" I asked.

"Yes, Ray, if you will forgive me as well," she said.

"You don't know how much I've wanted to hear that, and yes, I do forgive you, Lori. Things are going to work out somehow—I can't figure in what way, but they will."

"I love you, Ray," Lori said. "And as much as I can help, I will."

There was complete silence and after a sharp intake of breath I said, "I love you too, Lori, and I love you, Diane."

"I love you too, Ray," Diane said sincerely.

"That's more than I ever expected either of you to

say right now even though I needed to hear it. I also need to know if you really mean what you said? I mean not just that you love me."

Diane spoke up. "Ray, what are you talking about? We've said so much over the past few months."

"I mean about making room in your lives for me. I'm getting my life in order here so some changes can be made. I need to know what direction I should be moving in," I said.

"Yes, we meant it, Ray," Diane says. "If things come to that. Everything is up to you at this point. We want this to work either way. It's a lot for us both to accept a person physically. It's easier to get to know a person mentally on a surface level—but striving for something deeper seems to mean allowing for absolute trust. There's so much involved with being intimate with a person. I mean outside of body part to body part, we're talking, kissing, licking, sucking or whatever! I can't see me doing that to just anyone, things being the way they are," Diane said. "Why do you think I had us wait until April for you to come here?"

"I thought you were giving us time to get to know one another," I answered.

"Yes, that's true, but we were also giving you time to make decisions in your life. It gave you time to decide what you really wanted. We knew once you did that, your expectations for yourself would become higher. Only then would you truly feel that you deserved to have a better life or fulfill your dreams and also to be with us as more than just friends," she said. "Ray, tell us what's going on, maybe we can help…."

I told them what had been going down and then I told them how my day started. I had a talk with Janese and asked her if she wanted to stay with me or with her grandparents and visit me on the weekends. What I didn't want was to hold on to her, especially if she felt more comfortable with her grandparents, just because I fear losing her. Her answer was enough for me to know that I should continue to fight for her.

Lori and Diane switched into gear. Diane asks for me to get a pen and some paper.

"First," Lori said, "fax me a copy of the documents you have for your case and let me see what can be put together on this end. Second, go to the police station and tell them what happened with Shawna. I believe there is some kind of report they can fill out for it. I believe it's either criminal mischief or fraud. I'll check with my boss tomorrow so I can be sure. Submit the report to the gas and electric companies and to your landlord. The companies will have to turn the services back on without the hassles they've been giving you. Your landlord will keep watch for strange requests or strange people lurking around your apartment. She'll probably be more understanding if you're late with next month's rent."

"Lori, I've already done the obvious things and put security codes on my utility and bank accounts. I made sure that it's not a number that's common to anyone close to me."

She said, "I was just going to suggest that very thing. Come to think of it, your recording equipment is still under warranty so if you send it back to the manufacturer, they will probably fix it at no cost. It might be something minor that was done to it. It will be a lot cheaper to repair than purchasing new equipment."

Diane quickly offered her help. "There's a clothier called Elvin's at the Mart, ask for Brother Elvin and tell him Ms. Dee is still wearing his favorite watch. He'll provide you with whatever you need because he owes me a major favor. Brother Elvin gets there at 7:00 A.M., so you can go there on your way to work. I only ask one favor: please keep my location confidential. I know he's going to ask you and if he does, just let him know that I'm doing well and send him my love.

"I promise, Diane. I'll be careful. I'm sure that looking like a million bucks will give me the extra confidence I need to sit down and talk with my boss. I want to explain the situation, not in great detail but paint enough of the picture for him to grasp that it's not my inability to do the job, it's the recent upheaval in finances.

Diane said, "Be upfront and to the point and let him make a decision from there. Look in the mirror when you're done talking with us tonight and say, 'The Lord is my Shepherd, I shall not want.' State the outcome of what you want to happen. If you truly believe that you shall not want, then your life will show it. You said that you were willing to change, and your life now reflects that. You also said that you deserved everything good that comes to you and it should reflect that too. Believe it and watch and see what happens."

Diane was right. Before I was just speaking the affirmative statements and not believing them. It was time for a change. "I'll be right on top of things," I said. "You've both given me another source of inspiration today. I'll call you and let you know how things are going. Now I can stop shaking my head in disbelief, and start moving my ass to get some relief."

Lori laughed and said, "Well at least your poetic side is still in working order.

"And that ain't all," I said, laughing with her.

Lori's voice changes, "Really? Do tell?"

I immediately sober up. "Lori, don't start with me. I don't need to be thinking with *that* right now! I heard both women laugh, and I joined in. Their laughter is something that can always lift my spirits.

That night I made my own list of what I wanted to

happen and what I wanted to experience. I started saying my affirmations with a lot more power and force than I had been. I also made a list of the people who mean the world to me. I started feeling lighter. I knew everything was going to be alright.

I woke up first thing the next morning and was ready and raring to go. Unfortunately Janese was a little groggy and was moving kind of slow. I had things to do so I had to usher her every step of the way. I looked in the mirror and said, "The Lord is my Shepherd, I shall not want. Today will be a peaceful and successful day for me. I deserve everything good that comes to me. Thank you for my daughter, for Lori and Diane and my mother and my aunt. They are truly blessings in my life, and I am a blessing to them."

On that note, I felt ready to conquer the world....

Chapter 15

GOT MYSELF TOGETHER

RAY

*T*he day has been full-speed ahead and I felt like I was flying. Things have been happening in ways I never imagined.

Lori's boss called a friend of his in New York to take my case, and Lori forwarded my information to her and promised that she would handle any document preparation or research. My lawyer, Ms. Bestone, filed an appearance to inform the court that I had retained a private attorney, and I wouldn't be handling the case on my own anymore. She then filed a motion to vacate the judgment against me and asked for a continuance to give her time to review my case and build a strategy. It did a lot of good to know that she's one of the top lawyers in family practice, with a better reputation than the one Angel's parents hired. Things are definitely looking up!

When Ms. Bestone asked my intentions, I told her that I would like to retain full custody of Janese and if possible, I would like for Janese to be able to spend time with her grandparents if they can be friendly about it. They were really being mean about things because in some way they blame me for Angel's death. Angel and I were going to be married before Shawna came into the picture, and

Angel's parents felt that if I wouldn't have broken up with her, she would never have been with the man who killed her.

Her parents are making me pay for Angel's death, and it's not fair. I loved Angel, but the truth is we should never have thought about being married, even for Janese's sake. We were not mature enough to handle the responsibility of marriage, or for that matter, raising a child, but the child was already on the way. Marriage would have made an unexpected situation worse and complicated the situation. We just weren't ready for it. We were breaking up before Janese came, and when I found out Angel was pregnant, I stayed in the relationship two years longer than I should have. One thing is for sure, I love my daughter and want to do what's best for her. She wants to remain with me, and I will fight Angel's parents for my right to do so.

Ms. Bestone listened intently and after I was done explaining, she said, "Would you be open to sitting down with Angel's parents and their counsel and expressing that? I can set up an informal mediation and maybe we can all come to some common ground rather than dragging everyone back and forth to court. If they're not willing to do this reasonably, then we'll hit them with everything we've got. I'll let them know that I'm the lawyer who can give you a fair shake."

I appreciated her strategy. It showed that lawyers are human too.

After completing the other tasks on my things-to-do list, I also made an appointment with a doctor to have some tests done. Even though I didn't believe that I had any sexually transmitted diseases, testing was part of Lori and Diane's requirements. With everything that had been going on lately, I wasn't as sure of the results as I was a few months ago. Lori was right, men don't see the doctor like they should, so I also decided to get a test done for diabetes. Lori told me how her brother died. He went into a diabetic coma and never came out of it. She said he never went in for checkups so he didn't know that he had diabetes. Lori had urged me months ago, and I hadn't. If I'm going to live, I want it to be in the best health possible and part of that is knowing what's going on with my body.

The plan was to have the lab forward my test results to Dr. Gervais—Lori and Diane's doctor in Chicago. Lori and Diane's test results were to be forwarded from the lab to my doctor in New York. It took forever to find a doctor that would work for me. Believe it or not, I chose a female doctor. I figured if anyone needed to see the "real me," deliver my results, or handle the family jewels, it had to be a woman.

All was going well in Dr. Taylor's office until she said, "Turn around and bend over." I immediately took steps to cover my ass (literally). She laughed and said, "I only want to check your spine alignment." Now you know I thought she was trying to check something else—and that wasn't happening.

I know that Lori and Diane have stated that when I come I will be visiting them as a friend this time, just to get to know them. But I'm becoming more like them. I like to plan for what I want to happen. When they receive the results, they'll know that I'm serious.

I was down to the most dreaded thing—speaking with my boss. I have to tell you that I was not looking forward to it. I was about to give him a full serving of what he didn't take to kindly—bullshit.

I looked at his nameplate on the door for a few moments and said my affirmations. I walked into his office, and he asked me to have a seat. He looked me over for a few minutes before he said, "What's on your mind, young man?"

I took a deep breath and silently said, *I deserve everything good that comes to me* before opening my mouth. "Mr. Irving, I asked to speak with you today because I wanted the opportunity to explain some things. I missed the sales meeting in Memphis due to some unforeseen financial difficulties. Someone I trusted decided that my credit was her credit and maxed out my cards and wiped out my bank accounts. I really wanted to be there with my team, especially since I was the one who made initial contact with that company."

Mr. Irving's facial expression became thoughtful. "Hmmm. Sounds like woman troubles."

I could only smile inside. What would *he* know about it? He might have been a hard-line in the office, but he's been married for thirty years and his petite five-foot-one wife, Therese, ran everything outside the office. Let her tell the story, there was no trouble as long as Mr. Irving recognized *her* authority.

"Yes, it's something along those lines, Mr. Irving," I said.

"Well I hope you learned something from this and be careful where you place your trust, Ray. I'm sorry that it affected your attending this trip. I really wanted to see the outcome of this meeting. You know, Ray, I've been thinking…"

Damn! I thought to myself, *here it comes.* I calm myself by silently saying, *I deserve everything good that comes to me.*

"…I remember how the clients in Chicago had glowing reports on your presentation to them. They said you seemed inspired and motivated to make things work. [If they only knew that Lori was some of that inspiration.] You worked every angle to get the deal done. I never really got around to acknowledging your hard work there."

Mr. Irving settled back in his chair and twiddled his thumbs. "Ray, after careful consideration, I'm going to give you a promotion, and a bonus based on a percentage of the Chicago contract, as well as a raise retroactive from November. I'll make sure it gets taken care of today." Mr. Irving gave me a figure and said, "I think that's fair...."

I don't know if my mouth dropped open or what. But for the first time since I started this job, I saw my boss roar with laughter. *I never expected this!* I finally pulled myself together and said, "Yes, I think that's more than fair." After a few minutes, he was still struggling not to laugh at me. He could tell I was having a hard time taking it all in. With a straight face he said, "I can respect that you approached me in this manner. You expressed your commitment to sticking with what you start. It shows loyalty, and that's one of the qualities I admire in all of the people here. I look forward to more good things from you, since the Chicago trip proved a great deal."

That word *Chicago* triggered an idea so fast that I didn't give it much thought before speaking. "Mr. Irving, speaking of Chicago. We're getting a large client base there, and our team spends a good majority of time flying in to maintain old accounts and to develop new ones. I believe the clients' interests [and mine] would be better served if we had a branch office in Chicago. It would allow us to venture into the outlying areas as well."

"Not a bad idea, Ray. Someone would have to pull the research and figures and put a proposal together for a Chicago office. Of course, you have someone in mind for that project, Ray? [Was that another smile from Mr. Irving?]

"Actually, Mr. Irving I was just sitting here calculating the extra time I would need to put in to have that project done by the end of the week. I have a couple of contacts that live in Chicago who would be excellent consultants for this project. They are very familiar with the market and the area. One of them worked at a major communications company before a merger not too long ago and is currently in the legal field. These consultants can help pinpoint what we need as well as help define a good marketing strategy. I was planning a vacation to Chicago for the last week in April and while I'm there we can narrow down our choice of locations." [Notice that I switched from contacts to consultants. Contacts are favors, consultants are paid—Lori and Diane deserve it.]

"Very well, Ray. Make sure your consultants submit an invoice for ther services and, we will compensate them for their time. It seems you have the resources, determination and the motivation. Ray, if you're willing to do that, the company will pay for your vacation expenses as well. We can consider it a business trip. We're going to need someone in Chicago who knows the intricate workings of this office. The vice president there would need to have experience in all areas of the company...."

I'm sitting there silent as he makes his decision. I don't have to sell myself on this one, I've worked here long enough. Eventually after he lets me stew for a minute, he looks at me and asks, "Would you be willing to relocate to Chicago and head that office once you've established it and staff it with your own team?"

I quickly said, "Yes." Maybe a little too quickly.

Mr. Irving stroked his chin and said, "Ray, if I didn't know any better, I'd say you have an ulterior motive here."

I smiled at him and said with total confidence, "Mr. Irving, this project will be to everyone's advantage. I see a lot of prosperity in our future."

I left that office with a raise, a bonus, a promotion, a vice presidency in the near future and an all-expense-paid trip to Chicago, all thanks to the helping hand of the Creator, belief in myself and advice from my friends. I truly feel that I deserve everything good that comes to me. After recent events, things were finally moving in a direction I could appreciate, but it was happening in a way that was truly only the Creator's touch.

I can't wait until I'm on the plane to Chicago! There's so much work to do, and I'm ready for new challenges instead of reliving the old ones all the time. I was tired of focusing on bills and debts (and the little nasty-grams that come with them). It's time to focus on prosperity, living well and enjoying life! I know that there are a lot of good things that await me in Chicago. I already have friends there, and after my test results come back, I need to see if I have lovers as well. I didn't know it then, but I didn't know everything I needed to know about the women I'd fallen in love with. I also didn't realize it, but my trip to Chicago would turn out to be an eye-opening experience.

Chapter 16

Day 1: Anticipation...

RAY

I watch Lori looking at the flight status board. She's absolutely beautiful! The whole package is a winner! Lori's complexion is medium-brown, she's about five-feet-seven, and I'd say about a size eighteen, with microbraids swept into a love knot. She has a figure that makes the aqua-colored dress she's wearing look like pure dynamite. Her sensuality has its own raw power. *What a woman!*

She looks at her watch and then looks in the direction of the last few passengers getting off the plane. I was supposed to be at that gate, but there was a problem with instructions from the tower, and the passengers that are coming through right now are actually supposed to be at the flight gate I just came from. She holds her head, and the set of her shoulders shows her disappointment. Lori thinks I didn't come.

I haven't said anything because I'm taking in her beauty, her grace and her sensuousness, all of which show in her walk and the way she carries herself. I'm also afraid to open my mouth for fear that all I can do is stutter. She takes a deep breath, composes herself and then she walks right past me toward the exit—without even seeing me.

I call out to her, "Lori," and she turns and looks in my direction, not really seeing me at first. She's not expecting to see me where I am. The realization hits her and she asks, "How? What are you...? Ray?"

Her voice is so breathy and sexy that I can feel myself stir. I can't say anything so I hold out my arms to her, and she comes into them. Lori is beautiful inside and out. She is all woman, and there is no mistaking that. *Good Lord!* What I feel when this woman is in my arms means that there is no way that we can ever just be friends. I want her in every way! Lori and Diane have been there for me when no one else has. I notice the looks that people are giving us but I don't care. I'm taking in the scent of Pheromone perfume, the sweet, sensuous smell of it is really doing things to me. I can feel the heat coming from her and the slight trembling of her lips and body.

"Ray, we can't be this close again while you're here. Okay?" she whispers in my ear while pulling away from me.

Thank God, I'm not alone in what I feel! I know that this was supposed to be a friendly visit, just to make sure there's no pressure on anyone. Lori and Diane have my test results and know that our options are unlimited. They said we could all decide if there needs to be a return visit for a more intimate encounter. I want to let Lori know that I understand their point, but I need more than just friendship.

I pull her to me again and brush my lips across hers and I feel her take in her breath. I run my tongue across her bottom lip, asking them to open for me. I plant my lips softly on hers, and she responds. Then I kiss her as if I'm savoring a good meal—slowly, completely and passionately. There's the taste of strawberries on her lips and chocolate inside them. *Lord, have mercy!*

We finally break long enough for her to say. "It's

so good to finally see you, Ray. Welcome to Chicago…."
Lori makes a quick phone call and judging by the
conversation, it must be Diane. I'm standing a slight
distance away from her, but I hear the words *prepare*
yourself and then she looks in my direction, "He's changed
the plans, and I think we're in trouble. This man is
magnificent! He's six even, about 220 pounds, muscular
and all of him is pure milk chocolate! He's also very
handsome. Can you change from a room to a suite by the
time we get there?" Don't forget to move the items from
the kitchen too…"

The drive to the hotel is really trying. My friend
keeps wanting me to start something right in the car. It
doesn't help that I can't stop kissing Lori either.

We finally arrive at the hotel and Lori is leading
me to our room. I'm a little nervous at the prospect of
seeing Diane. She wouldn't send me a picture or give me
a detailed description. I only know that she is different
from Lori in color, shape and size. What if the attraction I
feel for her is different? What if I don't feel the same way
about Diane as I do about Lori? I knock on the door and
hear a familiar voice call out, "Yes."

"It's Ray." I hear a slight movement as Diane comes
to the door. She peeks out of that little glass and slowly
opens the door….

Wow! This woman is beautiful too. She's slender,
but not thin, curvaceous, about five-feet-eight, one hundred
thirty-five pounds of honey-brown heaven. Enough to wrap
your arms around and feel the fire. She looks dynamic in a
black leather pantsuit! She's sporting a chin-length bob,
and it frames her face just right. Diane is wearing a
mischievous smile as she watches my reaction. All of a
sudden her expression changes and she meets me halfway,
and we embrace. It feels good to hold her and after a few
minutes I pull back to kiss her. To taste her. It's a deep,

probing, searching kiss. My friend below is giving me a very hard time. For the second time tonight I would like to abandon the program and start being wicked. Diane is wearing Destiny perfume, and the floral fragrance blends well with her chemistry.

I love the way she feels in my arms. I pull back and take her hands in mine and kiss her forehead. She reaches to put her arms around my waist again and she holds me and rests her head on my chest. I stroke her hair and her curves. *Lord, can I get enough of this?* She pulls back and places her hand over my heart, looks into my eyes and then kisses me again. I place my hand over her heart, and I kiss her.

I turn and see Lori watching us, and I extend my hand to her. Lori comes to me and places her hand over my heart, right next to Diane's. I place my other hand over Lori's heart. We don't have to say anything because we've just said everything.

I finally get a look at the room. The colors, the candles, the music and their warmth…it's all so beautiful, and I let go of my thoughts for a moment. The only thing on my mind right now is them. I take in the sounds of Alex Bugnon's "Missing You," and the timing is just right. Yes, I've been missing something—I've been missing out on the type of love every man needs to experience at least once. Real love…unconditional love.

I pull both of them back into my arms and hold them. Their fragrances are intoxicating and I'm getting a little heated while Lori starts trembling. Diane can see that the two of us are in trouble so she says the one word she hopes will bring us back into focus. "Dinner." I realize Lori's trembling is from another type of hunger, but now is not the time. Alright, dinner it is…

They take me to Don Pablo's Mexican Kitchen in Merriville, Indiana, and let me tell you, the food was something to write home about! I let them order for me since they are familiar with the cuisine. I start with a pina colada topped with toasted coconut and then Lori and Diane introduce me to a tender, tampico steak cooked over mesquite logs, beef enchiladas, Spanish rice and charra beans, ending with an apple pie sitting in warm brandy butter topped with vanilla-bean ice cream.

The meal is delicious within itself, but what makes it sensuous is watching them eat. Each women has a hearty appetite and is not afraid to indulge in front of a man. They have a graceful way of doing it, with none of the "Oh, I must show extreme ladylike behavior and leave half of everything on my plate because a man is here." I can tell that they take great pleasure in a good meal. I find out later that a meal isn't all they take great pleasure in.

Conversation is light and the mood at our table is one of anticipation. I am trying to stay focused on the meal, but I am not getting much cooperation from certain parts of my body. Even though the food was really good, I can't help thinking about what might take place later this evening.

I open the driver's door and look at Diane, and Diane looks at Lori. Diane wants Lori to drive because she had a few drinks. Maybe we should have kept the limousine. Lori jokingly looks in my direction and smiles. I smile back as if to say, "Not me, I'm new here! I need to be in the backseat where it's safe." A certain part of me really wants to do some driving. I relax my position so no one can see the hard-on I'm sporting. It sends the message that I am too tired to drive anyway. I hold open the door for Lori and she sighs and gets behind the wheel. I then open the passenger door for Diane and watch as she settles in. Alright! My not-so-secret is safe for now.

As we travel back to the hotel, we all remain silent. The smell of leather and perfume is quite arousing (as if I needed help in that area). I close my eyes for a moment, and then feel a hand brush my face. I open my eyes to find Diane smiling at me. I reach forward to brush my hand across her face and then take her hand in mine.

Lori is a fast driver, and we make it to the hotel so quick, it was like we never left. If I didn't know any better I'd say there is a reason that she wants us there so fast. The thought crosses my mind that it's been a few months for me, but it's been more than a year for them. As I open the door for both women, Lori steps to me for a kiss. Here we go! Diane is caressing me, and I practically lose my mind. After several moments out in the open, we finally make it into our room…

They both change into very seductive lingerie. Diane's skin glows with touches of bronze, and Lori's skin has a pearl essence shining through. They look so beautiful. I've always been proud of my sexual ability, but for the first time, I don't know what to do. Which woman do I take first? Will it make the other feel left out? I don't want to take both of them at the same time. Not for the first time. I want to savor each woman individually. Diane and Lori look at each other and then take the decision totally out of my hands. Was my confusion that obvious? Lori seats herself on the chair next to the bed. Diane gives me a smile that could only mean, "*Ahhhhhhhh*, me first."

The food, wine and environment have me totally relaxed and what Diane does next only makes things worse. This woman's hands are dangerous! I whisper, "Diane, don't make me too relaxed, I have to stay awake enough to take you both."

She says "*Shhhhhh*! Just lay back, Ray. It'll be alright."

"Diane, do you know how long I've wanted both of you?" I ask.

"Not tonight, honey. It's our turn to explore you.

Will you let us do that? Will you let us touch, taste and feel you? I mean you are dessert. All you have to do is lay back and let us take care of you tonight."

"Diane, that's not fair," I protest.

"You're right, Ray," she agrees, "but it's unfair in your favor this time. Let us please you."

I'm not too happy about it, but her hands are working me to a point that stress and tension are leaving me, and I can't resist her even if I want to. I'm given no choice in the matter—I'm in their hands tonight. I wonder exactly what that means. I'm used to being in control in all of my sexual encounters. Not because I want to, but it seems to always work out that way. I have never experienced a woman's lead before. After tonight I will never have a problem with this aspect of sex again. With Lori and Diane, there are no better hands to be in...

DIANE

As I start unbuttoning Ray's shirt, he lifts my red chemise slightly to stroke my bottocks. With each button I open, I place a gentle kiss on his chest. I remove his shirt, unzip his pants and pull them down. His hands are on my shoulders as I bend over so he can step out of them. As I rise, I place my hands on the outside of his boxers and slowly pull them off. He is rock-hard! I place his hand in mine and guide him over to the bed. I ask him to lay on his stomach and use a pillow to cradle his dick. He gives me this strange look and asks, "What are you about to do?" I laugh as I tell him, "You'll see."

He lays on the bed and I reach over to the nightstand and get a feather and some Honey Dust. The dust is edible, so I'm in for a treat too. I position myself on top of his buttocks. I apply the dust all over his backside and then with a firm touch, I start to massage his shoulder muscles in a rhythmic motion. Ray says, "Diane, this feels

152   NALEIGHNA, VEE DENISE AND KEVIN KAI

great. Please don't stop." I use the palms of my hands and stroke his neck and shoulders to release the strain. He has a gorgeous body, and I can't wait to explore all of it.

I tenderly move my thumbs up the small of his back, pressing on the muscles along his spine. He lets out a deep sigh and asks, "Baby, could you please do that one more time?" I do exactly as he asks and then move down slightly so I'm able to reach his lower back and that beautiful brown ass! His skin feels so good against the palm of my hand and his body responds to the rhythm of my touch. With each delicate movement, he moans with pleasure. I begin to glide my fingers down the sides of his body and over his buttocks. My hands part his thighs and I use a circular motion to stimulate his inner and outer thighs.

I stroke down to his ankles, and then back up his legs and calves. He says, "Diane, you're spoiling me. I won't want to move after this."

I lean forward and whisper in his ear, "You don't have to. This is your day to rest and be pampered."

"Baby, you are doing a wonderful job of that!"

I ask him to turn over and then stroke his face, chest and stomach. Finally, I take his hard-on in my hands, and I stroke and caress him until he reaches his first orgasm. I take the feather and dust his entire body once again. Lori has other plans for him…

I rise and Lori walks over to the bed, and I say, "It's your turn. I want to watch."

LORI

I'm standing before him in a royal-blue chemise. The anticipation is killing me! It's been so long for me, and I've wanted him so much. My stomach is doing cartwheels. Where did my courage go? I take in the wonder and length of his body, while he's doing the same to me. There are no obstructions to viewing that milk-chocolate skin from top to bottom. This man has a beautiful body!

I walk over to the bed and notice Diane is going to sit in the chair. I look back at her, and she smiles.

I straddle the outside of Ray's thighs and use my fingers to search his skin. I move forward to stroke his navel, stomach, chest, nipples, shoulders and finally his face. Such a beautiful face. He looks like an angel, but Diane and I know there's pure wickedness inside. I hold his face in my hands and search his eyes for a moment. I lean forward to kiss him and run my tongue across his bottom lip, and he stirs slightly. I gently suck and nibble on his bottom lip, and he moans. I love it! The salty taste of his skin mixed with the Honey Dust totally agree with me. I work my way back to the hairs surrounding his jewels. Boy, is it standing at attention!

I move down some and bend over to kiss his inner thigh and then his hardness. My fingertips stroke it, tease it and then I kiss it again. It's calling me, saying "Please put your tongue where your fingers are." But it's not time yet. He tries to reach for me, but I won't let him. I tell him, "Relax, Ray, I have this covered."

I place his hands back down to his sides. I'm so hot that my juices are dripping down on him, making him want to be inside me even more. I would love to place him inside me but it would be too quick for me. Between jet lag, dinner and the anticipation of it all—it's best if we wait until tomorrow and stick to the appetizers tonight. I linger on his beautiful, full lips—no mistaking him for anything but a brother!

I stop long enough to give his nipples some attention and suck them until he moans again. I put my hands under him to grip his buttocks and caress them. I'll have a longer conversation with his buttocks a little later. Now, down to that part that distinguishes male from female—it's still holding its own. Do I: a) kiss it again? b) suck it? or c) straddle it? Decisions, decisions! I look at him and ask softly, "Honey, what do you want me to do?"

His breathing is ragged but he manages to say, "Whatever you want to do. I'm in your hands." He's putting the decision back on me. I look at the entire length of his body and decide to go over it one more time with my lips and tongue. The Honey Dust mixed with the saltiness of his skin tastes so good. I cover almost every inch and then I'm back at his center. I lick him from tip to base. I take his balls into my mouth and suck them gently for a few minutes. He almost jumps from the bed. I remove his balls from my mouth so I can lick them, and my tongue goes up from the base until I reach the tip. His moans turn me on so I concentrate on this area for a few moments. I gently nibble, suck and lick on it and then I place my tongue in the hole at the tip to gently stretch it. His hands reach up to hold me, but I put them back down at his sides.

I ask him, "Do you like that, baby?" All I can get out of him is a moan but it will do! As I continue to lick him, I find that I'm ready to take him all the way into my mouth. I slide the top part in and gently work him along the insides. In this way, I'm letting myself adjust to his size because I can already tell he's not average. I slowly take him in to reach toward my throat. He moans loudly, and he runs his hands through my braids, pulling the pins out to let them fall down over my shoulders, and I take both of his hands and hold them down. Looks like I'm going to have to do this with no hands since he won't cooperate. I want all of him, so I lean forward and go all the way to the base, taking his entire length into my mouth. I hold him there and let my tongue and jaws go to work.

There's this little sound he makes from deep within his throat. It's just short of a growl. I love it, and I know he does too! I continue tasting up and down the shaft, stopping to concentrate on the tip occasionally. I remove him from my mouth and treat his dick with soft, wet licks. Finally, I position my lips and grip his buttocks, then I bring him all the way back into my mouth with one smooth motion. He's so hot and hard that I can feel the blood pulsing through him. He gives so easily when I wrap my lips around him. He tries to hold on to me, but I won't let him. Is he going to cum? As I suck him, I touch his balls and they're pulsing. Yes, he's going to cum.

I position my mouth in the shape of a tight little *o* and suck in my cheeks to give him the feel of being inside the walls of a woman. I cover my teeth with my lips as he thrusts in faster and faster. His moans get deeper so I work my jaws in a wavering, contracting motion and use my tongue to seal him to the ridges on the roof of my mouth. I pull him forward all the way into my mouth again and again and again. My mouth meets his thrusts, and our rhythm matches. When he releases, his body tenses as he grips the sheets and lifts from the bed. I lick my lips and stroke his thighs and then straddle his waist again. I reach forward under the pillow for a chocolate mint and put it in my mouth. I'm preparing for our next kiss and to get him well-acquainted with my lips and tongue one more time.

Diane applauds our efforts. I forgot she was here...

Chapter 17

Day 2: Getting to Know You

LORI

 Dawn begins to break. It's so hard for me to sleep with such a beautiful male specimen lying next to me. I feel his body leave the bed, and I'm missing his warmth already. He had a nice, soft grip on my hips, and his face rested slightly in my hair. I know he thinks I'm still sleeping, but I'm thinking about what happened yesterday. Last night was a total tease, and I'm still aroused. I was able to bring him to completion once more in my special way, before Diane put him to sleep. He fought her every inch of the way, but no one can resist Diane's massages. With my eyes half-closed, I watch Ray walk away from the bed. He's such a strong, handsome black man, with such a perfectly shaped ass! He makes a side trip to the chamber and after a while comes out sliding into his robe. He's shaking his head as he looks over to the bed. He must be thinking about last night too. He grabs a towel to dry his hands and then I watch him bustle around in the kitchen trying his best to be quiet. Whatever he's cooking smells good, and he seems very comfortable in the kitchen. He doesn't notice that I've shifted my position to get a better view of him.

 After he's done making breakfast, he walks toward

the bed. Ray abruptly turns and walks back to the kitchen, and I see him go into the refrigerator. What is he doing? I see him smile, and I know he's up to something. He's coming this way, but he stops to take in the sights. What does he have in his mouth? I can't open my eyes further because he'll know that I've been playing possum. What is he up to? He comes closer to me, so I close my eyes completely. I feel his breath on my breasts and then...I feel a sudden cold moisture. *What the hell!*

I quickly open my eyes and find that he's dripping strawberry juice onto my breasts. He then leans forward to suck it off as I stroke his head. "You wicked man!" I say.

He raises off the bed once more and signals for me to follow him into the living room. He takes a blanket that's lying next to the bed and closes the bedroom door. This time is strictly for us. After my own personal freshen-up trip to the chamber, I walk toward him on the sofa. He motions for me to lay on my back and then lays right on top of me. He kisses me passionately and prepares me for what he wants to do next.

RAY

As I begin to remove her chemise, she starts to protest. She wants to keep it on. At that moment, I realize that men have been more than willing to just sex her. She might have experienced some pleasure from them, but none had truly made love to her. I also realize that for years I've been playing at it myself. Maybe I hadn't found a woman that I could give myself to totally. I can't do anything about what I hadn't done in the past—but I can change right now.

"Lori, I want you totally bare before me," I say softly. I didn't understand it before, but Lori was self-conscious about her body and size. Even though she is comfortable with herself, for herself, it's different when I'm the one looking at her. I slowly pull the chemise over her head and now we're skin to skin. I can tell that she's switched perfumes and this one is lighter and sexier. This is our intimate moment, and I want her to know that I love every part of her body. This is who she is, and I want her and love her. I kiss her passionately as I pull her thighs around my hips and grip her buttocks. She's so wet that I really want to plunge right in, but I hold back, and I'm right at the tip. As I prepare to enter her something makes me look in her eyes…

If the eyes are the windows to the soul, then Lori's soul is right there on the surface for me to explore. I can see exactly what she's feeling. Her eyes and face are so expressive. If I am reading her correctly, Lori's soul is asking for healing. I look in her eyes so long that she closes them to try and keep me from reading them. It's too late, I saw everything I needed to see. Some say that a man makes love to every woman the same; and a woman makes love to every man differently. It was definitely time to change. What I first thought of doing isn't the way to go with Lori. I had to make love to this woman's spirit as well as her body. Not just to make her feel good but to make her feel whole. I can't let Lori close her eyes and shut herself off from me. I want her involved with every part of our lovemaking. I don't want her making comparisons or thinking of the past. I want her here with me right now.

"Baby, keep your eyes open for me. Will you do that?" I ask. She opens them and looks up at me. First there is a slight hesitation and then a frown. I say, "No matter what, keep your eyes open. Do you hear me, baby?" She looks uncertain, but I receive the answer I want to hear. "Yes," she says. I kiss her face, lips, eyebrows, forehead, temples, cheeks and chin. No part of her beautiful face goes uncovered. I want her to see this and know that I accept her completely. Somehow I know it's important.

The first rule of making love is know your territory and this was some woman. While other men concentrated down below, I was more than willing to go the distance. Lori is fully undressed and exposed to me. She doesn't want me to see how afraid she is. Lori isn't shy or timid when it comes to making love—her oral performance last night was truly the work of an experienced woman! I realize that her fear comes from what has happened in her past. She is waiting to see the signs of disappointment or rejection. She won't get that from me. Not now. Not ever. I lean down and slowly run my lips over her neck, shoulders, breasts and arms, and end with her hands. I pull away to kiss her stomach and navel. I love the taste of her skin and the smell of Mystic perfume. I'm already hard, and getting harder every second. I look up just in time to see Lori close her eyes. "Lori," I say gently, and her eyes open quickly as she says, "I'm sorry, Ray."

"Don't apologize, baby, but try to keep them open."

My hands massage her stomach and sides and then I caress her buttocks and back. I touch and linger mostly on the parts she's tried to hide from me. Finally, after a few minutes of massage she begins to relax and tears form in her eyes but they don't fall. She watches me discover her body and still looks in my eyes, expecting to see something that will never be there. I know how the average man claims to feel about women over size fourteen but I can't agree with him. This woman is luscious and she hasn't been made to feel that way. I love her just the way she is, and I have to show her this. I whisper in her ear, "No more of the past. Let it go. Lori. Please let me love you in my way."

The tears finally fall. She's been holding them back a long time. Longer than even I can know. I kiss her tears and taste them on her cheeks and embrace her. My dick is straining to be inside her. I want to be as close to her as humanly possible. A woman can enjoy foreplay for hours, but brothers are a different story. I've never had to wait this long before, but it's still not time yet. Lori needs this, and I need to do this with her. I never knew how much power there is in helping a woman to heal. I watch her slowly open herself to me, and I know that I can take her where we need to go.

LORI

I hear him ask, "Are you ready for me, baby?" I look away from him, but he gently turns my face back to meet his. He looks directly in my eyes and asks again, "Lori, are you ready for me?"

Oh, God, I'm not sure. I thought I was before. What do I tell him? I can't answer and I try to look away again but he won't let me.

"Baby, don't be afraid," he whispers. "I want you to know my touch, my feel, my smell and my taste. I want you to need this."

That's what I'm afraid of. I don't want to need him quite so much. It feels so damn good being in his arms! As he continues to talk to me, he runs his hands and lips over my body.

"Lori, you are my woman completely," he says and stops to look into my eyes. "Lori, do you trust me?"

I look at him and say, "Yes."

He strokes me softly as he says, "That was years ago. Let it go, baby." He holds my face in his hands and says, "You're stronger now, and no one can hurt you, baby. I won't hurt you." He kisses me, and it's all I can do to stay sane. He pulls away to whisper in my ear, "Relax, and let me take you with me, Lori."

I let go and bury myself in him and wrap my arms tighter around him. I'm not thinking of anything else but Ray right now. I pull back slightly to look in his eyes. He kisses me and slowly pushes himself inside me. I take in a deep breath, and he places his lips on mine. As he parts my lips to kiss me, I hear a low moan from within him. His tongue plays in my mouth, and the heat is flowing over me in waves. After a few moments, I can feel my cervix shifting, allowing him deeper access, and he keeps going. I hear a small whimper escape my lips, and a moan follows right behind it. I hold on to him as if my life depends on it. He responds by wrapping his arms even tighter around me, and he goes even deeper. I moan this time because it hurts, but it also feels good. I haven't been penetrated in more than a year. I should expect it to hurt. Maybe not quite this much. This man is definitely not average size! I whimper once again and he stops his movements and looks at me and asks, "Lori?" Was my body built to handle him? He's only most of the way in, and I can't feel his balls tickling my clit, which means there's more. "Are you with me, Lori?" he asks.

"Yes, I'm with you, Ray." He starts a slow rhythm, working me without pulling away. We're still holding each other close and I join his rhythm. Good Lord, this feels wonderful! He pulls away just enough to watch my face, and I look back at him. He can tell that I'm enjoying this now. He smiles and then kisses my forehead. After a few minutes, he decides to change the rhythm from teasing to moderate. My body has accepted as much of him as it can, and still there's a little more. He keeps pulling out slowly and working his way back inside. I grip my thighs into his buttocks and cross my legs directly behind him. I move my hips to meet his thrusts. After several minutes of a slightly faster rhythm, he runs his fingers through my hair. He pulls my head back slightly, not enough to hurt, but enough to distract me from what's happening down below.

He's forcing my eyes to meet his. He slowly works his entire length inside of me, and I lose my breath. What comes past my lips is a low, wavering moan. The pleasure is too intense!

With tender, searching kisses he touches my face, my neck, my breasts, covering as much of my exposed body as possible. He pulls slightly away but keeps himself buried as far inside of me as that last plunge will allow. My body trembles violently, and I can't control it. Would I really want to?

He puts his lips to my ear and lowers his voice to say, "You're my woman, Lori. All mine. Every inch of this is mine to please. Do you understand me, Lori?"

I can't answer because I can't breathe. God, what is he doing to me? I can feel him pull out and work his dick all the way in, and I'm shaking as the heat washes over me.

I finally manage to say, "Oh, my God, this feels so damn good!"

"Do you hear me, Lori?" he asks again.

"Yes, I understand," I say in a resigned whisper.

"Don't ever forget it, Lori." The power of his words penetrate my thoughts. I realize that one thing is for sure: I won't ever forget it.

RAY

I don't know what's come over me. When I see her pleasure, I want her to know that I don't want any other man inside her. I feel her heat, how tight and wet she is and then I see the signs of her first orgasm. It's in her eyes before her thighs start trembling. Then it works its way up through the rest of her body. Her orgasms are the most beautiful things to watch. Lori's body is like liquid in my hands and holding her so closely I feel it inside and out from beginning to end. Damn! *This is heaven!* She takes her breath in short gasps and what comes out are these little whimpering sounds. I didn't stop moving inside of her during her release and she manages to flow with me. I love every minute of it!

I keep working her body and she is right there with me. A few minutes later I feel her body tense as another orgasm comes over her. Women don't know how blessed they are. Multiple orgasms back to back to back! I want her to have as many as her body will allow. I hold her close to me as her body trembles once again...

LORI

I can't stop crying. I don't want him to see me like this. I feel so vulnerable. You'd think I'd never had some decent sex before. It's been good, but it's *never* been like this. My body is humming a precision tune! I need to get away from him so I can compose myself. I unwrap myself from him and make a beeline for the chamber.

Unfortunately, I'm not fast enough because he's right behind me. He pulls me to him and brushes his lips on my neck and I feel his hard-on right on my buttocks. I'm caught.

"Where are you going, Lori?"

I can't voice it at first because there's a tightness in my chest. I finally manage to say, "I need to be alone for a while. I just need to be alone."

"Why?" he asks softly.

"I don't know. I feel like crying and I want to be by myself. I just want to be alone right now."

"Lori you don't understand. There is no alone for you anymore. I won't let you do it this way." He turns me to face him and kisses me deeply and pulls me to him, and I slowly give in. There's nothing else for me to do. I don't feel the need to hide from him anymore. I'm not sure that he would let me even if I wanted to.

RAY

I watch as Lori buries her face in her hands and her body starts shaking uncontrollably. Her hands fall to the side, clinched into tight fists. She throws her head back and her face looks toward the ceiling. The sound that escapes from her lips tears into my soul! There's only one word that can describe it—*wounded*. I wasn't expecting this. This woman's pain runs deep. So deep. It's a release for her, and it isn't sexual. I run my hands over her back and shoulders and end by loosening her fists to hold her hands in mine. I look into her eyes as the tears flow freely. She's never been exposed like this. I know right now that I'm sharing something no man has ever witnessed. I will take special care with Lori because I love her. I hold her and rock her in my arms for a moment, until I'm finally able to lead her back to the sofa. Her body continues to tremble, and I tell her that's it's alright to cry. It's alright now. It truly is.

As I comfort her, I shift my position on the sofa and pull her with me. One of my legs is on the floor, with the other stretched out on the sofa. Lori is sitting in the opening with her head resting on my chest. I want to explore more of her, but right now is not the time. This time is strictly for her. She leans up to kiss my chin. I draw the blanket over us and I talk to her as she closes her eyes. I'm stroking her hair, face, back and hips. I want her to feel cherished, loved and conquered. She says in a voice that's just above a whisper, "I need to feel your strength. I'm so tired of fighting, I've needed this for so long. I want to surrender my spirit to your protection just for a while and not think of anything."

I know it takes a lot for her to say this. I kiss her forehead and say, "Rest, baby, I'll be right here. Her eyes are closing, but I must tell her before she goes to sleep

completely. "I love you, Lori. Don't forget that either."
Her eyes open once more as she takes that in. Tears flow
once again as she closes her eyes to rest.

Her heart, her mind and her body all have
experienced pain. Then it hits me: *this* is what I contribute
to the relationship. Comforting, loving and protecting her
are more valuable than *anything* I could buy her.

DIANE

I come from the chamber and find Ray and Lori
stretched out on the sofa. No wonder sleeping was so
comfortable. I had the bed all to myself. Ray blows me a
good-morning kiss, and I send one back. He points in the
direction of the kitchen, and I notice there's an excellent
spread of items to choose from. Ray must have fixed
breakfast because none of the items I see would be Lori's
choice to cook.

I help myself to a plate and motion to Ray and ask
if he's ready to eat. He nods, and I fix him a plate. Lori
looks comfortable and her breathing is slight. I can sense
that I've missed something but I don't feel bad about it—
although, they could have let me watch. I smile to myself
as I think about that and bring his plate. Judging by his
position, it looks like I'm going to be feeding him. We
begin to talk in low tones. I ask him, "What would you
like to do today, Ray?"

He has this wicked look in his eye as he says, "What
did you have in mind?"

I ignore his true meaning and smile as I tell him,
"Maybe we should take in some of the sights in downtown
Chicago: Buckingham Fountain, the Magnificent Mile, the
Sears Tower and then drive north on Lake Shore Drive to
the B'Hai Temple in Wilmette and from there we can play
it by ear."

He tells me that it sounds like a plan, if we can

wait for Lori to wake up. I look at him, and it's in the way he looks back at me that lets me know that whatever happened between them was good for both of them.

* * *

RAY

We're driving back to the hotel. Chicago is really a beautiful place to be. There's not nearly as many people downtown as there are in New York. People actually have room to walk.

My mind wanders back to a conversation I had with Diane a few months ago. I asked her if she fantasized. She told me that she didn't now as much as she used to. "My husband and I always had a normal sex life, but sometimes I wished for a little spontaneous action. My husband thought he reinvented the missionary position, and it was years before he would entertain any conversation of letting me be on top. I became accustomed to the way he did things but I always wished that making love was more eventful and fulfilling than it was. If I were younger I would probably try something new, but now…"

Age really shouldn't be a factor at all. I had to remind myself at times that I am several years younger than she is. That's why she's always so calm and patient. She has the looks of a woman ten years younger. Diane had years of traditional sex with her ex-husband, and it was time for a change. She was the adventurous type and age hadn't taken that from her. I wanted to show her just how wrong she was….

It's pouring-down rain. We're driving past a forest preserve when an idea hits me. "Lori, pull into this place." She parks, and I ask Lori and Diane to exit the car. They look at me as if I've lost my mind. Lori says, "It's raining cats, dogs and a few other animals, and you want us to do what?" I extend my hand and say, "Please, come out of the car, both of you."

Not one person is in sight, and I'm not sure it would matter if there were. I lead them to a picnic table. I turn to face them and begin to remove my shirt keeping my eyes on both women the whole time. They both look at me, then the surprise and shock factor leaves them, and they both smile and shake their heads. No words are spoken, but they both know exactly what I'm thinking, what I'm wanting and what I'm hunting for. Diane begins to discard her clothes, but I stop her and say, "No, I'll take care of that." I touch her face to feel the rain against it. She gently kisses the inside of my hand accepting what we are about to do.

I slowly bring Lori in for a kiss, and she looks uncertain, and I know what she's thinking. I tell her, "Keep your clothes on, Lori. You can watch this time." Is that relief I see in her eyes? She's not ready for this yet, but eventually she will be. I grab Lori by the hand and position her to sit on the table. I remember something Lori said in one of our conversations. She told me that she's always wanted to watch a sexual encounter as it happens. Well, here's her chance. I kiss Lori and then ask her, "Are you sure you don't want to watch this from the car?"

"Are you kidding? And miss all the special effects?" she says. "No, I want to see it all—up close and personal."

It's raining harder as I slowly turn Diane to the table and position her head and back on Lori's lap. I rip open her blouse to expose her bra. I look into her eyes and kiss her as I slowly remove her bra. She has the most beautiful honey-brown breasts, and they swell as every drop of rain touches them. I begin to suck and tease them. Diane grabs the back of my head as her buttocks quiver. I slowly begin to work my way from her breasts down to her belly button. I begin to lick and nibble at the small puddle created by the rain. I hear her say, "I never knew the rain could be so much fun." We all laugh but I quickly go back to what I am doing. I lower her jeans far enough for me to see those beautiful emerald silk panties. I pull her panties down for me to see the hairs leading to my treasure. When they are down far enough, I begin to lick the outside of her lips, but knowing where I was going with that, Diane grabs the back of my head to prepare herself for my tongue. I look up at her and smile. I slowly wrap my hands around her buttocks and begin to squeeze them. She gives a short sigh and a moan, fully accepting what I'm about to do. I place my tongue at the bottom of her stomach and begin to catch the raindrops as they fall there.

My finger glides slowly down to her center. She isn't expecting that, and she trembles slightly. I slowly circle her belly button with the tip of my finger. I work my way down to her clit and tickle it, placing one finger in her center at the same time, until I feel that sweet juice between my fingers. I stop and stand up. They both look at me. I take my fingers with her juices still on them and place them in my mouth to taste every drop. It's time. I take off her jeans totally and as I lean into her center, I'm ready to take off. I hear Diane say, "Ray, wait!" but it's too late, I'm already in there! I begin to put my lips and tongue everywhere my mind can think of: her breasts, her navel, her thighs, and eventually I nibble on her outer lips once again, and I work them out of my way and thrust my tongue into her center. I suck with such gentle intensity that she grabs the table and almost breaks off a piece. Diane lets out this loud, wavering moan as she cums. I begin to drink her like a vampire drinks blood from his victims. I look up with my face wet from the mixture of her juices and the rain. I turn my face up to the sky and let the rain fall on my face. I've always wanted to do this.

It's raining harder now and the thunder and lightning are somewhat intense. Our clothes are wet and sticky, but I'm not done yet. I pull Diane to me and turn her around so her back is to my chest. I begin to caress her and hold her close enough for her to know that there is a nice, hard piece of chocolate waiting for her. I begin to slowly lick and nibble on her ear. I discard the rest of her clothing. Her body is very wet from the rain. It's intoxicating! I turn Diane around to face me and pull her to me so I can circle her lips with my tongue. She opens her mouth to give me her tongue but I pull back. I place my finger gently over those sweet, full lips. "This is my time, baby. You'll get your turn."

I lift Diane, and our bodies press together as we engage in a soft but passionate kiss. I balance us both by bending my knees slightly. I lift her up higher so I can place her thighs over my shoulders. I then begin to run my tongue down her inner thigh slowly to her knee. She grabs the back of my head, "Don't tease me, baby," she says in a breathlessly sexy voice. All of her sweet, intoxicating juice is right there for me! Before I take it, I run my tongue slowly, circling her lips and then licking her center until she begins to quiver. Caught up in the moment, I thrust my tongue into her wetness. She lets out a deep moan of pleasure. I feel I am still not getting enough of her so I cup her buttocks and bring them forward so I can push my tongue deep inside of her. Diane is holding on to my head for balance and she wraps her thighs around my neck for leverage. I begin to nibble and suck on her clit, and she tastes so good. I feel her body begin to twitch. Can it be? Yes!!! She is beginning another orgasm, and I am *soooooo* thirsty. Another deep, sensuous moan leaves her lips as I begin to drink every last drop of that sweet juice that comes trickling down to me. Keeping my balance, I turn to face Lori with Diane still in the air, and my lips buried deep in that place. I slowly walk her over to the picnic table and lay her once again on Lori's lap.

The rain is easing up slightly. Diane watches me take off my clothes to reveal a serious hard-on. She sits up to take me into her mouth but I stop her. I smile as I tell her, "You can't taste me just yet." She looks at me and bites her bottom lip as if she's wondering what I plan to do next. I lower myself on to her and I grab her legs and lift them slowly into the air. I glide my tongue down the back of each leg, still teasing her. I leave both legs on my shoulders. I take my dick and circle her lips gently, slowly. Then as I insert myself inside her, a hissing sound leaves her lips. I begin to work her with slow, deep movements. She follows my lead as I plunge in deeper and deeper. She purrs like a kitten that's found its place to rest for the night. With perfect timing I quickly pull out as she begins to cum. I thrust my tongue back into her to catch every drop. "Oh, God!" Diane yells as she cums real hard, clinching the table in her hand. After another drink, I take her breasts into my mouth.

Still quivering from her orgasm, I feel her reach down to fondle my dick, and the atmosphere changes quickly. Lori is kissing and licking my chest as Diane takes me into her mouth. Lori works her way down slowly to join her. I begin to moan louder than I ever have before. Lori has taken me into her mouth while Diane pays close attention to my balls. I can't help but tell them, "Damn, that feels good!" Lori uses soft, wet strokes going down to the base and slowly back up to the tip. Diane has taken both balls in her mouth, and she starts working her way to join Lori, licking the base as Lori comes back down from the tip. I can't take it! The intensity is too much! I know Lori and Diane are not going to stop until I cum. At that moment, I release.....

Lori turns the heat to the highest setting in the car. Diane and I spread our clothes over the front passenger seat—we'll put them back on at the last possible moment.

Lori is driving in her blouse (and not much else). She informs us that we'll take the scenic route back to the hotel, which will give us some time to warm up.

Diane and I are seated in the back, and I'm cradling her in my arms. I whisper softly in her ear, "I enjoy taking you like this. You don't have a problem with it, do you?"

"Oh no, I like it like this! I want it just like this!"

She's ready, willing and Lord knows, she's able. I kiss her forehead and whisper, "There's so much more to come, because you're my love and my woman."

Diane looks up at me and says, "Yes, I am." Her words mean a lot to me, but her eyes say so much more.

I'm getting more possessive by the minute.

Chapter 18

DAY 3: TIGHTEN UP ON YOUR BACKSTROKE

RAY

*W*e're just leaving Skyway Bowling Lanes and I've found that bowling isn't a strong point for me or Diane. Lori just thought she would remind us of that fact. I can't believe how badly Lori beat us! But we had so much fun.

Earlier, Diane and Lori took me to Leona's Italian Restaurant, and they ordered for me once again. I really feel the pounds adding up! Five-Cheese Lasagna, Fettucini Alfredo, Kick-Ass Garlic Bread (yes, it really says that on the menu), hot wings, and a Strawberry Hurricane. We didn't have room for dessert. These women know how to enjoy life!

At the moment, we're driving in a direction that I don't recognize. "I thought we were going to the hotel," I say.

"We are," Diane responds. "We're going back there tomorrow. We have something in store for you."

I don't know whether to be afraid or excited. I think I'm a little of both.

We end up in front of a place called the Essence Inn. "Interesting," I say. Lori leans over to Diane and says, "Maybe we should have used a blindfold." We arrive in our suite. This place is fabulous! It's laid out with a fireplace and a

Jacuzzi. "What are you two up to?" I ask. They both laugh and give me one of their wicked smiles. "You'll see."

I'm standing in the middle of the room with Lori behind me and Diane in front. They begin to undress me. Diane works the bottom and Lori works me up top. They try to take off every stitch of clothing I have on but when they come to my boxers, I put up a *very minor* protest. "Help! Rape!" They laugh at me because they're not having it. They begin to caress my body and massage me for a few minutes. They point me in the direction of the Jacuzzi. I step into it and slowly sit down, eager to see what happens next. The water is hot and bubbling, and my dick is responding to the water and what my eyes are taking in. Diane undresses Lori all the way down to her bathing suit!

The look on my face makes them laugh. "No fair, you're cheating!" I say. "And your point being?" Diane says. I laugh in return. Lori steps into the Jacuzzi and then I lose sight of her for a moment. She goes under the water and I feel the pressure of her mouth on me. She slides her mouth from tip to base, letting the water flow around me. "Damn! No, you didn't!" I say. She lifts her head, shakes the water from her braids and says, "Oh, yes I did!" I can barely keep my eyes open, but I see her go back under leaving those tiny braids floating on top of the water. I can't believe how long she can hold her breath and continue to do this. She comes up for air long enough to give me a kiss and then goes back to what she was doing, licking my balls and dick, and stroking my thighs. *I love this!*

Lori's body is laid out flat and it's floating on the water. Suddenly, she raises up to kiss me again, and I slowly begin to take off her bathing suit. I watch her the entire time and there's no resistance, but she's watching me very closely. It will take some time for her to get used to me looking at her. I lift her, and she wraps her thighs around my waist, crossing her legs behind me as I guide myself inside her, starting a slow rhythm as she gives several soft moans.

Her arms wrap around my neck, and I bring her forward for a kiss. She pulls away and whispers in my ear, "You want it like this? Then come on with it!" It's that wickedly sensual look in her eyes that makes me take control. I grip her buttocks and then turn to push her to the walls of the Jacuzzi. This feels so damn good.

I thrust into her deeply and pull out and thrust again. She tries to move away so she can regain the lead, but I'm gripping her buttocks as I hold her in place. She can't move unless I let her go. I have no intentions of releasing her until I'm done making her cum. Every thrust from me makes her whole body shake with the force of my power. Her buttocks are pressed deeper into the walls—there is no place for them to go.

Lori looks directly in my eyes as I watch every expression. She's enjoying this. She tries once again to stand up, and I pull her legs back around my waist. I keep thrusting until I feel her start to cum. I thrust into her another time and hold that position. Lori's moans are enough to keep a man hard all the time.

Out of the corner of my eye, I see a naked Diane entering the Jacuzzi. I hope she's not there to lend Lori a helping hand. They're dangerous when they double-team me. As Lori continues to cum, I start thrusting into her again, and I don't stop until she's done trembling. After a few moments of this, I pull her close and hold her tightly. She lays her head on my shoulder and I rock with her for a while. While I'm still inside her, I feel her muscles contracting around my dick. *Hot damn!* I finally lower her legs so she can stand but I continue to hold on to her for a few more minutes as the water flows around us. I look at her and see her face is totally flushed with color. Just as I think I'm done...

DIANE

I place my hands on Ray's shoulders and kiss him as he turns to bring me into his arms. Lori kisses him and then walks to the other side of the Jacuzzi. He kisses me passionately and then I take his hand and guide him over to Lori. She's standing slightly away from the wall. She holds out her arms, and I bend my body over them and let my legs float to the top. I'm laid out on the water using both arms to brace myself away from the walls. Lori supports my stomach to keep me floating on top of the water. My legs have reached the surface. I look back at him as if to question. Well? He then takes my legs and positions himself in between my thighs. He says, "I can't believe this!"

It doesn't matter because I know he's going to do it anyway. He's positioned and aimed right at my center. I moan as he slowly pushes himself inside of me. I like this position—wheelbarrel style! (He's not the only one with ideas!) He pulls out and grips the sides of my thighs. He stands still and moves my body back and forth on his dick. My elbows bend slightly with each push. It's a smooth fluid action, with the water flowing against my body weight. He keeps changing his gripping point from my thighs to my buttocks and then starts to move in a slightly faster rhythm. I have a hard time holding on. I'm losing strength and I can feel my release is near. My hands let go of the walls as he thrusts into me harder and I start to tremble. I'm gasping for breath and my eyes close, and yet he keeps going—even faster now. Finally, he allows my legs to fall so I can use them to balance—but my hips are still in his hands and they are the focus of his grip. We both cum at the same time, and the sound he makes is almost...criminal! He reaches for my shoulders to pull me up against him. My back rests on his chest as he rocks me and holds me. I smile as I think to myself, *I can never get enough of this man.*

* * *

LORI

I leave the Jacuzzi and spread a blanket before the fireplace. Ray is holding Diane's hand as they come to join me. He takes a towel and dries us off and then lays on his back with one of us on each side as he caresses us both. I run my hands over his chest then I pull away from him and try to rise. He keeps my hand in his as he asks, "Where are you going, Lori?"

"I'll be right back," I say. He still won't release my hand.

"Where are you going?" he asks again.

"I'm going to get a pillow for your head," I say calmly.

"Why couldn't you say that in the beginning?" He laughs as he says, "You always have to be so damn stubborn!"

I join in his laughter. "Look who's talking!" I say. I place pillows under his head and Diane's. I'll just use his chest.

While he's holding us, we begin to talk. He tells us that he's really enjoyed our time together and that he doesn't want it to end. As we lay together, we talk about the new house and the visit that we'll take tomorrow to see it. We start on simple things, but when he makes a statement about relationships, I didn't know that the conversation would turn deep and take us to a variety of subjects. I didn't realize that this trip is going to be more than a sexual experience, it's a learning experience as well.

RAY

"This trio is amazing to me. I truly thought that all women want monogamous relationships," I say, speaking my thoughts out loud.

"Most women do, but not us in this case," Diane said. "All of us are in agreement on this relationship and everyone benefits. Everyone has to do what works for them. I mean, we're only taking one good man off the market instead of two. I'm sure our sisters could appreciate that. The process of finding another man like you would take a while."

Lori lifted her head from my chest and said, "Personally, if the numbers were different and there were more men on the planet than women, I would feel it was my God-given right to have at least seven."

"Damn!" I say. But the more I thought about it, the more I felt it was the truth. Lori and Diane could probably handle multiple partners. Over time I might be up to the task as well, but as much sex as I had over these few days, even though it was fulfilling and pleasurable, I was wishing I had a spare dick! They were wearing out the one I was born with (but I was enjoying it anyway!).

DIANE

"Actually the only drawback is a woman having more than one man means that at times no one could really be sure of a child's paternity. Every child has a right to know at least that, because the mother is a given. So it might not serve the same purpose for women to have more than one man or husband, but I'm alright with women who do. A woman has to do what she must, especially if it's something that completes her.

"Sex was originally for procreation purposes and a man could impregnate more than one woman at a time, making repopulation a given. The Creator made sex feel so good, to make sure that we would replenish the earth (whether we wanted to or not). If it weren't planned that way, human anger being what it is, there would be a lot less people on the planet. Because the first thing people in a relationship withhold from each other when they get angry is sex. Sisters put it on lock down and brothers decide they're the ones having the headache. As Lori and Ray break into laughter, I say, "Think about it, sex is used more for recreation than procreation these days. How many times have you gone into it over the years with the intention of creating a child?

"Although I have to say, just for fun's sake, I'm with Lori on the numbers issue. But I'd have to make it nine, with two extra in case one of the regulars give out."

Lori laughs heartily, but Ray was looking a little unhappy at my last statement. I realize that a man doesn't always appreciate when the tables are turned. It's hard for anyone to consider things from a different point of view if they've only been exposed to one side. Ray doesn't have a problem with the trio concept because he believes he doesn't have to share. But if this trio were two men and one woman, I'm not so sure he'd be as willing to be involved. I decided to flip the script on his butt and give his ego a little shake.

"Ray, there have been many types of cultures in addition to the ones that are commonly known—including ones where women had more than one husband. It's called polyandry, and the financial and power base are with the women. It worked well for two reasons: either there were more men than women or their society supported it because the ruling structure was created by women. Women chose who their mates were, supported the family, and the children carried the family name of the women."

Ray shifts his position, and his eyebrows draw

together. When he looks back at me, I realize he understands where I was coming from—it was very close to home—especially the "women chose who their mates were" part. I continue by saying, "Today there are many different cultures and relationships existing right here in the States, We just don't take the time to really look at it. We know of women who have a man on the swing and another on the slide. No one raises an eyebrow about it these days. Since women have a choice now, we make our relationships according to what *we* need. Where before, our choices were very limited and forced upon us. Today, we either share our men at the same time without knowing about it, become celibate, wait until a man becomes available, chose an alternative lifestyle or settle for less man than what we really want.

"The trio concept as we're embracing it is definitely nothing new. Our history, before our time here as slaves, was built on men mating with more than one woman [polygamy]. Our men had more than one wife, and men were only powerful or rich if their *wives* were. The women brought wealth into the marriage. The more wives, the more wealth. So for some, having more than one wife became a part of their culture and for others it became a part of their religion. For some it was about the money or status that the woman brought into the marriage. Either way, this system only worked because people chose for it to.

"Even in the Bible, men had more than one wife. I'm sure most women these days would argue, "Well, these aren't biblical times." Each culture handled the effects of war, disease and famine differently, and that's how it was handled back then. Every woman was cared for and secure in some way or another. Women paid for that 'security' with the inability to choose the fate of our lives. Women weren't allowed to provide for themselves in order to maintain the balance, or rather imbalance, of power. They were forced to accept rules, husbands or lifestyles that didn't agree with their own personal approval. So after all this time, things are pretty much the same.

"Just like during biblical times, today there are the same, as well as other factors that lead to a shortage of desirable men—war, imprisonment, abusers, addictions, alcoholism and men who prefer other men. What's different in how we handle it today is how we view relationships and because we were brought into a society that put a high emphasis on monogamy, while really supporting the opposite. So already there was a contradiction on what was *law* and what was *acceptable*.

"Monogamy has never really held true for men in this society. Some men have always had multiple women in their lives, whether they are labeled mistress, concubine or paid companion, whereas women were bound and gagged by monogamy laws. During slavery, black women had to be, in a sense, monogamous to their masters and white women had to be monogamous to their husbands. And now, society has changed but the rules secretly require that women stay monogamous or otherwise bear the label of slut or whore. Men on the other hand who are not monogamous are generously labeled playboy, player or mack. Let's be real, today, women aren't going for it!

"There is, however, a shift currently taking place spawned by the fact that women are seeing financial progress and opportunities. Black women in particular are moving rapidly toward financial, physical and mental freedom. We have taken control of our own fates and bodies. We don't want to be trapped in loveless, dominating and abusive lifelong relationships. We want the ability to love who we want without fear of disapproval. We also don't want to be bound into a marriage because of the inability to care for ourselves or any children we produce."

Ray shifts his body, but he's listening very closely. I can see we're going to be on this subject for a while. I really want Ray to always consider more than one way of looking at a situation. I don't want him to settle for just a traditional view of things—it will not work in this relationship. It's important he knows where we're coming from. It seems we've covered a lot of ground before now, but there's a few more things he needs to know about us. How he views things can affect how he sees us and treats us, or it just might bring an end to our relationship.

"Ray, it's a fact that these changes haven't been welcomed by everyone. People who are on top want to stay on top, and it takes staying in control of the money, standards and population to do so. During slavery, laws were laid down to ensure that children of mixed lineage were discredited. Today, some cultures are mixing into others so thoroughly that they aren't repopulating enough to replace themselves. So with things being as they are, people with that 'I'm superior' way of thinking had better wake up and see that drawing the lines on color and sex will soon draw them right out of the picture. Things can change at any time and what's law or acceptable can change too. Especially if the majority rules and the majority in the states, and most other cultures are women. All it takes is stepping away from tradition or conditioning to make it happen.

"As it stands on a global level, the people who consider themselves the majority here, are the minority everywhere else if you take a *true* count. That's why germ warfare and chemical weapons are so important. Those weapons can kill groups of people without destroying the land or resources in the process. It still is used for the purpose of keeping one group or sex ahead of another.

"Ray, there are so many ways of looking at society, race relations and sexual relations, but the one thing we must remember is that we now have a choice. We can choose to have a lifestyle that suits us, which means, some of those relationships will not be along traditional lines. And it will mean that men will not have the comfort of automatically being in control." I paused at this point for effect. "That will take some men a little time to get used to. The words *equal* or *even* haven't reached some of their vocabularies or if they have, they aren't something they really believe. Some men just humor women when women mention a balanced relationship, but in reality they still view things in the old way."

Ray is silent as he ponders what I said. He then asks, "So you think we're moving toward a matriarchal society or female-dominated culture where women run things?"

Ray sits up and looks toward both of us. We have his full attention now. Lori decides to give her views on things. "Let's hope we're moving toward a more balanced society, Ray. The balance of power should be shared between women and men. In a matrilineal or matriarchal society, the wealth, decision-making power, property and land stay with the women and their daughters. It's still a better alternative than the society that we've bought into. All this society has done is divide sexes, cultures and religions where most people tend to be opinionated, judgmental and selfish. It also further divides us according to economic differences, and people that don't meet the physical or societal standards. No one looks at the overall picture, and a lot of people are unhappy deep down inside.

"If you really look at it, even though there are more women on the planet than men, men are in position of political, social and economic control in every country that we know about. Why is that if women are the majority of the population everywhere? We're so unhappy with the way things are being done. Women like a peaceful existence, so war is virtually against our nature. We wouldn't believe in vicious methods to conquer land and people for selfish reasons. Because we are the ones to produce new life, we also have a greater appreciation of it. And yet we still wait for the tide to turn instead of making waves. It's evident when mentioning women in places of financial control or political control. Some women will say, 'We're not ready for a female president.' Well, I haven't seen where the men have done all that great either. So, why not a woman? Why not at least be able to picture it. Some can't because they've been taught not to.

"Things are slowly returning to a point that women are now the heads of most households. We are also finding our way into the top positions of corporate America or becoming entrepreneurs. So right now the economic and spiritual development of the black family rests with the woman. We shouldn't have to do it alone. There needs to be a balance in the household where both the male and female energies work together to accomplish what they will. It doesn't necessarily mean that it has to happen the way we've always known it to. Sometimes having positive male energy nearby—maybe not every given moment—can be enough to bring some women and children the balance that's necessary.

"We should each find a way that brings individual balance, and that will lead to peaceful family relationships and intimate relationships as well. That will be better for all of us. So much emphasis has been placed on color, sex, finance and religion, but if we truly look at things, it shouldn't be about that. We just have to understand how people work. We know where most people's belief systems are. Certain people think they're superior because they've been taught that. Others think they're inferior because they've been taught that. Certain people think that their way or belief system is the only way. And others give up their belief systems even when what they're changing to doesn't truly agree with them. It's just to please others or to be accepted, and it's all a state of thinking.

"Yes, a system is in place that keeps one group on top and continues to cater to them. It's the law of survival. If we were in control and from the line of thinking that they are, we would probably do things in the same way unless we came from a spiritual-based view. That's why when Harold Washington became mayor of Chicago, it was such a problem here. When he got into office the people who always ran things here saw that he tried to shift the balance from being one-sided, to where everyone got a piece of the pie. I admired him for that. Everyone that has the mind to do it, will. It's a fact that people on top can't stand to envision themselves not receiving more than others, but people on the bottom can always envision themselves on top and doing things in a better way because they know firsthand what hasn't worked. Spiritually, we should want things to be more in balance, and in order to do this it means some of us will have to change our thinking. Not everyone will be willing or able to do this.

"If women don't think about ways that relationships can be useful and beneficial to them, a lot of them are going to be unhappy. Whether they are the wife, fiancée or other woman. Everyone thinks that the wife, fiancée, or girlfriend gets the short end of the stick in a shared situation. Sure the wife or fiancée, gets the man's money and most of his time, they also have the most work of seeing all aspects of the man's character at once. It only seems like the other woman tends to get everything else from him. There's also pressure on the other woman to present herself in a way and manner that keeps the man interested in her or lose whatever security he provides her. That means there's pressure of some type on both sides when there shouldn't be any pressure at all. In a European society that works, especially since it's all about money, control and power. But with most black women today, now that the finances are falling in place, it's about the affection, comfort and security, and we seem to be missing out.

"In turn, if women would take time to require that men be more responsible toward them by creating a continued relationship rather than a *hit-and-run,* everyone could find some contentment. A man would make wiser choices about the women he gets involved with based on the fact that those women will be a factor in his life for a longer period of time. It would be better for the women, if they chose, to work cooperatively for health and peace reasons. In this way, the work of the relationship is not on the women, it's up to a man to do what it takes to keep the balance. It's been on us and against us for too long.

"If men could really be honest about things, they could handle relationships well and be stable. There wouldn't be brothers sleeping with different women every night trying to find fulfillment strictly in pleasure alone. Men would be more careful about the women they choose because an environment has been created that he finds peaceful. He doesn't want to destroy it by indiscriminately sticking his dick in just any woman. He will actually get to know her and become involved with her in a way that benefits everyone. I don't think the average woman would see it that way. We've decided that a trio works best for us. It's a choice that works for *us.* Not that monogamy is bad, it's just that there are different strokes for different folks."

RAY

Lori and Diane have a damn good understanding of history and politics! I realize I'm going to learn a lot from them. I've been struggling all of my life just to "make it" and never really took time out to learn about things that affect me and my family on this level. They have put a lot on my mind. I know that I have a lot of reading to do. I like learning from Lori and Diane, but it's only a start. I want to research and learn for myself. I didn't know it then, but in a few days I was going to learn almost everything I needed to know to understand them. As much as I prided myself on it: I didn't know as much about Lori and Diane as I thought I did.

I reflect on one comment that stuck in my mind: "If there were more men than women, I would have at least seven." The thought of either one of them with someone else disturbs the hell out of me! This has to be a *man* thing. I know I've done some growing, but I can't entertain the thought of sharing them. I never felt this way about any other woman I've been with. After all is said and done, I feel the need to ask them one more thing. I'm a little reluctant to voice this request, especially after this discussion, but it is very important to me. Reflecting on the episode with Chris and Shawna taught me that I need to voice this to Lori and Diane. I haven't asked for much in this relationship. They always seem to give me what I need. But the more I'm here with them, the more I'm beginning to understand what I want.

"This might sound a little selfish, especially behind the conversation we just had, but... I don't want to share either one of you with another man. I know that you both have made allowances for me because of the distance and my previous situation. But if this is to be a permanent arrangement, you must be totally mine—both of you. Am I wrong for wanting you all to myself? When I'm inside you, the only one I want you to be familiar with is me— my size, my feel, my taste and my rhythm. When I taste you, the only one I want to taste is you. I don't want you to be with any man but me. The thought really irritates me, and I didn't really consider it until we talked just now. Can you agree to these terms?"

Lori starts to explain. "Ray, it's not a problem. We've always stated our position on that. We're alright with staying with one man because it works for us."

"I know, Lori, but it's different now, and I want to hear it when there's no sexual pull between us. I have to hear you say it again right now."

Lori looks into my eyes and tells me "Ray, I'm your woman. As long as we're together you'll be the only man inside my heart, mind and body."

Diane shakes her head and remains silent. I know she's thinking *Were you listening to us at all?* She lets out an exasperated sigh and says, "I can't believe we're going through this."

"Diane, I heard everything you had to say, but I also just went through something a few months ago that makes me ask this. It's about my safety too. I know you and Lori will keep any promise you make to me—that's the type of women you are. I haven't asked for much."

"Ray, I won't allow another man to take your place..." and then she looks at me evenly, "at least not until we have finished our course." I understand Diane's position and realize that with her, that's as good as it's going to get—for now.

I breathe a small sigh of relief and hold them closer. Something they just said doesn't sit too well with me either: "As long as we're together" and "...until we have finished our course." I really want to say something about it, but now isn't the time. I can't push for too much too soon. I'll bide my time. I kiss each one of them in turn and say, "I can't believe how much I love the both of you. How much I want the both of you. I'm relieved to hear Lori say, "I love you, too, Ray. Everything will work itself out."

Diane says, "It's the same for me, Ray. I love you

too. I hope you'll keep it foremost in your mind."

Lori tries to rise again. I grab her hand again. "Lori?"

"Ray, I'll be right back, really," she answers quickly.

"Didn't we go through this already?" I ask.

"Yes, Ray, but *this time* I won't tell you what I'm doing," she says without even looking at me.

"Oh?" I say. "And what makes you think you won't?" I challenged jokingly.

Her eyes lock on mine. "Because I'm asking you to let me go." I release her hand immediately and watch her walk away. I have to learn the difference between when she's running away and just walking. I never like watching either one of them walk away from me. I like it when they're next to me. I feel…I can't even describe it.

Lori slips on a robe and then washes and dries her hands. She reaches into a bag they picked up just before we drove out here. I've been curious about it for a while. They wouldn't tell me what was in it (and you know I asked several times). She heats up the carry-out containers. The food smells wonderful, and I'm sure all of us worked up a hearty appetite.

As Lori comes to our area, she asks me to close my eyes. Diane says, "No peeking!" After a few moments, I feel the fork near my mouth and I open wide. Lori places the fork on the tip of my tongue and I use my lips to bring it all the way in. I taste it, open my eyes and say, "No, you didn't! No, you didn't!" They know this is my favorite! Damn, and it's good too. Jamaican food! Peas and rice, jerk chicken, beef patties, salad, plantain and ginger beer. I look at the menu that was inside the bag. It's from Jammin' Jamaican Jerk Chicken, and I have to say, this is really good!

"Thank you so much," I say, sincerely. They're laughing with me. I love to see them laugh—they are so beautiful. I think about how knowledgeable these women are, how they pay attention to detail. Their goals, my goals, eventually they will be our goals. Lori and Diane will be successful in whatever they decide to take on. I'm glad they decided to take me on and I now have the mind-set to be successful too.

They both take turns feeding me this late-night snack. I'm not going to miss a bite. I have a feeling I'll need the strength....

Chapter 19

DAY 4: DRIVING ALONG IN MY AUTOMOBILE

RAY

We've just taken in a few of the black sites of Chicago. We've visited places that are dear to Lori's heart: the DuSable Museum; Regal Theatre; ETA Theatre; Harold Washington Library; The Salaam Resturant; Mosque Maryam; Christ Universal Temple Church, School and Banquet Hall (the pride Lori and Diane felt for this place was obvious because it was built by a black woman); Chicago Vocational School; Lori's grammar school; PUSH headquarters and newly constructed homes by black real estate and construction companies. Lori and Diane also took me to the home where Lori grew up and to the place where they worship. There were a few more places but I can't remember the names. We also visited several places that Lori and Diane thought would be excellent locations for my company. We narrowed it down to the one that would work best. I prepared a new proposal and faxed it to my boss. So that's my work for this week...now back to the real reason I came here....

We stop by Disco Don's Music Emporium to pick up some CDs Diane ordered for me. She's always full of surprises. Lori's brother, Donny, has always loved music and decided that he wanted to spend his life surrounded by music. So he opened a record shop and a night club. (Sounds like a plan!) That song "Missing You" will be on my mind for a very long time and Alex Bugnon's CD is one Diane bought me. As we shop around, the sound system plays a smooth jazz piece, Art Porter's "Inside Myself." I like it, so I bought that too.

Lori and Diane's taste in music is so different. Diane prefers contemporary jazz and straight R&B. When Lori is driving, she listens to one of Jye Brown's underground house mixes and prefers dance, hip-hop and rock.

They tell me of their visit to a club in St. Louis. Lori said Jye had the music and spirit so high in that place that no one was sitting. He now sends them a live tape every week. Lori said while they were there she danced for two hours straight and her side started hurting. All she could manage from that point was putting one hand in the air and turning it from side to side. I pictured it and started laughing. I know that music can do that to a person.

Lori

Diane is driving while Ray and I are seated in back. My head is lying in his lap, and he's stroking my hair. He's telling us a little more about himself and some of his life stories have us laughing so hard my head hurts a little. I'm listening to him while I watch his mouth as he forms his words. Ray's hand travels under my blouse and reaches under my bra to cup a breast. He starts to play with the nipple, and I adjust my body for better access. He has this devilish smile on his face as he looks down at me. Diane notices how quiet we've become and looks through the rearview mirror to see what we're up to. "What are you two doing back there?" she asks.

We both laugh as Ray switches to the other breast. I'm getting really wet now, and he's watching as I bring my thighs close together. He reaches between them to gently push them apart. He wants to touch me in that place. Oh no.

"Not here. Not now," I whisper.

"Yes, here. Yes now," he whispers right back. He reaches for the waistband of my panties and pulls them down some. "Lift your hips, Lori."

I raise them and allow him to take off my panties. He runs his fingers along my inner thigh causing me to tremble a little. Anticipation is a motherfucker! Ray plays in the surrounding hairs and eventually parts my lips. He runs his finger along my clit, and I nearly jump out of the car! He pulls me back down on his lap and continues exploring me. His finger traces the outline of my opening, and he teases me for a little while. *This man has no mercy!* Ray loves watching me squirm and tremble. He cups his hand over the entire area and then pushes one of his fingers inside me to begin a slow, teasing rhythm. I arch my hips to meet his fingers. It feels too good! He pushes his finger deeper inside me. I forget how long they are. Two of them put together feels like a…well, *you know*.

I love it. I really do. His fingers are probing me, searching me, trying to find out all of my secrets. I start to shake a little harder, and I grip his hands to take his fingers out of me. He's not having it. He uses his thumb to manipulate my clit. *I can't take it!* I raise my hips toward his fingers, and I cum while he's smiling down at me….

I turn on my side and bring my knees toward my breasts. I watch as Ray seperates his middle and index fingers and the juice glistens between them. He puts his fingers directly into his mouth and sucks until they are clean. The way he does it gets me aroused—again. It's always amazing to me that a man can savor the taste of a woman, just like I love the taste and feel of a man.

After I regroup I decide that it's time for a little payback. I'm already lying in his lap so I slowly unzip his pants and place my hands inside. He lightly smacks my hands away. "Oh, no you don't, Lori." I smile at him because I still have my hands inside his pants trying to work my way into his boxers. "Those damn boxers!" I whisper. "Couldn't you be naked sometimes and make it easy for a sister!"

He smacks my hands again and laughingly says, "Will you cut that out?"

I'm not hearing it, though. I finally make it inside his boxers, and his friend is really glad to see me. I can tell because he stands up to say hello. I decide to greet his friend in my own special way.

With my head still lying in his lap, I begin to have a gentle conversation with the tip of his dick. I like it there because it's so sensitive. I caress it with my tongue and then softly lick up and down his shaft. He begins to moan and the moan escalates to a growl. I keep licking and sucking until the entire area is wet. I purse my lips, and I run them over every inch. Finally it's time to pay a little attention to his balls. I lick at them and pull back and wait for his response. He looks down at me and whispers, "Woman, quit your clowning!" I let out a wicked laugh.

I lick at him once again and the car stops abruptly. Diane says, "Alright, you two!" I guess our moans and the smell of sex have really gotten to her! She pulls over to the shoulder of the expressway and gets out of the driver's seat. Diane exits the car and opens the back door. She taps me on the shoulder and says, "You don't mind do you?" Of course not. I laugh as I lift up and straighten my skirt. I look at her as I say, "He's all ready for you." I look back at Ray, and he has this look on his face that says, "unbelievable."

I get up and move out of the car as Diane climbs in. My panties are on the seat and I reach down to take them with me. I turn just in time to see Diane straddle

Ray's lap. As I get into the driver's seat and signal my way back onto the expressway, I hear them moan and then Ray takes a deep breath. Diane is working him, watching him, and working him even more. He moans even louder. I look at them ever so often, through the rearview mirror and I smile to myself. So much for a smooth ride home....

RAY

When we finally make it to the hotel...

"Lori, I need to speak with Diane alone for a few minutes. There's a personal matter we need to discuss," I say.

She looks over at Diane and then says, "Alright."

I know that Lori's favorite pasttime is bathing, and our actions in the car have her thighs (and other places) a little wet. *Let me stop thinking like that.* I watch Lori get into the tub and tell her that I won't be too long. She touches my face and asks softly, "Is it that serious?"

"I believe it is for her, but it won't be for long," I whisper in her ear. I kiss her lightly to reassure her.

* * *

When I walk out of the chamber, Diane looks at me. The tight way she's holding her body lets me know that she's already on the defensive.

"Diane, why aren't you divorced?"

She winces, but she is looking at me intently as I continue, "It's been six years now, and it doesn't seem part of your character to wait this long to do something that important."

"I just haven't gotten around to it," she suddenly tells me.

I remain silent and just look at her because that's not the answer. After several minutes pass, Diane finally tells me. "I'm trying to find a way to do it without my husband finding out where I live."

That was not the answer I expected to hear. "You're *still* afraid of him?" I ask because I find it hard to believe.

Diane looks at me, and she doesn't answer right away. After a few minutes of silence she says, "Yes, I am."

Diane is a strong woman, and it took a lot for her to admit even that to me. She likes to think that she's not afraid of anything. I guess all of us fear something, and it's unfortunate when that fear rules your life. And it has ruled Diane's life. I go to hold her, and she returns my embrace. I lead her to the sofa so we can talk.

DIANE

Ray wraps his arms around me, and I begin to relax. This is something I haven't discussed with anyone, not even Lori. Ray really wanted to know, and I feel that it's alright to talk about it. "When I was younger, Ray, I would have picked up a gun and threatened him right back. I realized that he had changed and that would not have worked. If I felt it necessary to pull a gun on him, I would have to use it and not just threaten him with it. I appreciate life now, and I know how precious it is. I wanted my freedom, but I didn't want to spend it in prison. There are many women who did what I thought of doing and the court system isn't too fair about it. If my husband killed me, he would spend a lot less time in jail than I would If I did the same. I had already spent years in a type of prison, I wasn't going to trade one for another.

I didn't want to go home and get my family involved. When it comes to protecting one of our own, no one in my family has a problem with picking up a weapon and taking care of business. I didn't want any of my family members to spend time in jail for this either. I made the choice to stay with him after all that happened between us in Houston. I thought that Melvin and I had reached an understanding.

"I understood your need to stay in your *comfortable* relationship, Ray. I stayed with Melvin because I was used to him and thought that all I had to do was fight back to assert myself sometimes. I thought marriages worked like that. I learned that sometimes fighting can't keep you safe. I stayed with *comfortable* so long that it became *dangerous* instead. When he beat me, and I couldn't move for those four months, I laid in bed, and I felt something that I hadn't felt since I woke up under the porch that night. I felt helpless. With that feeling of helplessness came fear. I knew he would really kill me.

"I should have left him the first time he hit me. At least then I wouldn't be in fear for my life. His behavior, his anger and his jealousy all came shining through again when we moved away from my hometown. I never thought of it as abuse before we moved to New York.

"I hate being afraid, Ray. For the first time since grammar school, I was afraid of someone else. I didn't like that, and I began to dislike myself. The more afraid I became, the more I didn't know where to turn. Every day I would dread coming home from work. I had a drink in the nearest bar and kept a serious stash in the house. I had no one to turn to in New York, and I didn't want to go home where he would follow me and endanger everyone else. I turned to cigarettes, weed and alcohol to get me through the day. It was perfectly alright with Melvin because I was right where he wanted me—under his control. It only took the threat of death to accomplish it."

Ray held me close to him, and it felt so right. I knew I could tell him what I felt. Ray would never use this information against me. "I recognized that it wasn't just a threat to him. Control of something became important to him because so much else was going wrong in his life. Control of me was something we had always fought about.

Well, he had it, and I was not the same woman anymore.

"For a while we stopped having sex, especially when my lack of enjoyment was obvious. After a while it didn't matter to him if I enjoyed it or not. He liked it. Every time it happened, it was just like reliving a nightmare. It was painful because my body didn't want him, and I was never prepared mentally or physically. What's more is that he knew that it hurt me. We had more sex during that period of time than I could ever remember before. I would lay until he finished and then no matter how long it took me I would make it to the chamber the best way I could to clean myself up. My body, my mind, my heart and my spirit were so unhappy. I was hurting so bad, and he didn't care.

"There was a man from my childhood that came to New York, and I ran into him on my way to work. He had been in love with me all of his life. I didn't tell him what was going on but he could tell I wasn't happy.

He asked me to leave my husband and marry him. Unfortunately, he had a serious cocaine habit, and that would have been a whole new world of problems. This was my cross to bear, so I handled it the best way I could and came to Chicago. It was the best decision I ever made. The people here love me and accept me for me, and they are as good as their word. I love it here, and Lori's family treats me like one of its own. Especially her mom. She calls us 'her girls.' She always says 'my girls' do this or 'my girls' do that.

"I can go home to Houston as much as I like and can come and go as I please without anyone clocking me. Lori always encourages me to go out and make some friends of my own, but I like being at home, and I don't venture too far away."

Ray says, "I was wondering why you hadn't seen some of the places we went to."

Ray's hands were stroking me, and I felt safe. I

told him, "I don't go out very much. I was in the Nation of Islam for a long time and I know a lot of people from there. This is where headquarters is located, and I could run into someone I know. If it made it back to the mosque in New York, Melvin's bound to find out because there's a good chance he still attends there. Even though the Nation wouldn't condone the way Melvin treated me, I didn't feel comfortable telling anyone there what was going on. I stopped attending, and I really didn't know any of the members from the Mosque in New York to begin with. I didn't understand that a great deal of Melvin's frustrations came when he got disappointed by the actions of some of the members in the mosque.

"Melvin isn't likely to give up being a member. He joined the Nation when it was under the leadership of the Honorable Elijah Muhammad. I joined a study group in Houston when Minister Farrakhan decided to stand up and bring the message to the people once again. Melvin and I were some of the first people to stand up with him when he came forward. We also made sure he had ample Texas-style protection to back him. Things were volatile back then because there were some people who were not happy that Minister Farrakhan was starting things up again. So once again, I secretly became familiar with Smith & Wesson (I carried it in the middle of one of my study books. The minister would not have approved of the guns, but we lived in Texas and had to keep it real. We already had lost our study group leader under mysterious circumstances). If anyone was going down, trust me, it wouldn't be us or the minister. I liked the discipline and learned a great deal while I was in the Nation. The words *do for self* are ones that totally agreed with my spirit. I also liked the fact that I could question any of the teachings and get some answers.

"I was raised a Baptist and when I was a child if I

would question things in the Bible, depending on my timing, I was either told to shut up or slapped. I was always curious and felt that I wanted to understand something that I was supposed to believe in. It had to make sense to *me*. Whether it's church, temple or synagogue, everyone comes for a different reason—and truth can be found in every teaching. I saw the Nation just like I saw any other church: as a great big washing machine: some people came to get cleaned up, some came to watch all the spinning going on and some came so their stains could rub off on someone else. All those people and their reason for being there have an effect on one another. Either way, everything always comes out in the rinse cycle.

"The first thing that was put into force for members of the Nation was the use of common sense in all dealings. Melvin forgot this and allowed himself to be used so many times that he became bitter. He stopped listening to me when I felt someone or something wasn't right. All that was happening to him made me pull away from the people in the Nation. Eventually I stopped going altogether, and Melvin was highly upset. It was a major problem between us. He would pressure me so much that I finally gave in. Then I would embarrass him enough to stop asking me. I would show up to the lectures but I wouldn't be in traditional dress or have my head covered. This created quite a stir, and brothers would be on Melvin's case about 'putting his wife in check.'

"The Nation was not about women being 'in check,' it was about self-awareness and spiritual development. People's egos tended to make them forget the Nation's *original* purpose. Well this individual no longer felt that she could grow there, and my husband should have respected that. Some brothers felt that my independent, rebellious and enterprising spirit would be a bad influence on their wives. Those same brothers never seemed to have a problem when their wives came to me for ways to make money. Then I was respected. I enjoyed what the Nation offered, but I felt that for my own peace of mind that I needed to leave. Melvin had become so absorbed with some of the *people* in the Nation that he forgot the *purpose* of the Nation.

"About a week after I got to Chicago, Melvin called and threatened the people at Lori's job, the karate school and members of her family. He must have requested copies of the bills from the phone company. Everyone in Chicago had been told what was going on and no one, not a single, solitary soul gave up any information about me. I was so grateful to them for protecting me. No one gave the impression that I was even here. I thought by now he would have had time to cool off. He's still looking for me. He called my dad earlier this year and a few other family members to see if they knew where I was. He said he just wanted to talk. Actually, my dad wanted to *talk* to him too.

"My dad never forgot what he said to Melvin years before, and he happened to be oiling his gun at the time Melvin called. He joyfully told Melvin to come right over. It must have been my dad's tone of voice, because my husband didn't show up." Ray tensed when I said those last words and I can't quite understand why.

"Even though I probably could have found a way to hurt Melvin, I didn't want to. I loved him once. I loved him so much, I forgot to love me too. I forgot the rules of love: You love yourself first and then share yourself with others. I asked Melvin so many times if we could leave New York. Our marriage, if it could be called that, probably would have survived a little longer if we had. Things always happen for a reason. He had always wanted to live in New York, and he never listened to me because he loved the place. It's perfect for hustlers because it's so populated that anyone can maneuver and make some money. My husband didn't mind living like that but my hustling days were over. When I left Melvin, I left behind mostly all of my personal items. They didn't mean more to me than my safety. I had to go.

"Lori made it easy on her end, and she changed her life to make sure I would continue to stay safe. Not many people would do that. I mean, we met over the phone, Ray. Almost like we met you. She had only seen me that week that I came to visit. I don't know many people who would extend themselves to a stranger. They say if you can make it in New York, you can make it anywhere. That's true, but I was tired of just *making it*. I wanted to enjoy what I was making.

"When I left Melvin, I knew one thing, I wanted to live, Ray, not in a loveless marriage, not in jail and not in New York. I just wanted to live." I looked Ray in his eyes and said, "I want to love too. And I don't think there's any reason why I shouldn't receive love and give it too. I don't want to be afraid of someone I love."

RAY

"Diane, I love you, and you know that. I would never raise a hand to you. I don't have it in me to hurt a woman, and I love you too much for that. I love you, baby. *I love you*." I kiss her forehead and her lips. A thought comes to me, and I share it with Diane. "Personally judging by the *skillet* story you told me a few weeks ago, I need to be concerned about the same thing. I don't want to be running down the Chicago streets in nothing but dick, air and opportunity." The laughter that rolls from her was contagious. I had to let her know that her ex didn't take her power. She would fight again, this time for something she wants. Lori and I will be standing with her to keep her safe.

"Diane, every time you say the words *my husband,* it irritates the hell out of me, because it doesn't mean me. You should go ahead and file for divorce. I'll fly in when you need me to be here. I'm thinking of some things that need to happen, and I want you free and able to do them. I don't want some man coming back to lay his claim on you in any way. I need you to be mine in every sense of the word."

Diane smiles at me and says, "Ray, you're getting more demanding every day."

"Is that a problem?"

"As long as you continue to love me and respect me, there won't be any problems between us," she whispers.

Her eyes speak volumes. I hold her and kiss her as I say, "I give you my word." I give her another kiss and that is the seal to our agreement. Love and respect were the deepest of my feelings. Diane can't know that I am preparing the way for an even bigger request that would have a greater impact on all of our lives.

Chapter 20

Day 5: Anytime, Anyplace

RAY

Brandon is competing in an interschool karate tournament today. Lori never misses one of his tournaments. I've learned enough from watching Brandon in action today to know that he's going to be a powerful young man when he comes of age.

It's also amazing to see little girls my daughter's age performing very complex movements. They make it seem so easy. Brandon is a blue belt, which means he is an intermediate rank. He explained that the other colored belts signified the person's rank—the darker the belt, the higher the rank.

Because his skill level is much higher than the other ranks in his age group, Brandon is placed with the adults for Kata. Kata is going through a series of movements as if you're fighting an imaginary person. It is really something to see. It is miraculous that Brandon beat the higher ranks and took first place. I didn't understand it. Not that I doubted Brandon's ability, but I thought the higher ranks, having more knowledge and experience were supposed to win. His instructor explained to me that while the adults just went through the motions, Brandon actually looked like he was fighting. He had the right facial expressions, sounds and movement and that counts for everything. Sometimes things don't happen the way we think they should. I'm still getting used to that concept.

Later in fighting, Brandon, who is thirteen, is teamed with the fifteen-to-seventeen year olds. They tower over him, and I really think it is unfair. It looks like a rematch between David and Goliath. Only this time David doesn't slay Goliath, but he sure tries like hell. One of the competitors is disqualified because he keeps using illegal techniques on Brandon. No matter what, Brandon always gets up and stands ready to fight again. I am truly amazed. Karate is reinforcing a lesson in self-confidence. Brandon doesn't seem to be afraid just because the others are higher ranks, older, heavier or taller. He stands up to fight each person, and I am as proud as if he is my own son.

I watch as he fights the last opponent. This is the fight for first place. Brandon scores a few, but not enough. He loses by one point and takes second place, but he's smiling about it. He brings his second trophy of the day to Lori and Diane, and they hug him. He's smiling from ear to ear as he walks in my direction. I give him a handshake and pull him in for a manly hug (yes. there is a difference). As he pulls away, I congratulate him. "That was some fight. That trophy seems like first place."

He says, "It is first place for me. I did the best I could." I couldn't have agreed with him more.

"Brandon, I'm really proud of you."

I look at him and what looks back at me are Lori's eyes. "Really?" he asks.

"Yes, you looked great out there. No matter who stood in front of you, you didn't back down."

"Man, but I was kind of afraid on the last one," Brandon revealed. "He did some unnecessary damage to a student last year, and they took him out of competition for a while. It really doesn't seem like he's learning the lesson on this one. The sponsors and judges will not let him participate in tournaments again."

I told him, "I would never be able to tell you were afraid by the way you handled yourself. Sometimes all of us are afraid of something, but we have to overcome that fear and fight anyway."

He says, "Yeah, it happens almost every tournament!"

I laugh as I tell him once again, "You did great, Brandon," and he gives me some dap (you know what I mean).

"Brandon, I want to talk to you while I'm here," I say as we walk away from the other competitors.

He looks a little uncertain. "Sure, what's up?"

"I love your mom, and I love Diane. How would you feel if my daughter and I came to live here and became a part of your family?" Brandon is quiet as he listens closely.

"I'm thinking of asking to make things permanent between the three of us, and I just wanted to get your take on things, being the man of the house and all." Brandon's chest puffs up a little on that last note so I keep going. "Brandon, you know I'm going to need your help. I mean, Chicago is a whole new world for me and Janese. You know more about it than I do, so I'm going to be coming for your opinion sometimes."

Brandon looks back at me and says, "Okay. I think I can do that. I mean help out and all. I don't have any problems with you coming here as long as you treat my mom and Diane right. And I've always wanted a little sister. How will Janese feel about having me for a big brother?"

He really looks concerned, so I said, "I think she'll like you. She'll probably become very close to you because this place and the people will be different than what she's used to. She'll become comfortable a lot faster, especially if you show her some of your karate moves."

Brandon laughs. "No problem, man!"

We walk to the refreshment stand, and I buy him a soda. As we're walking away from the hungry mob, I say, "I care a great deal for your mother and Diane and would never do anything to hurt them. If things work out the way they should, I'll bring Janese with me in a couple of months so you can meet her."

"That's great!" he says. Then he frowns, and his eyebrows draw together. He looks me straight in the eyes as he asks, "What do you mean '*If things work out the way they should*?'"

I forget whose child I'm dealing with. "I have to convince your mother and Diane to marry me first."

Brandon stops dead in his tracks, both eyebrows go up and his mouth falls open. "Whoa! Marriage? Whoa!" He shakes his head. You have to *convince* them? Let me tell you, they can be really stubborn. I have a hard time getting them to change their mind if they told me no when I ask to do something."

I think to myself, *That's what I'm afraid of.*

Brandon continues his point. "Sometimes I ask the question several times or in different ways hoping to get a different answer."

"Does it work?" I ask hopefully.

"Nope." He must have seen the expression on my face because he changed his statement—a little. "Well, sometimes—it depends on how well I can convince them that it's something I want to do and that I can keep up with my schoolwork and chores, and that I can handle myself." He gives me a mild warning. "I can tell you, it's going to be rough, but try and try again."

I say, "I'll give it my all, no matter what. I learned that from you tonight, Brandon. You are truly special and

I look forward to getting to know you better." His smile was enough to light up the place.

I have one more thought to share with Brandon."I'd like to ask you something, and you can give it some thought. No matter what happens between your mother, Diane and me, I want you to know that you've got me in your corner, and we'll always keep in touch. Okay?" Brandon didn't say anything, and I can tell he is really thinking it over. "I'd like to think of you as my son, and it won't take being here to be there for you."

He blinks twice, and I swear Brandon even has Lori's mannerisms. He says, "That's alright with me. I'd like to think of you as a father."

He hugs me and says, "Thanks, Ray." And when he pulls away, he asks, "By the way, does Janese like roller coasters and waterslides? There's this place called…"

I know then that Brandon and I are going to get along fine. I know my hardest work is still ahead.

In celebration of Brandon's victory, we pick up Lori's mother, Paula, and go to Suresh's East Indian Kitchen. This is a whole new world to me. I thought I loved Jamaican food, but East Indian is giving my favorite food a run for its money. Lori and Diane order all of their favorites and make sure I taste each one. I came in thinking that everything would be heavy, spicy or filled with curry, and it is nothing like that. I loved the Tandoori Chicken. It's red, baked in a clay oven and tastes like it came straight off the grill; We also had Chicken Makhani in a red sauce, Lamb Curry, Creamed Spinach, a well-seasoned vegetable soup, a crispy bread with potatoes and onions inside called Masala Dosai, Lentils and Mushroom Curry. None of it is too spicy, but all of it is delicious.

It's the desserts that have my taste buds on edge. Lori's favorite is Rasmalai, a cottage-cheese cake in cream sauce with pistachios. Diane's favorite is called Khir, a rice pudding, which has raisins, almonds and seasonings in a sweet, creamy sauce. I smile to myself as I think *two different women, two different tastes*. The employees have to roll us away from the table.

As we're leaving the restaurant, Paula pulls me to the side and says, "Son, take good care of my girls. They're special to me." She looks me level in the eye and says, "I cut up a chicken real well and a human your size would be no trouble at all."

Her eyes say everything. I can tell that Paula didn't make idle threats. "I love them, Ms. Harold, and I'll do right by them. I just have to find a way for them to accept me in a more permanent arrangement," I said sincerely.

After looking me over for several minutes. She looks me square in the eyes once again. She relents, but only a little. "Think long and hard about what you want, son. They're strong women, but they have their weaknesses too. Don't use their weaknesses to hurt them. Show them how you can help make them even stronger. They can respect that. If you can do that, you won't have a problem making them yours. But also show them that you're theirs too. It cannot be a one-sided thing. They know what they want, and you must be something special if you've made it this far. It's up to you now to have the strength to make this go further."

She hugs me and then looks up at me and says, "I lost a son last year and sometimes the Creator has a strange way of giving you back what he's taken. I'll treat you just like I would treat my own son."

I look down at this lady, and she reminds me of how strong my own mother is. I want to make sure I have Paula on my side too. I reach in my pocket and pull out a small box and show her what's inside. She chuckles and says, "Now that's the spirit!"

Brandon goes home with Paula. She's staying at Diane and Lori's home for the week of his vacation and theirs. I enjoyed getting to see both of them, and my talks with Brandon and Paula give me some inspiration to fight for what we all need.

I'm driving, and Lori is sitting in the passenger seat. I must have been a little too quiet on the trip home. Lori has been watching me closely, and she finally asks, "Ray, what's wrong?"

"I think your mother just threatened my life," I say jokingly.

"Oh, she wouldn't do that." Lori says confidently.

Diane and I both look at Lori and say, "Yes, she would." Lori is silent and thoughtful for a few moments. All of a sudden she bursts out laughing. She says, "I guess she only threatens those she cares about so she must have liked you."

I say, "Yes. She made her point absolutely clear." We all laugh.

I ask Lori why she doesn't compete in the tournaments. She tells me, "I only take karate for self-defense, and tournaments are not my thing. Actually, my skills came in handy one day. My niece was highly upset that I wouldn't take her bowling with me and while I was driving her to my mother's house, she reached from the backseat of the car and tried to hit me. I put up an instant block. I didn't even have to think about it. I parked the car in the middle of the street and would have given her a half-order of ass-kicking right then and there. She should have been grateful that I gained some patience. The year before, I would have given her a full order at no extra charge, without a doubt."

We're halfway to the hotel when Lori reaches over the stick and fondles my dick. I smack her hand away. She laughs and goes back to that area anyway.

"I knew I should have let Diane sit up front," I say out of frustration. They are unbelievable. One would think we haven't done a thing all week.

Diane starts to run her fingers through my hair. I can't believe them! "Oh, no, Diane. Not you too!" I pull the car off the road and park. "Look, ladies either the both of you stop, or we won't make it home."

They look at me with these devilish smiles and Lori says, "So, we don't make it home."

I can only laugh and shake my head. "You little hellions!"

Lori says, "And since we're already parked..."

Diane interrupts, "Wait I have an idea!" She whispers in Lori's ear. I'm totally left out of this, but I can tell it's something wicked. Lori turns back to look out at the traffic. Lori looks at me, smiles and says "Okay, it's safe for you to drive now. I'm directed to a place on South Shore Drive near the lake. They keep their hands to themselves the entire time. They are being a little too good. What do they have in mind?

DIANE

We're at Lake Michigan, and it's late and a little chilly. The water is really beautiful, and the Chicago skyline is breathtaking. Ray specifically asked me to wear a dress today. I'm still trying to figure that one out. We're parked, and I'm sitting on the car looking out at the lake. Lori is sitting next to me on the car. Ray is standing facing both of us. He positions himself between my thighs and unbuttons my dress. Ray wraps his arms around my waist and kisses me. Lori stands directly next to him blocking anyone's line of vision. He pulls away and kisses my forehead and goes back to my lips for another kiss. He unhooks my bra and takes both of my breasts in his hands. He kneads them and strokes them and quickly bends down to kiss them. Then he kisses my lips again, and Lord knows he's an excellent kisser! He lingers on my mouth while stroking my back and begins to remove my panties to get a better feel of my ass.

I'm exposed to him, and he pulls me to the edge of the car. Ray parts my thighs with his knee and enters me oh, so slowly. When he's all the way inside me, he stays there without moving a muscle. He looks into my eyes and holds my buttocks. I start moving on him in a slow, slight rhythm. Not enough for anyone else to notice, but more than enough for him to feel. I whisper to him, "I can work you like this all night. Can you handle it, honey?" He kisses me and that's my answer. I stop for a moment and let him feel my muscles rippling on him. I feel the tightness in his thighs and work with him rhythmically until we cum…

After our release, he says, "Lori, would you like to try this in the water?" She smiles and asks him, "How good is your backstroke?"

LORI

We're in the car, and I think we'll actually make it to the hotel this time. It seems all we do is eat, make love and sleep. I don't think Ray or Diane have a problem with it. I sure don't! I mean he started it. Didn't he? I didn't take him up on his offer of lake sex. Actually, he let me off the hook on that one. We park, and Ray signals to Diane, and she goes into the hotel. As I leave the car he pulls me to him and kisses me. He scouts the area by looking left and then to the right. What is he up to? In one smooth motion he lifts my skirt, pulls down my panties, spreads me and thrusts himself inside of me. *Oh, Lord!* He pulls out and thrusts again. Then he pulls totally out and his oversized shirt covers his hard-on as he walks away zipping his pants. He turns back to me and says, "Take your panties off. Now!" He walks into the hotel. I slowly remove them, but I'm still in shock. *What the hell did he just do?*

As I walk into the lobby, I don't see him. From out of a shadowed corner, his hand reaches out and pulls me to him. He kisses me as he lifts up my skirt again and enters me. He moves inside me and thrusts twice then walks away toward the elevator. I'm left standing there once again in total shock. I must have this stunned look on my face. He looks back at me, notices my facial expression and says, "Well, bring it on!"

There's no one in the elevator but us. He pushes a button on the panel and slowly turns my body to face the wall and lifts my skirt to expose my naked ass. Ray puts his thigh between mine and spreads them apart. He bends me over slightly as he grabs my ass and pulls me toward him. He takes me twice from this position, and I'm getting real frustrated with this. "Ray, will you stop teasing me and fuck me!" I demand.

He smiles at me and asks teasingly, "Are you sure you want me to? Here? Out in the open?"

The elevator stops and as we exit—wait a minute, *this isn't our floor!* He's heading for the stairs, and he beckons for me to follow him. I enter the stairwell, and he places me against the wall and kisses me as he lifts my skirt to finish what he's started. As I cum, and that juice makes its way down my legs, I fall to my knees and take his dick into my mouth and tease it until he's just about ready to cum. *He wants to play?* Then let me show him how it's done! I gently squeeze the base of his dick to keep him from releasing.

I stand up and back away from him with a smile. I give him my sexiest voice. "You want to do it like this, honey? Let's go back and start this over again—this time it's my way! Are you ready for me, Ray?" He smiles as I take his hand and lead him down the stairs....

LORI
10:30 P.M.

We try to wake Diane but she was in a deep sleep and positioned comfortably on the sofa. After several attempts we have no choice but to leave her there.

Ray and I decide to watch a movie we picked up earlier today. We're lying in bed and Ray's head is resting on my breasts. I stroke his face and the other parts that are within my reach. He wraps his arms tighter around my waist. Ray fits so comfortably between my thighs as he listens to the sound of my voice—the voice that he swears he's addicted to. As I stroke him, Ray is having a hard time staying awake. I tell him how much I love him, appreciate him and that I enjoy him being here. Ray buries his head deeper between my breasts and closes his eyes completely. He says softly, "It feels so peaceful here with you." I use my voice to comfort and relax him as I tell him, "Allow your mind to rest, and your body will follow." His breathing changes to long, slow intakes. He's struggling to stay awake. I whisper to him, "Rest my love. Rest now. Everything's all right. You're in good hands. Stay right here with me until morning as I watch the rise and fall of your chest and the fluttering movements of your lashes."

I feel him relax his grip on my waist, and his body grows lax. I adjust my body so that my thighs wrap around him, and he stirs immediately. His hands move down to my hips and hold me. It's a subconscious move and I understand. He wants me right where I am. I want him right where he is too. "Rest, my love and let your spirit fly. Let me love you in this way."

Chapter 21

Day 6: A Little R & R

Ray
9:23 A.M.

I awake and daylight hits directly in my eyes. I feel revived and unfortunately, my body is telling me that I can't sleep a moment longer. I lie there just long enough to hear the shallow breathing from Lori and the total silence from Diane. Diane must have joined us sometime during the night. I listen to Lori's heartbeat and stroke Diane's hair. They're both resting comfortably and I don't want to wake them. I reluctantly remove myself from the comfort of Lori's embrace. Nature calls.

After a side trip to the chamber, I slip on my robe and walk to the living room and sit on the sofa. I make a call to New York to talk with Janese. I call her every day and the first words out of her mouth are, "Daddy, when are you coming home?" I switch on the television and flip through a few channels but nothing interests me. I turn off the set and look at the video game at my feet. It doesn't interest me either.

As I sit in silence, I look at the end table and notice there's a familiar book on it. I pick up *Speak It Into Existence* and read a chapter that always does me some good. It talks about appreciating what you have and blessing the people in your life. I think about my life as it was before Diane and Lori and how much changing I've done. Even my language. I don't feel the need to curse as much as I used to. I think back over the events that have brought me to where I am right now. I think of the women in the next room. How different they are but how in tune they are to each other.

This is the first time since I've been here that I've had a few moments to myself, and it feels a little strange. It's like there's always someone to watch, talk to or touch. I thank the Creator that I've been given this opportunity to love these women in every way. I ask the Creator to please give me the strength and wisdom to continue to provide them with what they need, because my prayers have certainly been answered.

Once I was through running the games in my younger days, I found that I like being in a stable, one-on-one relationship, but I enjoy the flexibility that this relationship offers. Lori and Diane want a man who could handle this type of relationship but not too many woman can handle this like they have. I knew all along that I was going to be the one. I wanted them badly enough, and they have certainly been worth the risk.

Lori and Diane are so wise, so strong and independent. Each woman is an excellent choice individually, but having them both is truly a gift from the Creator. Each woman mirrors a particular side of me. Diane's nature is nurturing and she's sexually spontaneous, while Lori is conservative sexually and needs nurturing.

I am many things with these women, and none of what I am is wrong for them. It's a first for me. They're not trying to change me or alter who I am to fit some ill-defined notion of perfection; they're existing with who I am, as I change myself for the better. I can live with that. I must say that it's something a man could get high from.

It doesn't cost me anything to love completely or to be honest with them. This relationship doesn't require anything but time and energy, everything else seems to follow.

I know Lori and Diane say that it doesn't matter, but I want myself in a position to give them what they need financially as well. I know they would rip into me for thinking this, but it's a personal thing with me. I've always felt this way and there are certain things about me that do not bear changing. They should have the best, not because they expect it, but because they deserve it. The vice president's position will be a start, but ultimately I will use the experience and finances I gain there to start my own business. My promise to myself is that from this day forward I will use my time and life more wisely and spend it enjoying, growing and building myself and something lasting. My reward in this relationship is peace of mind, restful nights and a mind that's ready for new challenges. I feel more grounded. I wish all brothers could experience this type of peace. Not all of them would be willing to come to terms with themselves and see the value of a woman in this light. Not many women can see the value of a man in this way either. I'm glad that I've come to this realization early in life. I can spend my time getting things accomplished instead of struggling to find my way.

I have so much to be grateful for: my daughter, Lori and Diane, my mother, my aunt—all in good health —and I want them to enjoy life the way they should. I want to do right by these women. My women. Because in doing so, I do right for myself.

They say it's a man's world, but the universe is the woman's playground.

I hear a stirring in the bedroom and then Lori walks out of the bedroom and into the chamber. She comes out and looks in my direction and smiles. "Can't sleep?"

I smile in return as I tell her, "I have a lot on my mind."

"Alright," she says and continues to walk toward the bedroom.

"Are you really ready to go back in there?" I ask her.

"No, but I thought you might want to be alone right now," she says seriously.

"Woman, what's with you and that damn word? Please, come over here and talk to me." Lori sits on the floor and lays her head on my thighs. We're both looking at the televison's empty screen as I stroke her hair. She moans. "*Mmmmmm,* yes, I like that. What are you thinking about?" Lori asks.

"You," I say.

She smiles. "Okay, then what *were* you thinking about?"

"You and Diane. My life. Everything that's happening. It's so incredible. I feel blessed. Thank you for giving me something that I've needed for so long."

"Ray, I thank you for giving me what I need too." She closes her eyes, and we sit in silence as I continue stroking her face and hair. I break the spell by saying, "Lori, I want you up here next to me." She changes her position and comes into my arms, and we kiss. I could kiss this woman all day long! I realize that of the two of my women, Lori needs the most attention. She's so strong but she's also very soft inside. She's not used to people seeing her soft side. I hold her tighter and notice... "Lori, are you losing weight?"

Her body tenses, and I realize that I've hit a real touchy area. She looks at me and says honestly, "Not on purpose."

I kiss her forehead and say in my gentlest tones, "Baby, I'm just making an observation. I can tell the difference already. You've been eating the same things as we have, and I think it's totally unfair that you're not gaining like the rest of us."

Her body relaxes. She laughs and says,"It must be that new exercise program that I started on Monday."

I chuckle at that one. That brief moment of insecurity lets me know that I have to protect this woman's heart at all costs. I can't put her through any of the bullshit that she's been through before. She doesn't deserve it. Lori doesn't have to tell me that she's happy. It's in her eyes, and I want to see it there all the time. I want her happy to be with me, because the feeling is definitely mutual. I've never truly experienced the love of a woman in this way, and it brings me a great deal of peace. I have to help reinforce the love Lori has for herself. That's really important. I don't care what size she is, I care about her. As I kiss her forehead, I tell her how much I love her.

I will never be able to say it enough.

RAY
10:45 A.M.

I hear Diane taking a shower and decide that I'd like to watch. I position Lori, who has fallen asleep, as comfortably as I can on the sofa. I knock lightly on the chamber door and walk right in to take a ring-side seat. I'm getting aroused watching that beautiful honey-brown body as the water flows down onto her. She takes special care in soaping herself. The lather is thick on her breasts, arms and buttocks. She bends over to reach her thighs and legs. Eventually she starts to lather between her thighs and that's where I join in.

Diane is startled when I touch her. Evidently, she didn't hear me knock and didn't know I was watching her. I remove my robe and step into the shower, and she turns to me and places her hands on my chest. She begins to lather me using her breasts to do the job. She slides them over my upper body and eventually bends down and uses her hands to lather my legs and thighs. The water is pouring down on both of us. She lathers the hairs and my balls, saving my dick for last. She strokes it and caresses it. Diane reaches behind me to soap my back from nape to knees. She passes the soap to me and I return the favor.

As the water washes over our bodies, we kiss and embrace. I love making love to this woman in water! She turns her back to me and allows the water to cascade directly onto her buttocks. She braces herself against the wall as I part her thighs. She is totally open and exposed to me, and I know what she wants and how she wants it. I am more than willing to give it to her. The water is pouring down on her back and rolls onto my dick. I enter her slowly and she pushes herself back into me. Between the water, the pleasure I find inside of her and her movements, our release isn't far away... *Mmmmm*, what a wonderful feeling!

LORI

I wake to find myself alone on the sofa. I didn't even feel Ray leave that time. Ray and Diane are playing a video game. I try to distract him by stroking his buttocks. He laughs as he slaps my hands and tells me to cut it out. I continue anyway. What a nice ass! I swear some brothers have it like that! Maybe I should get a little oil? Later! But for now, I feel it's my right to stroke the backside of his body. I look at the kitchen and find that they've already fixed a light breakfast, but I'm starving and I'll have to fix something extra. I decide to shower first. From the looks of Ray and Diane, I'm the last one in there today.

RAY

We had a full day of viewing more of Chicago and the place where Lori and Diane plan to build their new home, excuse me—mansion. It's breath-taking! They do

not think along small lines. That's for sure. We haven't
eaten since breakfast, and I'm starving. I'm watching
Diane and Lori fix my dinner. Both of them are moving
in total harmony in the kitchen. Lori's adding more butter
to the crust of the peach cobbler she's making. My mouth
is watering! My father used to fix a kick-ass peach cobbler.
Come to think of it, the last time I had some, was when he
was alive. I look at my watch. What time did they say
dinner is?

It's going to be a full menu: glazed turkey ham,
green beans and potatoes seasoned with smoked turkey
wings, homemade honey-wheat rolls (dripping in butter),
candied sweets and macaroni and cheese. A traditional
Sunday dinner on a weekday! But it's the peach cobbler
that has me shifting from cheek to cheek.

I check my watch and ask them, "What time is
dinner?" They laugh and Diane says, "When it gets ready."

As I watch them, I realize these women are doing
this for me. My women. I say those two words over and
over to myself so they quickly come to mind and I know
these words as truth. They aren't *these women* or *the
women*—I'm possessive like that. They are *my* women.

Just thinking of this makes me want to go over to
them and embrace them. Nope! I don't want to distract
them from this labor of love. It's taking enough time as it
is. It's been said that the way to a man's heart is through
his stomach (actually it's through his mother, but that's
another story). With the smells coming from the kitchen,
I'll be happy to let them work through my stomach! Lori
decides to give me a sample of her famous macaroni and
cheese. Damn it's good! I ask again, "How long until
dinner?"

They both laugh at me because I'm acting like a
child. *Hell, I feel like one!* I want dinner *right now*! The
scents, the seasonings—I can actually taste the food and

picture it going into my mouth. I ask Lori if she would bring over a taste of her peach cobbler. "No, you'll have to wait on that," she says.

I'm still savoring the flavor of that one measly teaspoon of macaroni and cheese—*hmmm*, what was in it? Did I taste garlic and onion powder? Black pepper? Seasoned salt? What was that slightly sweet taste? Was that nutmeg? In macaroni in cheese? Damn that was good! How many cheeses did she say it was? Four? I hope I don't pay for this later! You know I think they're moving slow on purpose. I breathe a loud sigh of frustration. "Ladies, if you don't speed this up, I will put you both on the table and..."

"Ray, just a little while longer," Diane says laughingly.

"You said that a little while ago," I reply.

"No, I said that a few minutes ago," she says.

"That's what I meant." They both laugh at me.

Diane says, "You are so impatient."

After what seems like an eternity (which was actually six minutes), the serving dishes come out of the cabinet. "Finally!" I say. Diane asks me what I want my portions to be.

I'm quick with my answer, "Don't hold back, baby. Feed me!" You would think I haven't eaten all week. (We all know differently—don't we?)

They bring the plates to the table and ask me to pour the wine. We hold hands to say grace, and they look at me. I understand. As we bow our heads, I'm the one to give thanks for all of us. No disrespect to the Creator, but I do make it brief.... Amen! I look at my plate, and I don't know what to try first. I notice that something's missing. "Where's the peach cobbler?" I ask.

Diane answers after savoring her first forkful, "It's still in the oven."

"But I thought it was done," I say.

Lori answers with a wicked smile on her face "It is. I'm just keeping it hot for you, honey."

"It can stay hot right next to me on this table," I explain.

Lori uses one of her most soothing tones and pats my hand. "I promise, after you eat your dinner, Ray." I realize they're both humoring me and my antics so I give them something else to smile about.

"Just like a woman," I mutter, "always making me wait."

* * *

DIANE

Ray has been awful quiet, and he seems thoughtful. I would ask, but I know he will tell us in due time, so I'll wait.

After dinner, we're lying on the floor playing dominoes, and all of a sudden Ray asks us to sit on the sofa. Then he hits us with a bomb. "Will you marry me?" The question is directed to both of us, and we're in shock. I'm the first one to recover and answer him....

"Ray, I'm not looking for a spouse, more like a soul mate. Why would you want to be married anyway?"

He says, "I want both of you, and I need it to be in a way that will always stay in your minds and will be respected by all of us and our loved ones."

I take in a deep breath before I say, "Ray, I've had thirteen years of marriage, and I personally think Lori would be the best one of both of us to consider it. She's never done it before." If looks could kill, the one Lori gives me would have put me six feet under, without a proper burial.

RAY

I decide not to argue my point with Diane because I know where she's coming from. She was also thinking along the lines I had considered in regards to the *physical act* of marriage. Diane would still be my wife in a way that it mattered between the two of us, and I'll bring that point out a little later. I look at Lori and she does something I should have expected: She gets up and walks away. She doesn't get far. I calmly say, "Lori, don't go. We need to talk about this." She stops, and after a few moments she turns and looks at me. Her eyes regard me with total defiance. If she walks away right now, it could mean a great big "fuck you." I begin to wonder if she really loves me. Staying means that she is at least willing to compromise. As I wait, I don't even realize I'm holding my breath. I want to go to her and hold her. I can't this time. It's important that she comes to me on her own.

I know it's going to be an uphill battle. I see her expression change from defiance, rebellion, fear and doubt, and then start the process over again several times. We can talk through all the other emotions, but fear is going to be a major problem. People don't tend to let their fears go easily. I watch it all and I'm relieved when the doubt turns to understanding. Then her face holds no expression at all. That's when I hold out my arms. As she slowly walks to me, I say, "We need to talk this out now, baby."

I hold her in my arms as I look at Diane. I can't understand why Lori is shaking so badly. Fear of commitment? Damn, women go through that too? They love me unconditionally, I have no doubt about it. But the idea of marriage frightens them both. This is going to be a problem because marriage to both of them is something that I want, and I will not settle for less. I know only one of them can legally be my wife, but I want the other woman to know that she will equally be my wife in every way that it counts. Neither one of them has considered marriage as an option. I can't help but feel disappointed and eventually I get frustrated. It hurts to realize that maybe everything we have planned is only going so far. After thinking about it for a few minutes more, I realize one thing: They are trying to put up barriers, and I'm not having it! I am not going to give my all in another relationship, especially one this deep, without some serious commitment from all sides. There is too much at stake.

I turn to Diane and extend my hand to bring her into my arms and say, "I see that 'gentleman' you were married to put you through a lot, and I feel for you. I do know what men are capable of. I'm not trying to ignore what you feel, because I can basically understand it. In my opinion, you shouldn't look at it as a marriage issue but a man issue. Thirteen years is a long time to be with someone and end up mistreated and unloved. But I have to know, Diane, what you are asking of this relationship? Is it only supposed to be for a few months? A year? Two years? Are you going to humor me for a little while and then kick me to the curb to start over with someone else?

"I thought we were trying to build something worthwhile and permanent. Is your commitment level that limited? If you're up to the challenge of making this work then you should be willing to go the distance. If not, as much as I wouldn't like it, we can end this right now. I just hope the two of you can find someone that can love you for you *and* accept your limitations, because in this case I will not be the one for either of you. I have to have some permanency with this too. I have my stability to think of, and I also have to think of my daughter. If we're in a marriage, it shows that all of us are serious about this relationship. Not saying that we aren't now, but that ring and ceremony with our family and friends accepting it and understanding us, means a lot to me, and it will complete our trio."

Diane looks at me and says she will keep it on her mind. That was a start. I won't push further with Diane because she isn't the type of woman you push. You have to give her time. I release her from my embrace, and she goes to sit on the sofa.

Lori tries to follow her, and I catch her and gently pull her back into my arms. "No, baby, not this time," I whisper in her ear. "Lori, while I understand where Diane is coming from, she also has a point. You have never been married, and it will be a first-time experience for both of us." I look into her eyes and say, "I need this to work. Lori, I need to love you like this." I know why she is holding back, but I have to try.

"Ray, I could never give myself totally to a man in marriage because I know what men are capable of firsthand," Lori says in a resigned whisper.

"Lori, what you went through with your father was a tragic experience and should never happen to anyone. He wasn't right in what he did to you, but you must realize all men are not like that." Then she says the words that let me know exactly what else she's holding on to. "If I hadn't run away from home, it would never have happened." The tears and her pain come to the surface.

I hold her closely and Diane quickly comes to hold her too. Diane remains silent, sending Lori her love with a tight embrace.

Lori can't do this to herself. I have to let her know this. I kiss her forehead and lift her tear-filled eyes to meet mine. "Baby, it wasn't your fault. You have to know that. You have to believe that. Lori, you left home trying to find someplace that would be safer than where you were. Your father couldn't do that for you, and I can see that what happened has destroyed your trust in all men. To my knowledge you haven't told anyone the full story, and I won't press the issue right now. But if you haven't shared it with Diane either, then we need to find someone you can talk to. I'm here for you if you need me in that capacity, and I will listen and won't judge you. When you're ready, just let us know."

Lori's body is tense and still as she tries to hold

the tears and keep the pain within. I move my lips to her ear and whisper, "Lori, keeping it inside won't help you, and it will cause your emotions and feelings to worsen. That won't be good for any of us. When you heal, it makes you better, and overall that will be better for the relationship. We've become so in tune that if you're experiencing anything, it affects me and Diane too. We can help. That's what we're here for, baby. Let us at least try.

"Lori, if you're still holding back because of those other men who were in your life, let them go. What you went through is what a lot of people have been through. I understand because I put women through the same pain and have also endured that pain. When I was younger, I did play the games, but I'm older now, and I know what I want. I also know I won't hurt you, Lori. I love you too much for that. I'll keep that foremost on my mind."

I raise her face so I can look into her eyes. "Lori, we're supposed to learn from our mistakes, not deprive ourselves to prevent them. That was years ago, Lori. I'm pretty sure you've learned a lot about men since then, even though you haven't been with a man for the majority of the time. I believe you know enough not to make the same mistakes. It's the fact of seeing through the bullshit, finding out what's genuine and what's artificial. Lori, I know you're scared because marriage is not something you can just walk away from. It takes a lot more effort to become disentangled, and you're used to having that freedom. I'm scared too. You don't know how many times I thought that I couldn't handle this and that I wouldn't be enough for the both of you. I'm wiser now, and I damn sure don't want to deprive myself of the best this relationship can offer all of us."

I look at both women and make my case. "If you're both saying no, then I'm the only one that has done some growing these last few months. You've picked my brain, put me through your tests, and now you've made love with me. I've come out feeling stronger, balanced, confident and determined for this to succeed. You've brought out things in me that I didn't even know were there. It's time I brought out the best in both of you.

"You've both been talking about balance and equality in relationshps. Well, you're the ones that laid out the rules in the beginning and now that I have a few requirements of my own, you're going to say no. That's not right. I'm asking something of you that I think is only fair to me and my daughter. You can't have it all your way. I'm not like most men, and I've accepted things this far. I've also proven that I am willing to do my part, and I'd like to see you both do the same. The time for talking about things is over. You say you want this to work, then it's time to put up or shut up. Think about this, because I want an answer. You both started out as my friends and are now that and more. I can truly say that I want both of you as my wives. I want to be an obvious part of your lives. We can find a way to do this where each of us gets what we need. Come to me, Lori and Diane, and love me for me. Then you will make the right decision."

As I hold each woman in my arms, they are both silent. I can practically see the wheels turning and they actually look a little pissed. I'm sorry if I touched a few nerves, but I'm fighting for myself here too. They are very strong women and given the chance, they will take this relationship and make it into something that means I won't grow. I won't be able to be the man that I need to be. I can't go that route again, and we need to set this in place right now. My needs have to be taken into consideration. I don't think I've won completely, but I haven't lost either. I have gained some ground, and it's more than enough for now. I will try another approach when the opportunity arises and discuss with the each of them how this can work with our children. Maybe if we talk about it working, they will stop thinking of reasons for it not to work.

It's amazing, in the beginning *they* were the ones looking for this and now I'm the one trying to make sure that it continues to happen. I want them to see the benefit in what I am asking. I want them both, and I am ready to do the work.

STEPPIN'

Later that evening they take me to the most happening stepper's club in Chicago. More Than Enough is packed with wall-to-wall people. Lori's brother, Donny, owns this place, and we're escorted to a table immediately. (There are benefits to knowing the owner.)

As we walk toward our table, a brother steps up to Lori as she walks past and says, "Girl, how can I get with you? *Umph, umph, umph,* I'd love to have some of that ass!" Lori and I both spoke at the same time. I look at Lori and she immediately gets the message and remains silent. I notice the look on her face and realize that we are going to have to talk later. I turn to the man and say, "Brother, check yourself." My tone is enough to let him know that he is out of line.

"My fault, man," he says quickly, "I thought you were with the *other* woman.

"I am," I reply and watch as his eyebrows draw in as if to say "what?" The man goes back to the bar and has a conversation with a few of his friends. I whisper in Lori's ear, "Baby sometimes it takes a woman several tries to put a brother off, especially if they're as agressive as he is. I didn't want you to waste your time on him. I have every right to let any man know, who speaks to you that way, he's treading on dangerous ground." She looks up at me, and her eyes say that she's still a little pissed. As she opens her mouth to speak what's on her mind, I brush my lips across hers and softly swivel my tongue between the opening. She trembles in shock. End of conversation.

I make sure Diane is comfortably seated facing the door, which is her preference. She always has security on her mind. I didn't realize the chaos the two words spoken to Mr. Aggressive have caused. Suddenly I can feel all eyes turn on us. Obviously Diane and Lori feel a change in the air, so I ask them if they would like to leave. They both know why I am asking and say no. They don't care what anyone else has to say or think about it, but I don't want them to feel uncomfortable either. Just then the barmaid comes to the table. Lori orders an Amaretto Stone Sour while Diane has a double Vodka Martini. Evidently I'm the designated driver tonight.

I make a trip to the chamber and notice that the same group of men from the bar is following me. As I relieve myself, I notice the whole group watching. I look down. I don't have an extra dick and the one I have hasn't turned colors. What's up with these people? When I'm done, I walk to the sink and while I'm washing my hands, I can feel someone come up behind me. I look in the mirror and see a brother staring back at me. "How did you manage that?" he asks rudely. I know what he's talking about, but I decide to play dumb.

"The same way I've been doing it since potty-training," I say smartly.

The other men laugh as I smile. I grab a paper towel and turn to face him.

He looks pissed as hell as he says, "You know what I mean. How did you manage to get two fine women like that? They're not fighting or calling each other names and they sure don't look like hoes." All six-feet, two- hundred-twenty pounds of me step in his direction. The tension increases in the room as he backs up and puts his hands up to protect his face. "No, man don't get me wrong. I mean they don't look like they're from the streets, and they ain't selling it. They've got class. No offense, brother, but me and my friends are trying to figure out what the hell they see in you." I smile. I'm getting bored with this shit, but I answer his question anyway. "They see everything you don't see…" And I leave them all standing there wondering. My relationship with Lori and Diane is private, I don't have to explain myself to anyone.

I walk back toward my table but stop to look at both women. They are talking to each other and I watch their gestures, their style and grace. The guy was right, they do have class—not the snobbish "I'm better than you" type. They have the type of class that means they can go anywhere and handle themselves. I like it. What do they see in me? Everything I didn't see in myself…at first.

CHICAGO STYLE

A friend of Lori's comes to our table to speak, and he asks her to dance. Lori introduces me to Kevin as her man. The shock on his face says everything. He looks at me, takes the hand I offer and shakes it. He's still trying to take in what Lori has said. Diane just smiles and looks toward the dance floor.

Lori asks, "Ray, do you want to see how things are done in Chicago?"

I smile before I answer, "Anytime you're ready!" She smiles back, and I can tell she is about to say something smart, but decides to put her words into action. As they walk to the dance floor, Kevin looks back at me and the question is all over his face: "Who the hell did she just say he is? And where did he come from?"

When they make it to the floor, Lori transforms into this smooth-moving vixen. When I say she is smooth, I mean she is *smooooooth*! I can't take my eyes off her. Kevin is a good dancer, and they look good together. I watch Lori's hips and the smile on her face. The movements come easy to her. She has this sharp little rhythm that she changes every time he turns her. I look at Diane, and she has this devilish smile on her face as if she knows what I'm thinking. She says, "The fun of stepping is watching people's reaction to Lori's dancing. They're amazed at her style, and she's good at it." I look back at Lori and watch her turns, the rhythm, the smoothness. It's almost sexual. My friend below starts talking to me again. I will have to learn to step because I want to dance with Lori and Diane like that.

I ask Diane if she knows how to step, and she tells me she hasn't had the chance to learn yet. She says it's a Chicago thing and people don't step in Houston where she's from. Diane also tells me that Lori's brother taught Lori when she was growing up.

I look back at the dance floor and then watch the reaction of some of the men at the bar. Their looks make me want to get up to block their line of vision. *Lord, she looks good!* I didn't ask for it, but Lori and Diane have said that the rest of this day should be one without sexual activity. This is to give my friend a rest, but he is speaking very loudly as I try to calm myself *Down, boy! Not now. Please, not now. Damn, she looks good.* I'm not getting any cooperation from downstairs. If the Creator is listening…oh no, Diane places her hand on my groin. That's not fair! She's smiling at me as she massages me gently. She leans forward and whispers to me, "Would you like for me to sit on your lap, Ray. I could, um, keep it covered."

"Woman, are you trying to send me over the edge?" I ask.

"No, just over your limit." She laughs lightly.

"Diane, please don't do this to me right now," I plead.

"Do what, honey?" she asks innocently as she

strokes me. "You mean touch you like this, and this, and this?"

Lord, have mercy! Diane's hands are *dangerous*! I stand quickly and extend my hand to lead Diane to the dance floor. Maybe I'll be safe there. As I hold her close, I find that this isn't a wise choice either. Diane's fragrance, her touch and her beauty tonight have my dick still going in the wrong direction. Man, I'm in turmoil!

Unfortunately, Diane realizes what's going on. She can't help it. She asks, "Is that what I think it is?" Diane gives me another devilish smile and says, "Oh, my. We must do *something* about that." As we dance, she reaches down to touch me. She looks up into my eyes, and I can tell it is all she can do to keep from laughing. This is so unfair.

"Diane, please," I beg her.

"Please what?"

"Please stop."

"Oh, Ray, I don't think I want to," she says in her sexiest voice. "I love it when you're hard like this."

I used my last weapon. "I thought you were giving me a rest?"

"One part of you doesn't look like resting is an option," she counters.

She's right. My friend *does not* want his rest period. I'm in trouble once again. Diane leads me off the floor and toward the door. She stops briefly to whisper in Lori's ear. Lori doesn't miss a beat, starts laughing and nods, and we continue to move out into the parking lot. Diane unlocks the car door and we both get into the backseat...and the rest is something I can't even talk about...

Chapter 22

Day 7: Two?

Ray

I've been watching Lori and Diane, and I can't get something out of my head. They've been thoughtful ever since our talk of marriage. I'm not sure if it's my proposal that has them quiet or if it's something else. Lori is touching me a lot more now. It's almost as if she's acting like this will be our last time together. Will she say no to my offer? I hope not!

Diane keeps watching Lori, and it's obvious that she's worried about her. What's wrong? I can tell that they're keeping something from me. Diane can keep a secret but if you're watching closely, Lori's feelings always show on her face. Lori would probably tell me, and Diane must have said that she can't. What's up with them? I know them now, and I can read their body language. It's something they want to share with me but feel that they can't. Have they killed someone? Is Diane's husband actually dead? No, if anything, Lori's mother probably did it, but I don't feel it's that. I have to chuckle after thinking that one, remembering the threat Paula gave me. But I sober quickly as another thought comes to me. Is one of them terminally ill? No, they would have shared that with me. What is it that they're afraid to tell me?

Something's been in the back of my mind all week, but I haven't asked them. If I'm wrong, they will cut into me so quickly I won't have time to bleed.

As I watch how smoothly they work together, the gentle way that they handle each other. I get this idea that they are... *Oh, hell no!* That can't be. But then again, they've lived together peacefully for years, and they're very protective of each other. They move with a harmony that most friends don't have. There's always a kindness and consideration for each other's feelings. So I must ask... "How long have you been lovers?"

Lori drops the glass she's holding, and it breaks. She looks in my direction and closes her eyes. Diane finishes bringing a pan out of the stove and then looks up at me as I move toward them. Lori can feel me, and she opens her eyes. Diane is the one that answers. "Ever since my first trip here."

"Why did you feel that you couldn't tell me about this?" I ask.

"We know how some men feel about this type of relationship. Actually, how a great deal of people feel about it." Diane looks over at Lori, who is still holding her breath. Diane is breathing a sigh of relief. It's obvious that they were very afraid of how I would react to this news. How did they think they could keep it from me? Lori moves to stand directly behind Diane. I'm not having that! I gently pull Lori toward me and take Diane's hand in mine. As I stand between them, Lori looks up at me and says softly, "Ray, we never lied to you."

Lori is still tense, and I kiss the top of her forehead as I say, "I know, baby. You've never lied about anything I've asked you. It never even crossed my mind to ask about this. I'm hurt that you thought so little of me that you wouldn't tell me. It finally took really *seeing* you together for me to know. It's so plain to me that you love each other deeply. No one else might notice, but I know you now. Sometimes you look at each other and the love you have between you becomes obvious.

"Are you ashamed of the way you feel about each other? Are you afraid of what people might think about you?" I ask.

Lori looks at Diane and then back at me before she starts to explain. "No. When I made the decision to love Diane, I had to make sure within myself that I would do it without guilt or fear for myself. Being with her has done a lot for me. We have a good relationship, and it brings me peace, happiness and joy. I'm not going to spend the rest of my life loving her and feeling guilty about it at the same time. I believe that heaven and hell are a state of mind. If I'm wrong about what they are, then I love Diane enough to go to hell over this. I'm not willing to give her up for anyone." She looks directly at me as she says this, and I get the message. "We would be open about it because we can fend for ourselves but Brandon is another issue. We didn't want him to experience any problems growing up because of our decision."

DIANE

"How does he feel about it?" Ray asks.

"Brandon doesn't have a problem with it now. He loves his mother, but at first he didn't want her being 'that way.' We talked with him and found that he personally didn't have a problem with it. He was only concerned because of all the negative things other people had to say about it. He didn't want people saying things about me or his mom. He already has given black eyes to a couple of classmates when they commented on Lori's size. We didn't condone the severity of the beating that he gave those boys, but no one in their right mind has had the nerve to say it to him again. Boys have this thing about their mothers. If he's that way when people talk about Lori's physical makeup, how would he react when they talk about her sexuality? Imagine the ongoing problems he'll have if that came out. He'll be fighting every day because it's something that most people don't try to understand. I didn't want Brandon to spend his entire childhood fighting people about our decision. That would be totally unfair to him. He'll have enough things to fight about when he grows up. He shouldn't have to do any fighting now unless it's in self-defense. His life is already affected just by accepting his mom's choice. That's enough, and it's all we're going to ask of him.

"So we keep to ourselves, and the only people who know are friends and family that are mature enough to understand. It's not that we feel our choice is wrong, but we can't do that to Brandon. We're not obvious with our relationship, and Brandon has never seen us kiss or anything like that. He's never walked in on a moment of intimacy. When he's grown, it won't matter because then he will be able to fend for himself. We wanted to tell you, but could never figure out how.

"Ray, I never thought that you would ask us to marry you. I had my thoughts of how far this would go, but marriage wasn't one of them. It would have worked fine if you lived in New York and visited us on a regular basis. You probably wouldn't have known, and we could maintain our lives as they are now and still have the benefit of our relationship with you. I'm really sorry, Ray. We should have told you before now. We know this affects you, too, and it's something you should think about. Maybe you wouldn't want to marry women who are sexually involved with each other. Or women who have this type of bond."

RAY

I'm silent as I think about this for a few minutes. How *did* I really feel about it? I mean these are women that I love. I have to smile to myself. All this time I've been worried about sharing them with a man, constantly stressing I want to be the only *man* inside them, and they agreed to that. And here it is, everyone involved in this relationship gets a little of everyone. I stand corrected because in a way I'm sharing after all. I'm not angry or disturbed by it, and I find that it doesn't bother me at all.

I look at both of them and say, "It doesn't change the way I feel about either of you. A few months ago this would have been beyond my understanding. But now I know that a person can love more than one person at a time. I really do. And it doesn't matter that one of the people you love is female. I don't think you love each other because you're women, you love the individual. I love you both for who you are, and I know that you feel the same way about me.

"Now that I'm aware of it, I want to understand more about your relationship. How did it happen?"

DIANE

I walk to the sofa and sit down. Ray and Lori join me. I begin by saying, "When I would talk to Lori, I told her things about myself I thought I would never tell a soul. It was something about her voice that would calm and comfort me. It's one of the many things I love about her. I was so unhappy, and my husband and I had not been getting along. Sometimes her voice and encouragement were all I had to go on.

"After a while, I began to have feelings I couldn't explain. I didn't want to admit I was falling in love. I tried very hard to deny it, but my feelings for her were very strong. I didn't tell her how I felt. She told me about herself, and I was a very good listener. When she talked about some of the men in her life, even though she made the stories humorous, I sensed that she had been hurt deeply.

"Vacation time was coming and for the first time

in twelve years I decided not to take it with my husband. I let him know I was taking some time by myself to think about a few things. He didn't like it, but I believe he knew that if he made a fuss, things could get ugly. I don't think he was ready to end our relationship so soon.

"When I asked Lori if I could come to Chicago for a visit, she said yes. I was ecstatic because I would finally get to see her face-to-face. She sent me pictures so I would have something to go on when I came to Chicago. She didn't know what I looked like because I wouldn't tell her. As I walked through the airport, my heart felt like it was beating faster. I recognized Brandon by Lori's description, and he was holding a sign with my name on it. I hugged him and he told me that he made the sign himself. He was so well-mannered. When I came out of the terminal doors, I knew who Lori was right away. That beautiful smile and wonderful face greeted me. I embraced her, and the attraction I felt grew even stronger. Something I never thought would happen—Me? Attracted to a woman? As she helped me put my bags in the car, I couldn't help but notice the sexy walk she had. Lori moves so gracefully. She walks like she's thinking of sex all the time. You've seen her walk, Ray, so you know what I'm talking about. I thought to myself that she was absolutely perfect—all of her is pure woman. Lori never guessed how I truly felt about her.

"Lori had to go to work that week, and I rested, and it was the best rest I had in years. She came home the day after I arrived and said I looked ten years younger. I really felt it too. There was no stress, the pace here was so much slower, and I was in good company.

"We went a lot of places and one thing I can say, Lori knew where all the good restaurants were. I noticed that for a little guy, Brandon wasn't doing so bad putting away some food. Brandon was a very well-mannered child and had a sense of humor that was just like his mother's.

"Lori introduced me to the woman she calls her true mother, and I liked Paula immediately. Paula was very much like me in a lot of ways.

"The days were passing, and I still hadn't told Lori how I felt. My time to leave was approaching, and I was trying to figure out *what* to tell Lori and *how*. I was afraid of her reaction, and I thought I would lose a friend. But, my love for her was so strong I had to tell her.

"The last night of my visit, we were sitting in the living room discussing a variety of subjects. When we touched on the subject of men and sex, she explained to me how she felt about it. Lori thought she was frigid because she got sick when she thought of a man looking at her or touching her. I explained to her that she wasn't frigid, it was the men she had been seeing. I told her that I wanted to show her that she was alright. She didn't pretend to misunderstand me because she just looked at me and stared. I knew she was in shock, and I couldn't say anything else at that point. My heart felt like a hand was crushing it, and I knew I had made a grave mistake. I could deal with not having my love returned, but I didn't want to lose my friend. Was the risk of telling Lori worth possibly losing her friendship?

Lori

"When Diane first told me that she wanted me in that way, I was taken totally by surprise. I had never entertained the thought of sleeping with a woman before. I didn't see anything wrong with it, but I hadn't considered it for myself. I wasn't afraid or offended, and there was no pressure to do anything. We both sat in silence for a few minutes as I thought of what I wanted to do. I looked at her and realized that I actually wanted to experience it. I didn't know that the decision to try it would totally change my life. I didn't know what it would be like, but one thing for sure, I was truly unprepared for the pleasure it brought me. When Diane was done making love to me, I would have given her everything I owned."

DIANE

"I was afraid, but I held out my hand and a few moments later, Lori put her hand in mine. I led her to the bedroom, and I let her know she didn't have to do anything she didn't want to. Making love to her was very intense, and she was all tenderness, heat and softness. I thought of the many things she had told me, and I wanted her to feel beautiful and that she could be loved and cherished. It was my first time, too, so I used the pleasure that I experienced while making love to guide me. I knew what made me feel good, and she deserved to feel that there was nothing wrong with her. I enjoyed it immensely. There was nothing that I had before this experience that could compare to it. I was glad that I was already in love with Lori, because if I wasn't, I would have left my husband strictly for the pleasure this brought me. We made love several times that night and continued into the morning. It was a wonderful experience for both of us.

"As daylight came and we held each other close, I realized that I didn't want to leave, but I knew I had to. It would have been so easy just to abandon everything and never return to New York, but I couldn't do that. Not when there were so many loose ends to tie up, and my husband could come here and not just hurt me, but he could take his anger out on Lori and Brandon too.

"When Lori took me to the airport, my heart was aching, but I didn't let it show. The love I felt for her was returned to me. All it took was to look at her and see that Lori was happy. I could also see that she didn't want me to go either. Telling her how I felt was worth the risk, because it has truly paid off in every way.

"I made it home to my husband and…" The look on Ray's face makes me correct myself immediately "…actually, my ex-husband had this look of relief on his face. I guess he expected things to get back to normal. No matter how much I tried, I couldn't get back into the flow of things. Loving Lori had changed my whole outlook on life.

"The first couple of days, I was in turmoil, and I started drinking again to numb myself. I didn't have a single cigarette or drink while I was in Chicago. Not a one! I felt so free! So many thoughts were running through my mind. The one thing I knew was that I wanted to be with Lori. When I was with her, I was at peace. That's what I wanted more than anything else in the world—peace.

"It took a year for me to save money and put things in motion in preparation for leaving my ex-husband. Lori moved to several different apartments, changed phone numbers with each move and sent me a calling card to use. In this way my ex-husband wouldn't be able to trace her or me. We had to be very careful. I wasn't sure if he would think I was with her because that was the last place I visited, but I couldn't take the chance. Very few people know where she lives now.

While my husband was going to the Million Man March, I was on a single woman's mission to Chicago.

LORI

"After Diane left Chicago, I took off work for the next two days. I was in total confusion and couldn't get myself together. I thought to myself, *Is this why I have such a problem with men? Is this what I really am, and I've just been in denial?* I had never been attracted to a woman before then, but I also had never experienced this level of intensity when I was with a man. It scared me and I didn't know what to do with it. I enjoyed her entire visit and her friendship was special to me. I knew we could continue the friendship without the sexual aspect if I wanted to. When all was said and done, I had to think about how I felt and what I wanted. I had to think about the fact that this woman admitted to me that she loved me, and she truly meant it.

"I didn't think I could ever be loved and had given up on that. That's why it was so easy for me to abstain from sex all those years. I didn't want one without the other. It was so ironic, I had created a list of what I wanted in a relationship a few months before, and Diane matched all of the qualities I wrote down. I just hadn't specified a male. At first, it bothered me that love had to come to me in female form. When I really thought about it, I laughed like hell. 'Be *careful* what you ask for,' was more like 'be *specific* in what you ask for.' I finally came to accept her love, and I haven't regretted it since."

DIANE

"Our relationship was going well until years later, when I noticed a change in Lori. I would sometimes see her crying and that was unusual for her. I can't stand to see Lori cry, it tears into my heart. She didn't cry at all in our relationship in the beginning but after I had been here a while, her softer side started coming through, so now when she's frustrated or really pissed she might cry instead of raising hell like she used to.

"And let me tell you, Lori could raise some hell [and lower it or keep it somewhere in the middle too]."

When Lori cries, it's from the bottom of her soul. She tried to do this away from me but it's very hard for her to hide what's going on with her. For the first time in our relationship, she wouldn't tell me what was bothering her, and I thought something was terribly wrong.

"After several nights of this, I couldn't take it anymore, and I called a friend to take me out. For the first time since I left New York I had a drink. Actually, I had several. I was so worried about Lori that I hadn't slept in days. I rented a hotel room and stayed the night. I came home that next morning and Lori was sitting in a chair in the living room. It was obvious to me that she had been sitting there all night, worried about me. I sat on the floor at her feet and asked her to please tell me what was wrong. She finally let me know what was on her mind. She expressed her desire to have a man.

I thought to myself, *Is that all?* Thank God! I thought it was something life-threatening. I was hurt that Lori wouldn't tell me her feelings. She made sure to express that she didn't want our relationship to end or to suffer because of something she wanted. Lori also didn't want to change the way we had sex, she liked it just like it was— that was really important for me to hear because I also didn't want to change the way our sexual encounters were. She explained that it wasn't just the part that she was looking for, it was the entire package of a male—the touch, the taste, the smell, the hardness, the way men talk and handle things. She said 'Dee, I love you for you, and I wouldn't add anything to what we have. I love your softness and kindness, and I need that—and it can only come from a woman.' She didn't want to tell me because she thought I would be hurt by her having this desire. I love Lori, and I want her to be happy. I didn't mind her having a man, but he had to be a certain type of man. I didn't spend that time building her confidence to let some low-down, jack-leg motherfucker come and break her spirit down again. So it could not be a man like the ones she used to deal with."

Lori was wearing the only smile I've seen since we began this conversation. "Jack-leg, Diane?" she asks while shaking her head.

I have to think about it for a moment. "Well, you

know what I mean, Lori," I answer smartly. Ray was watching both of us and smiled as he waited patiently for me to finish.

"In the beginning I totally misunderstood what Lori needed. I still thought it was just about the dick. I watched Omarr for three months, and chose him as her 'fix.' The appreciation was evident because he couldn't keep his eyes off her. He watched her movements very closely, and it was obvious he was very attracted to her. I thought all she needed was a man who would appreciate her and make love to her real good. Omarr was extremely virile and sexy, and the man was very easy on the eyes. Actually, the man was *fine*!

"I didn't realize that sex from a male wasn't all Lori needed. While I knew Omarr wasn't a mistake, I now understand that Lori wanted something more than just sex. That's why she never really gave herself to him. It wasn't the part that she was looking for.

"That request was very specific. So I knew the one thing I wasn't going to have was some wimp of a man that didn't know what he wanted. My baby needed a real man, if she was to have one. This time, I understood that he had to be a man with certain characteristics and qualities. Lori told me about the list she created that brought me to her. This time we made sure to specify that it be a man. I wanted a man that would love her as much as I do. I didn't want Lori to be hurt again. Even though I have all the things I've ever wanted in my hands or within reach, if the man we chose could love me too—then I would be alright with it."

Ray

Diane looks directly into my eyes and says, "Personally I never thought that man existed."

I have to ask, "So you went along with this trio relationship just to keep Lori?"

Diane looks at me and doesn't say a word. It was a useless question. I know Diane well enough to know that she doesn't do anything unless *she* wants to. But judging by the way the story unfolds, it sounds that way. After a while Diane answers my question anyway. "As time went on, Lori met someone on the Internet. Lori started telling me about you, and you sounded interesting, *and* you were a brother, which was Lori's personal preference. She said after Juan and Omarr, she had done her part for international relations—she wanted a brother! I began to talk with you and learn more about you for myself. It had been a long time since a man captured my interest at all. I never thought it could be this way for me again.

"It's not that I hated men or anything like that. And even though my trust in men was low, that wasn't the reason that I didn't seek out a relationship with a man for myself. I had the love, the house, the family and peace of mind. I was content, and I still am today. But when I started talking and flirting with you, I realized that I enjoyed it. I didn't think I had a need as strong as Lori's, but I liked you, and my feelings grew stronger from there. I was perfectly willing to let Lori do this alone in order to complete herself. But now here we are, and I'm happy with it. I consider you a bonus in my life. You don't take away from what I already have, you add to it. I'm happy that my marriage didn't leave me bitter toward men, but it did leave me a little frightened and mistrustful. You taught me how to love in that way again."

I'm relieved to hear it. That means that Diane wants me for me and not because she is trying to please Lori. I realize that I'm alright with this for a very selfish reason. If they can please each other like this, then it isn't likely that they will look to another man to be with them while I'm trying to make my way to Chicago, if it comes to that.

They've been preparing me for this all along.

Understanding

I fix my women an exquisite dinner of shrimp scampi, angel hair pasta, Italian vegetables, salad and garlic bread. (Yes, I really can cook!) Diane makes strawberry cheesecake for dessert. Diane and Lori have just informed me that they will not let me be the dominant one this evening. "Your ass is ours!" says Diane, simultaneously slapping high fives with Lori. I mutter, "As if it wasn't already." We all laugh.

I ask what I think is a simple question, and the discussion gives me an insight into what they truly believe. "You are both such spiritual women and have a deep belief in the Creator. How can you be so spiritual when most religions are against this type of sexual relationship?"

Lori's fork is halfway to her mouth when I ask the question. She puts it down, looks at me and asks, "Do you want the truth, or the version that will let us remain friends?"

I say with a smile, "I want the truth."

Lori

This man knows how to take us to the deep end of the pool. What I have to say is going to take a lot of explaining. But I want to say it in a way that brings understanding without seeming to attack what he's known all of his life. Understanding is the key. Let me work from that end. I take in a deep breath before I begin. "First of all, we don't confuse spirituality with religion. Religion is basically a set of guidelines, a documented belief system or an interpretation of that belief system. Spirituality has to do with what's inside of us. That part of us that animates our bodies and experiences joy, pleasure, pain and emotions somewhere in between. Our spirit exists and needs nurturing, growth, as well as a means of expression. That expression can be a combination of religion, art, music, dance, sex, love, etc. Everyone chooses which combinations they need or don't need as they experience life and keep growing. That's why some people are brought up one way, and as they grow, they change their belief system from what they were raised in, to something that speaks to them at whatever point they're at in their lives. That can cause some hard feelings in families especially when some members believe that their way is the only way. Even if we don't set foot inside a church or temple, we still have a spirit that needs nurturing. It doesn't take being in a place or with a group of people to do that. I know what works for me, and I chose a spiritual path that feeds me. No one can tell me how to feel or how to be. My spirit directs me in that. I love and I live my life in a way that brings me peace. That's all I want is peace.

"No one outside of myself can make me feel guilty about the choice that I've made either. They don't know me, and they don't know what I've been through. No one can live my life for me, and anyone coming to me trying to tell me how wrong I am or where they think I'll spend eternity is in for a rude awakening. If I'm going to be judged for anything that I do or have done, it will be by the one who counts—my Creator; and at the time it counts—which is, when I return to my Creator.

"My life is right for me. Diane is right for me. She's everything female that I need in my life—she's my sister, my mother, my friend, my companion and my lover. You are also right for me, Ray. You represent everything male that I need in my life—you are my father, my brother, my friend, and also my companion and lover. All that I experience from the both of you completes me. I'm not going to love either one of you and feel guilty about it the entire time.

"For that matter, I don't have anything to say about anyone else's relationship unless it hurts or harms someone else or if there is an injustice done to a child. I recognize that people choose a path that works for them so other people's relationships are something I don't put my energy into. I have nothing to say about interracial dating, alternative lifestyles, young men with older women or vice versa. Who am I to say someone is doing something wrong? My opinion is just that—mine. Their opinion is just that—theirs. I mean society and people change their way of looking at things all the time. Or things are changed based on the culture or society. For example, Ray, you grew up with the Bible just like I did, right? Let me start from there. Check this: there are three different instructions on what to eat: first it was fruits and vegetables only (or things with seeds), then it was changed to include some of the animals, later it was changed to bless the food and eat anything you want. Why did it change? It took the needs of the culture or society being given the instruction into consideration. Also, there are two different ways of dealing with anger: an eye for an eye and a tooth for a tooth, or turn the other cheek. Now I only have two cheeks and when I run out of them, I'm back to the original formula because it makes people back up off of you a lot quicker."

Ray and Diane both laugh at that statement and Ray says, "I guess it depends on the situation. I've heard some people say, well by that method we'll all be walking around eyeless and toothless. But it's not fair that I'm the only one wronged and the only one missing an eye (or a tooth). I find that when someone has done us wrong, the majority of people don't just walk away. They deal with it in a way that sits right with them and then they move on. I never saw things from that perspective before. I can't just take one instruction and disregard the other. It has to apply to the situation. Ask any mother or father whose child has been hurt or wronged, and they will tell you that walking away from a situation doesn't always work. I mind my own business and maintain my own individual needs. I support my loved ones and that's all that matters to me. If more people thought like this, there would be a lot less trouble in the world. People should just let people be. There's no other way to put it. But it also sounds like you're saying that not only should people learn to accept others for what they are, they should also learn to love and trust themselves and their choices. A lot of people still don't have that ground covered."

Ray understands my point, and I'm glad for it. "Ray, I don't think you could have dealt with me before Diane and I had a relationship. I would have sent you through hell and back on the express train! Being with her has taught me how a relationship works: communication, caring, consideration, growth and developing, sharing the same goals and everything else that goes with it. I've never experienced it before. I'm also loyal to those who love me. I'm not the type of woman to say, 'Oh well, now that I have a man in my life, I can just kick her to the curb.' I still need what Diane gives me, but I need what you give me as well.

"I decided that the way I used to worship didn't work for me anymore. I didn't want to focus on fire, brimstone and fear anymore. I wanted to love the Creator because I want to, instead of being afraid not to. I started going to services at a place that teaches the principles from a variety of different belief systems: Science of Mind, Metaphysics, The Aquarian Gospel of Christ, Buddhism, Yoruba, Metu-Neter, King James Version Bible and a few other scriptures that agree with me. Sometimes a poem or a positive thought can become the subject of the day. Either way, it reinforces something I've always believed in—some truth can be found in *every* teaching. Even if that truth is as simple as 'God is.' I can take what I need from each one, and that which I don't understand or doesn't agree with me at the time—I leave it alone.

"I go to a place where I see results for myself and my family, and in the lives of the people I worship with too. Being there has helped me to work on what's inside my spirit— the hurt, and the pain. It's helping me to come to terms with everything, my nature, my past—everything. I can look on people and forgive and not be weighted by it. It's an everyday process.

"The more I recognize the Creator as my source, the more I am able to fulfill my needs and desires—not just material or physical, but the spiritual ones I've neglected for so long or didn't recognize were wanting.

"It's a small but powerful group of people, and they are about their own spiritual development. They accept me for me. My lifestyle isn't something that they focus on—they focus on me. Even if a few of the people there feel it is wrong on a personal level, they never show it in the way they interact with me.

"These people have a prosperous mentality as we all should. The first time I saw the collection plate—I tripped. People were cheerfully popping in fifties, hundreds and checks for more than that. This is more than I've seen happen anywhere else. Most places have to hold offerings several times and still don't see this type of faith in the plate. I've come to realize how blessed I truly am, and I started giving ten percent of my income. This is the only place of worship that I've *ever* wanted to do this. I want to give because I know now that even with everything that has happened to me that I've had a lot of good happen in my life. And I still exist because of—or in spite of— what happened to me. The Creator is still a part of me, and I'm still a part of the Creator, no matter which way I choose to worship or how I choose to live."

DIANE

I want to give Ray my own answer to his question and since Lori has his mind already open..."Ray, now you know I have something to add too. Are you ready for me?" He laughs because I'm throwing his words back at him. Ray spreads his arms wide as if to say: *well bring it on*. I guess by now he shouldn't be shocked by anything we say—or do.

"Ray, I've read that particular passage that speaks on same-sex relations. We know that King James altered the Bible to allow himself to get a divorce and to suit his rulership, which is why it's called his version. I'm also aware that quite a few books are missing from his version and many of the other popular Bibles. Why is that? I also noticed that all of the instructions in Leviticus 18 specifically speak to men, including the one on homosexuality. It doesn't follow up with the same instructions for women. The one exception is that verse regarding bestiality—*then* it specifically addresses the woman—I find it a little odd that it went down like that. It is the only reference to female sexual activities in the chapter. I'm not trying to use that to justify my lifestyle, because it doesn't need justification. It's just that people have automatically assumed that it's direction for both male and female. Actually the bigger argument has been that we were not included in that law because the *sin* that was attached to same-sex or masturbation act for men, was the sin of wasted seed. Women don't have any seed (or semen) to waste. So it wasn't as much of a concern with same-sex acts regarding women. Women like to be touched, held and loved, and our feelings were not always taken into consideration. Women probably turned their affections on one another. It makes sense to me that this might have been an outlet for women.

"I'm not saying that men who love men are wrong in what they do. The law of Onan was laid strictly to make sure that repopulation would take place. Maybe men were having so much fun by themselves that they weren't doing the job on the first instruction: be fruitful and multiply. Well, we don't have a repopulation problem anymore so the question is: Does this law carry as much weight as it used to? Is it just pure coincidence that allowed some instructions to change and not others? People live their lives and make their own choices. I won't be standing with anyone else when they meet the Creator, I'll be too busy doing my own explaining. I don't have time to get caught up in other people's lives. It's enough work just to maintain my own life.

"The point I'm making, Ray, is that we put a lot of stock in and alienate family members and friends on the word of a book that has changed meanings, purpose and leadership a little too often. Yes, there is still a lot of truth in the pure essence of the Bible, but we should be applying the words to make our own personal existence better. Not using it to downgrade, criticize and make people's spirits suffer or make them submit to the Creator solely out of fear. I thought the whole process of existence was growth, and the Creator wants us to have life, and live life, not be laden with so much guilt that we don't know how to enjoy what has been given to us. Life is too precious to spend it otherwise. It took me years to figure that out. But I've learned this lesson well and I hope you can too.

"I like where I worship and focus on my spirituality. I was tired of places that said women couldn't wear this or that, or 'we don't allow women in our pulpit.' Some people just focus on the external and take scripture too literally. It's hard for me to take a literal view of a book that has been used with ulterior motives, translated so many times and changed hands the way the Bible has. Especially when we all recognize that women made vital contributions and sacrifices in the Bible. Women were also a strong part of Jesus' ministry. When he first made his reappearance the first person he showed himself to was a woman. That should tell us plenty. A lot of what was added to the Bible regarding women and their role in the church or ministry was put into writing *after* Christ left. It was not spoken by him and was written into scripture based on a culture that did not hold women in high esteem.

"I wanted some place that would help me to work on what's inside. I like where I am spiritually, and I believe that whatever each individual believes in their spirit is what works for that person. When our hearts and spirits cry out to the Creator, by whatever means we use to express ourselves, be it Science of Mind, Metaphysics, Universal, Baptist, Methodist, Lutheran, AME, Apostolic, Church of God in Christ, Sanctified, Buddhist, Muslim, Hebrew Israelite, Ausar-Auset, Yoruba, Catholic or Traditional African or by whatever principles or name we call or serve the Creator, we are understood. We as a people have had the religion that we came here with taken from us. And because we have taken on the religions we've been taught, we don't even know what it is or was. Yet, despite this, we're still heard and still blessed for it. The Creator knows, and accepts us—regardless of what spiritual path we choose to take. No one can tell me otherwise, this is what I strongly believe. And I hope this answers your question."

RAY

Once again, I've been given a plateful of food for thought. I'm alright with this. What they believe and how they worship seems to mirror something that I've always felt deep inside. I also know that I need to read about each belief system they spoke of because some of them I've never heard of.

After our discussion, Lori and Diane excuse themselves from the table. A few minutes later, they call to me, and I find that there's a trail of rose petals from the dining room table to the bedroom. I follow the line of red and yellow flowers. I read the note that's attached to the door. WE'LL BE GENTLE, it says. They both look at each other and smile as I enter the room. Somehow I think they're not telling me the truth on that one.

They're both lying naked and covered with rose petals. "*Mmmmm*, a treat," I say. The discarding of my clothes begins! Like hungry, frisky kittens they come to me. Petals falling everywhere. An assortment of sensuous kisses and licks greet my body with every item of clothing they remove.

From head to toe, they are both exploring every inch of me. I react by moaning and then I glide my fingers down the line of their backs. They lead me to the bed, and the atmosphere changes as Lori takes my hands and pins them down on the bed. She firmly kisses and licks my lips. At the same time, Diane glides her tongue smoothly down my legs. From my inner thigh to my ankles her tongue caresses the area she is working. "Damn, that feels good!" I say.

"Does it, baby?" Lori asks softly.

Lori has that wicked look in her eyes again. I can tell that I'm in trouble, and this time I'm at her mercy. They both adjust their bodies over my dick. First, Lori takes me inside her, and she glides back to the tip and moves slightly forward and away. Then Diane positions herself above me and slides down on my dick and rises back to the top. They each take a turn thrusting their bodies down onto me one stroke at a time. Each stroke is a different woman, a different level of wetness, heat and tightness. *The feeling is unbelievable!* After several repetitions I can feel myself begin to cum. I am not ready to do that!

"Oh, damn!" I yell. I hold my body tight against Diane and find I can't keep from cumming. But I know that the both of them can help me. Lori, Diane, please...."

"Not this time, baby," Lori says as she watches Diane take the last stroke. I release with a deep, long moan as they both watch.

Lori says in her sexy, sarcastic tone, "Ooooh. What happened, baby?" I give her a devilish look. Giving me no time to recover, Lori begins to kiss my chest. I ask them, "Where the hell did you learn *that* move?"

Diane says, "Lori's mom told us about the Double Dip. They used to do that sort of thing back in her day. She thought it would be a good one to try on you."

My eyebrows raised as high as possible. "You know, I'm a curious person by nature, *but I'm going to leave that one alone....*"

I then whisper in Diane's ear, "Can I watch you two now?"

Watch us do what, Ray?" she asks.

"May I watch you and Lori enjoy each other?" Diane looks at me and then smiles as I say, "Ever since we talked I've been curious about it. I've also been curious about something else."

"What?" she asks.

"If you don't engage in oral sex, then what do you do to please her and to make her cum?"

Her eyes brighten and a knowing smile touches her lips, "Ray, I knew you would get around to asking."

"If you don't want to answer or show me how you make love, I understand," I say quickly.

"No, I don't have a problem with it. I told Lori from the start that we wouldn't have to do anything that makes her uncomfortable. What she doesn't like, I might like. What I don't like, she might like. We play it by ear, so we're open and receptive to each other's need. There are so many other ways to bring pleasure to each other—and we're really good at it. Most relationships like ours are more physical, but we do what works for us. Sometimes it's not the act of sex that brings pleasure. The touching, teasing, stroking and cuddling sometimes is more than enough. Not to mention that a wicked imagination and the right kind of equipment can bring a woman to her point," Diane explains.

"Are you sure you don't use a strap-on?" I ask.

Diane strokes my thighs as Lori massages my feet. "No, Ray, only hand-held equipment for us—Lori was adamant about that."

Diane smiles as she runs her fingers over my dick, but her eyes say so much more. I understand. Equipment is nice—but they want the real thing.

"Ray, you might have a problem with seeing us together like this," Diane says "Are you sure you want to see this?"

I didn't give it a second thought, "Yes, I'm sure...."

Diane rises and takes Lori by the hand, giving me room to get off the bed. Diane asks Lori to lay on her back, and it's obvious that Lori is not sure if they should do this. Diane begins by massaging, caressing and touching Lori's body. Lori can't manage to stay still. Diane caresses her breasts. She jumps in surprise and begins to speak. "*Shhhhh*, it's alright. He asked to see this."

Lori turns her head and looks at me. I blow her a kiss and say, "Enjoy, I'll join you in a minute."

Lori closes her eyes as Diane circles her tongue around Lori's nipples and then takes the left breast into her mouth. She circles the right nipple with her fingertips. Sounds of pleasure fill the room as Lori bites her bottom lip. She is enjoying every minute of this. It's such a beautiful sight. The two women in my life are pleasing each other.

Diane drapes her tongue across Lori's stomach and then she kisses her way down to Lori's navel and...

I understand why some men are jealous of women being together like this. I'm watching it being done, and I see why this is such a threat. The sensuality between women is something most men can't duplicate. There's a sweetness, softness and oneness to their lovemaking. It's a slow and gentle process, and a man could never make it this soft. I want to see more but I'm getting hard, and I can't take it anymore.

I walk over and touch Diane's back. "Don't stop," I tell her. I begin to place long, slow, soft kisses on her. Using the heat of my mouth, I run my lips over her back and then down each cheek of her incredibly, soft ass. I work my way down to her sweet, chocolate center and I take it into my mouth gently. Diane gives a deep moan of acceptance. I quickly stop and stand up. I'm rock-hard—again! I circle the lips of her center and find Diane is steaming hot and wet, so I submerge! Diane's reaction triggers Lori's orgasm. Diane leans her face deeper into Lori's breasts as her juices pour onto the rose petals covering the bed. With short, hard pumps, I stroke Diane, gripping her hips so she doesn't move. She begins to cum, and I thrust my dick in her to feel the wetness as she releases it. I don't have to tell you how much I enjoy this....

"Do you want more?" I ask softly.

"Yes," they both reply.

We change positions. I find myself on the bed again. Lori straddles me while Diane slowly lowers herself to sit on my face. I part Diane's lips with my fingers to expose her clit. I nibble gently there—very gently. Circling her clit with my tongue, I feel Lori is thrusting down on me more firmly and then she stays in one place as she works her muscles tightly around me. This woman's control is unbelievable! Watching me take Diane has aroused Lori even more. I have to try this with Lori. I know it will bring her pleasure too. I pull Diane close to my mouth, pushing my tongue as far as it can possibly go until my mouth begins to hurt from the strain, and I have to pull back just a little. We move to the same rhythm. Tasting, stroking, accepting with such intensity, I'm surprised the bed is still in one piece.

Chapter 23

DAY 8: THE BEGINNING

RAY

I wake up, and I feel that something's missing. Lori is not lying next to me. Where is she? Diane's body generates a lot of heat, and it feels nice. But I miss the comfort of Lori's body too. I smile to myself as I realize that I'm getting spoiled with this. I run my hands over Diane's breasts, and she moans and turns to me. I kiss her forehead and the tip of her nose. I reach over to the nightstand for a chocolate mint and let it work its way through my mouth. I whisper in her ear, "I have to find a lost sheep."

Diane wraps her arms around my neck and kisses me to share the sweetness. She tells me, "Lori never needs a lot of sleep. She always has so much energy, that normally with four hours of sleep she's ready to roll."

"Has she always been like that?" I ask.

"Somewhat, but even more so since I've been living here. This week is the most I've seen her sleep in all the years we've been together. She normally can't even force herself to sleep longer," Diane explains.

"I know the feeling," I say, remembering the many times I've experienced that this week.

This is the perfect time to get Diane's thoughts on some things that have me concerned. I want the relationship

between us to be as strong as the one I have with Lori—
or as strong as the one they have. I run my hands over her
back and shoulders.

"Diane, I can feel when something is really going
on with her. I never feel that from you, and I wonder why.
I want to be just as much in tune with you."

Diane touches my face. She pauses for a second
or two before she answers. "I don't show my feelings the
way Lori does. She's like that right now because she's
comfortable expressing herself when she knows that the
person truly loves her."

"What about you, Diane?" I ask.

"I'm better at giving love than receiving it, but Lori
gives as good as she gets and that's the beauty of it. When
she receives a little she gives back that much and more.
Ray, you seem to be the same way, but I'm still kind of
inward about my feelings." Diane shifts her position
slightly, and I can feel her breath on my chest. It is really
getting to me, but we need to cover this ground.

"Diane, is there a time that you will feel comfortable
enough to express yourself with me?

She lifts up so she can look me directly in my eyes.
"I can only hope so, Ray. Just talking with you is enough
sometimes," she said in a soft voice.

My next question has been with me for a couple of
days, and it was extremely important. "Diane, does it bother
you that Lori seems to get so much of my attention? I
don't want it to be a problem for us."

She kisses my cheek. "Ray, I know she needs it.
I've had twenty-one years of being with a man and that is
five times longer than most of the men she's been with—
collectively. She hasn't had the love and care that a man
can give. Even though it didn't happen during the entire
time, I did have it at some points. And right now I already
have what I want. No offense, Ray, but I don't feel left out

because I don't need as much from you as the average woman."

I kiss her gently. "You're definitely an above-average woman in my book, Diane."

"I know, Ray, both of us are." She smiles up at me.

I kissed her again before I say, "I don't think I could ever view you any differently. I really appreciate your understanding. Lori fights me so hard on small things sometimes. I feel I have to stay one step ahead of her."

DIANE

He's right on track with that, I know from first-hand experience. "I know, Ray. I've been there. You have your work cut out for you. She wants to love you completely, but she will not give in easy. When she fights you, she's fighting something from inside of her that's real for her. Trust is a hard thing to give, especially when someone has broken it the way it's been done with Lori or with me. I thought that there were a lot of things Lori should have let go by now, and I've helped to a certain degree, but I think that together we can help her heal the rest of the way.

"Outside of her mother and son, Lori has felt unloved. When I showed her that I loved her, she tried it at every opportunity. The only thing that gave me patience and strength was that I personally had been through some things that made me understand where she was coming from. Not everyone reacts to situations like hers, or mine in the same way. She's strong in a lot of ways, but she has her weak spots just like I do. I had to love Lori more than her fears.

"When Lori finally stopped testing me and started loving me back, I found it was well worth the effort. Lori has a lot of love to give and when it's the right person, the rewards are plentiful. Just like she has a need to be touched and held, she also has a need to touch and hold."

Then I ask him, "Ray? Could you imagine being in love with two women just like Lori at the same time?"

"Damn!" Ray said quickly.

"Exactly," I replied. "The difference in our needs is what will make this relationship work for all of us. I like holding you, making love with you and nurturing the both of you." I stroke his chest and kiss him softly.

"Diane, I love you," Ray says and looks directly in my eyes.

I feel him. "I know, Ray, and I love you too." Ray holds me and whispers the words *I love you, Diane* over and over in my ear as I caress him. As he speeds up the kisses and caresses, I laugh and say, "Ray, you can give me the condensed version of yourself. More like the *Ray Cliff Notes*. A little of you should go a long way." I give him one of my wicked smiles. "Even though there's nothing little about you."

He smiles at my comment and then his eyebrows draw together. Ray lifts my chin so that we're at eye level once again, "Diane, are you willing to take on the responsibility of raising another child? I mean, you're both almost done raising Brandon."

Good question. I know this is a serious point with him, and it's a question he should ask. "Ray, I've always wanted children, and I was elated to have the opportunity to raise Brandon. I would love Janese as if I had her myself. It will be easy to raise her with all three of us pulling together. We just have to make sure that she will not be affected by our lifestyle." Ray's eyes are watching me intently. He's paying very close attention to this answer, as well he should.

"Brandon can understand what's going on, and we always leave the door open to discuss anything with him. He has come to me and asked questions that he's too embarrassed to ask his mother. And that's the way it should be. I hope that we can create an environment that will allow Janese to become the young woman that she's supposed to. I want her to be able to experience happiness in all aspects of her life. The three of us can help give her the self-confidence and inner strength that she'll need to withstand any challenges that come her way. That's what I would want for a child that came from my body, that's what I want for Brandon and Janese."

RAY

Diane's answer lets me know that she's ready for the trio to be complete. Diane kisses me and pulls me to her breasts, and I rest there for a while. There's nothing like the comfort of a woman. You can't buy it, beg for it or steal it. A woman has to give it freely and when she does, it's pure heaven.

"Ray, go to Lori. She's feeling a lot of things right now and maybe you can help sort them out," Diane says softly.

I linger a few minutes more before I remove myself from Diane's embrace and stand up to stretch. I bend down to kiss her breasts and say, "There's no telling how much weight I've gained this week with all this good food."

Diane laughs, pats my buttocks and says, "Maybe some of these extracurricular activities have worked it off."

I certainly hope so...

* * *

I walk into the living room and find Lori sitting by the window. She doesn't hear me walk into the room so I call out to her, but she doesn't respond. I sit behind her and pull her to my chest. She doesn't resist, but she's not sitting comfortably either. "What are you thinking about?" I ask softly.

Lori shakes her head as if to say that it's nothing. I hold her close as I say, "Talk to me, baby. Tell me what's on your mind."

She takes in a deep breath, and she moves to rise as she asks, "Do you want something to drink?" I gently pull her back against me.

"No, Lori, I want to know what's troubling you." She is never able to hide her emotions from me or Diane and that makes things easy.

I turn her to look at me, and I can tell by the set of her shoulders that whatever it is weighs heavily on her mind. Today is my last day here, and I know if anyone would feel it strongly, Lori would. I can also tell she's on the verge of tears, but she's holding them back well. She tries so hard to keep them in. She doesn't have to be like this with me. She can cry all she needs to, and I won't see her as any less strong. Lori needs the release.

It's then that I realize something extremely important: Lori and Diane love each other so much that they didn't allow each other to really deal with what's hurting them. Lori would never have asked Diane to put an end to that chapter with her husband because Lori knew it was too painful for Diane to think about. Diane would not ask Lori for the full details of what happened with her father because reliving the pain would be too much for Lori to bear. So they loved each other and existed with their pains too. I love them both and I want to help them heal completely.

Lori's voice is just above a whisper, "I know you have to leave, I just don't have to like it."

She allows her body to relax a little. "Ray, it's hard for me to trust people with my heart and my life," she says. I hold her tightly as she continues. "I know we can plan and talk forever, but nothing is for sure. Diane is a certainty in my life. She's a woman that's true to her word, and that's one of the reasons we've lasted this long. Diane put up with so much from me in the beginning. I wasn't used to really loving and living with someone. I wasn't an easy person to be with. Sometimes I'm a solitary soul, and sharing myself doesn't come easy.

"If Diane were a man, she would have been out of here that first month. I think only a woman would have the type of patience it took to deal with me then. I didn't really know how to exist with someone else in my living space. I wasn't always considerate, maybe even a little selfish. Diane loved me enough to overlook those things and then I began to change. To accept her love for what it really was."

Lori plants a kiss on my lips. "Ray, I'm still thinking of what you asked me. I'm also thinking of what I want. Could you deal with living with us permanently? Would it be a problem if you had your own separate bedroom?" she asked seriously.

"To answer the first question—Yes. To the second—Why?" I couldn't imagine where this last question came from.

"Diane and I have our own rooms now, and it means we have our own space. It makes things peaceful with us not being under each other all the time. That's what makes it work. I think if you had your own space, it would work well too. You would have your own closet, your own bed, your own areas with your choice of colors. If you want to walk around butt-naked and dick-happy, you can."

I picture that and start laughing and after a few moments she relaxes and joins me.

"Ray, if you want to rant and rave about something, you can go to your room and lose your mind with no one watching you. Personal space is important," she explained.

"Lori, is that what you do when you feel the need to be alone?" I ask.

She let out a sigh and says, "No, I don't get angry like I used to but I do walk around in the raw." She smiles at the last part of her statement.

I don't understand how this works, so I have to ask. "What if I want to be with either of you."

"You can come visit either one of us, or we can come to your room. It will be like dating, and we won't become so 'common' to one another."

I never thought of it like that.

Lori goes on to say, "Another thing, I think you should buy your own home when you move here. I don't ever want you to be in the position you were in a few weeks ago. Even if you rent it out, you should buy some property for you and your daughter."

Damn, she just keeps coming up with stuff! "You're not trying to say that you don't think this will work out, Lori?"

"No, but I want to know that you're with us because you *want* to be, not because you *have* to be," she says.

I give in, just a little. "Baby, you have so little trust in people. Why do you always need assurances from me?"

"Ray, it's not just a matter of trust or assurances. It's a matter of your personal security. It's the same as when Diane came into my life and I checked her against my list. I knew she was the one. She had everything I asked for, I just hadn't been specific on the physical side. I just wasn't too thrilled that the person happened to be female. Now I'm presented with another person that meets the qualities of my new list, and you're requesting something that I didn't have on my list and wasn't pepared for. I never thought I would be married because I recognize my shortcomings more than anyone. I didn't think it would happen with me being the way I am because it probably wouldn't last. I know you're serious about us, honey, but I want you to always cover your bases," she explained. Lori still looked concerned, so I decided to help set her mind at ease.

"Lori, as we were driving around, I did see some property that I might be interested in. I want all of the people I care about in one place. So, if I can convince her, I want my mother out of New York too. I will buy some property for her. Not too close, but not too far away from us. You don't have a problem with that, do you?" I ask.

Lori looks even more concerned. "Ray, I didn't think about that. How will your mom take knowing about our relationship?" she asks.

"I don't know, baby, but she will have to accept my choice eventually. I'm making a wise decision here and won't have any regrets," I say seriously.

"I hope I won't have any regrets either, Ray. I could be satisfied with what I have with Diane. I thought I would live with her and my equipment for the rest of my life. I like the softness, the touching, caressing and cuddling, and sleeping next to her at night. Most relationships like ours are more physical, more sexually involved. And a lot of women who have same-sex relationships look down on us for that. But I like it the way ours is. I also love your taste, your smell and your touch. There's nothing that compares to you. I know some people would say to my choice to have a relationship like this, 'Oh, she's just confused or undecided.' But that's bullshit! I know what I need and what I want. I don't have to fall into what people have outlined for this lifestyle. We define that. I knew I could have both of you if I were patient and persistent, and it wouldn't hurt or harm anyone else. I thought wanting this would hurt Diane. It would mean that she was not enough. I love Diane and don't want to destroy what we have together. And it wasn't about the part either, if it was we could have accommodated that in another way. I mean, as it is, equipment is getting better all the time. They even have the kind that cums."

"What?" I ask in total disbelief.

She laughs at the expression on my face and says, "Yes, it's heated and uses some type of lotion, but it's not just the part I need. I like how you treat me and handle things. Our disagreements aren't shouting matches or tearing into each other. There's a strength that you have and a natural compassion inside of you. I need that. I can tell you really love me, Ray. I need that, and I accept that. I deserve you." She reaches for me and plants a soft, teasing kiss on my lips. I change the subject quickly.

"Lori, do you think if you would have put 'a male' on The List, you would have found me sooner?" I ask.

"Would *you* have been ready six years ago, Ray? Would *I* have been ready? That requirement was added immediately after my first time with Diane. It took me six years to find you, and now, I'm not willing to give up either one of you. Is that wrong?" Lori's expression is very serious.

"No, baby, I know exactly how you feel, and you won't have to give us up."

I decide that since we've covered a lot of questions and concerns, I might as well cover a few more. "Lori, consider what I've asked of you. That's the only way I can see it working for all of us. You want everything to happen the way you want it to. Sometimes it will take compromise and for you to be willing to give up something too. I'm giving up all that I've known, all that I'm comfortable with. All I ask is for you to let go of your old ideas. The fact that I'm here right now means I had to. We can define how things will be—the three of us. It can work, baby."

Lori rests her back against my chest. "Ray, are you really willing to take the risk of leaving New York and starting over here?" she asks.

I hold her hand in mine as I kiss her cheek. "Baby, even though it might not happen for months, I want to start fresh. I believe my daughter will be well taken care of here. I don't think that will happen the way it should in New York. Also, in addition to launching the branch office here, I also want to start my own business and get back into my music. You asked me before if I am willing to do the work. After being here, I'm more determined than ever. Yes, I'm willing to do the work, and I know it doesn't stop now. I want this to continue to happen. The real question is: are you willing to do what it takes to make it work, Lori? You both seem to know what I need. What do you need from me to make sure this stays right for you?"

LORI

I've been thinking on things for the past few days. I can only tell him what I see has worked so far. "All I ask is three things: 1) to make communication an important factor in this relationship, 2) for you to know I will never ask you a question that I don't want the answer to—so when I ask you something I expect the truth, 3) don't bring us home anything we can't live with."

Ray turns me to face him. "Lori, I think I know what you mean, but I don't want any misunderstandings. Please explain."

"Point one, if we can talk, we can exist peacefully and that's the whole basis of this relationship: peaceful interaction. Point two, if I ask you a question, it's because I want to hear the answer in your own words to confirm something I might already feel or something I need to know. If you lie to me and Diane then there's no belief or trust in us to understand you. Point three, we won't be the

ones to say that you can't do something you want to do,
as long as it doesn't put us in physical danger. If there is
someone you want to be with, and it's somehow necessary
for you, then do what it takes to make you feel whatever
it is that you need to feel. When I say, don't bring us
anything home we can't live with, I mean disease or drama.
Have enough care and respect for us to do this.

"One other thing, if you decide it's time to stop
loving us and start leaving us, don't bullshit about. Prepare
your things and go. If it's a choice that you've made, I'm
not going to stop you because I'm beyond begging and
pleading. Diane and I recognize that when it ends, it ends.
There'll be no fault in that especially if all of us have done
our parts to make things happen the way they should.
Separation hurts, but it hurts unnecessarily when there are
lies involved. There won't be any 'Oh, baby, please come
home, I can make it better.' Every time we interact, it
should be like it's our last time, so that won't be the case."

"Ray, are you sure marriage is the way you want
to go? Why don't you want to keep your options open?"

RAY

I run my fingers across her lips. "Lori, right now,
you and Diane are the *only* option for me. I have to put
my energies into making *this* relationship work. I have
more than enough to handle right here in my arms. I don't
need anyone or anything else. I appreciate the consideration
and all, but no. This is where my heart, mind and body
need to be, and this is where it will stay.

"Lori, I understand what you mean because I, too,
appreciate the fact that communication between us is real
tight. You're both true to your word. You are open and
flexible, and we all share the same goals." I look at her
and smile. "And, you both can cook." Lori punches me.
"Don't hit me, woman," I protest. She laughs and it lightens
the mood. "We blend well together sexually and are open

to new ideas, even though one of you is more inhibited than the other."

"Who?" Lori asks and looks at me like she's about to be pissed.

"Woman, don't even play," I say. "What happened at the lake?"

"You said I didn't have to," Lori exclaims as her eyes lock on mine.

I stroke her back and try to calm her before I make my next statement. "Lori, even though you put up a brave front, I could tell you were uneasy about it. I don't ever want you to do anything that makes you uncomfortable. There are too many other things to try."

She still looks a little concerned as she asks, "Then why did you start that episode in the parking lot?"

"Asking you is one thing, getting you invovled and taking you is another," I reply. "You had the opportunity to say no, or to stop me. You forgot to be afraid, and you let yourself go. If I took you in the water you would have been expecting it and would not have enjoyed it because of your fear. The parking lot was a total surprise, and it got you hot enough to say the hell with it. And you loved it. And you weren't the only one." I kiss her forehead and she relaxes against me.

I find that I'm not done wading in deep waters. "Lori, I know we've touched on this subject, but we need to talk more about it. How do you really feel about raising another child?"

Lori takes a deep breath and lets it go before she says, "Ray, I've always wanted another child, and Brandon always asks about a little sister. I just wasn't in the position to bring another child into the world, raise him or her right and then see that child long for the one thing that I couldn't give. Brandon wanted his father to love him so badly that the sadness, disappointment and anger seemed to make him a different child, and there was nothing I could do to ease his pain.

"Brandon would reach out to his dad year after year, and his father stood him up for Father's Day, with some lame excuse or another. Twice the man didn't bother to call and give an excuse. At least not until three months later when Brandon and I were visiting his neighbor and saw him by accident. He said, 'Oh, I was sick that day.' It didn't matter to Brandon. He wanted his father so bad that he'd give him a clean slate every year. I really wanted to speak up but it wasn't my place. As much as I love Brandon and want to protect him from pain, the decision not to see his father had to come from him. He had to make the choice that he didn't want to be hurt anymore. Sometimes we can't always protect our children from situations they bring into their lives. It was the hardest lesson Brandon and I learned.

"I never understood Brandon's need for a masculine figure in his life, until I had a need for a man in my life. Even though it was on a different level, it was still all about balance. Brandon needs a man because all of the people in his life are strong black women. He loves and respects us, but none of us has the body part that he does. He needs someone that he feels can understand him on that level. It would be nice if he could have a man to respect as well. All of us have a need for balance. This trio is mine.

"I didn't think I could trust a man in my household because I would always be watching for molestation from him. I was so happy Brandon was a boy. I still have to watch him, but I just felt that it was easier. I would love to be a mother to Janese."

I turn and Lori looks me squarely in the eyes. "Ray, if your daughter is with us, and she tells me that you've done *anything* to her, I will treat you as if I had given birth to her myself. I want you to know that. I don't think you're that type of man, but I have to say this. No one thought my father was that type of man. He was a police officer, and he told me that no one would believe me if I told them about the horrible things he did to me."

I know this weighs heavily with Lori, but it also lets me know that she will love and protect my daughter, and that's what Janese needs. I look at Lori and stroke her face "I know it's hard for you to take in, Lori, but I understand where you're coming from. Baby, you know I would never do anything to hurt you, Diane, Brandon or Janese. You can feel that in your heart, but once I'm here you'll eventually feel it in your spirit, and your mind will be at ease. If I could get you over what you've been through myself, I'd take you there right now. If I could get you to the point of being totally healed, I'd carry you myself right this minute. I'm fully aware that it's a process you'll have to go through for yourself, Lori, but I'll be here with you— holding you and loving you and helping as much as I can.

"Lori, it's so frustrating to know that it's something that's beyond my control. It will take time, baby, and I realize that and will be right here with you, if you let me. I want to be here, Lori. More than anything in the world. There's so much that we can accomplish together, and I want to be involved in the process. I want to live and live well and I want to love and love well. I want it for myself and for all the people in my life that I love."

Lori places her hand in mine and asks, "Did you have this conversation with Diane?"

"Yes, I did. I wanted to know that both of you are in agreement. Diane is flexible, and she's for this. We just need to focus how the household should run and work with the children."

LORI

I let out a sigh. Ray is really trying to get me to focus on the success of this relationship. He's not leaving me any room to say no.

"I was thinking on that, too, Ray. Janese is only used to sharing you with one person. Having to share you with three of us is going to be a lot for her to take in. I think she shouldn't know about the relationship between me and Diane. Maybe we can discuss it with her when she's mature enough to handle it. For right now, having her know that two women love her father is going to be a lot to handle. So for now keeping our relationship private is going to be best. We wouldn't want her to experience any problems from our decision either."

I have to let Ray know that I understand that there's a lot at stake here, but I can't give him an answer right now. I kiss him and then say, "I'm still thinking on what you've asked me, Ray. Marriage is not something to go into lightly."

It's obvious that he was hoping for a different answer. Ray calmly says, "Lori, our relationship isn't lightweight to begin with. Think about it all you want and take as much time as you need." He lifts my chin so that we're eye-to-eye and says, "But I want my answer before I get on the plane." Before I can reply, he pulls me in for a deep, passionate kiss. By the time he's finished, I am totally aroused. God, I want this man so much! I don't want to lose him, and the pleasure and comfort alone is enough to make me say yes. I'm taking everything into consideration, but I'm still afraid. Not of him, but of myself.

RAY

I can see the fear in her eyes. I don't want her to be there. I'm focusing on all the good things that can come from our relationship, and I hope Lori does too.

"Lori, there's something else I want before I leave. Somehow I've never gotten around to doing it," I say.

Her eyes narrow as she asks, "What?

I'm sure at this point I must be wearing my most devilish smile. I'm feeling frisky today, and I have this little idea, but I also have a small problem on how to execute it. Especially knowing Lori's resistance to certain things. I finally decide how to proceed, and I look into Lori's eyes and ask softly, "Lori, do you trust me?"

She looks at me, puzzled, but eventually says, "Yes."

Well alright! I quickly go into the other room and get a small pouch out of my bag, a scarf and a blanket off the bed along with two items from the fridge.

I re-enter the room and lead her to the kitchen table. I ask her to close her eyes and when she does, I gently place a blindfold over her. She takes in a deep breath. "Nervous?" I ask.

She quickly responds no, but I can tell that she is. I begin to lay her on the table and kiss her passionately. I take her hands in mine. I place her arms flat on the table and with my tongue I follow the path of her arm to the palm of her hand. I end that by gently tying her wrists together with a scarf. Enough to keep her hands out of my way, but not tight enough for her to feel bound.

I take a piece of ice into my mouth and began to explore her body with it. It melts quickly. I take another piece of ice and before Lori can realize what I'm going to do, I use my tongue to circle the outer lips of her center. Lori quickly closes her thighs around my head. She doesn't say a word, and neither do I. This is a serious Mexican stand-off! She's gripping me so that my head can't move, and my head being where it is means that she can't close her thighs all the way. She's not giving any ground and neither am I. I decide to talk my way out of this one.

"Lori, let my head go," I say in my most soothing tones.

"Ray, I don't want you to do this," she says. Her voice is barely a whisper.

"Lori, this has been done to you before," I say calmly.

"I know. It was years ago. The Professional was good at it. It was his signature service. When he did it, I wouldn't pressure him about the lies or I'd buy him anything he asked me for. It was a matter of control," she explained.

"Lori, am I trying to control you?" I ask pointedly.

"No, but it's still..."

I cut her off. "Lori, listen to me. The first time we made love, you agreed that you were my woman and that every inch of you was mine to please. Do you remember that?

"Yes, Ray, but I meant..." she begins to say.

"Every word you said, right?" I answer for her.

Lori was starting to get angry and her breathing was rapid. "Ray, don't twist my words."

I begin stroking her outer thighs and buttocks. "Lori, I want to please you in this way. I want to know what you taste like. I want my tongue to feel the trembling of your body. I need you to experience pleasure from this with me. Don't deny us this pleasure. Lori, open to me. She releases me and I move my head away from her body. I remove the blindfold and look at her. She's still uncertain. "Lori, if it gets to a point that you want me to stop, I will. But allow me the chance to do this at least once. Please?"

I gently part her thighs and there's no resistance this time. I glide my tongue along the insides of each thigh.

I follow this procedure again until I'm gently and slowly circling her lips with my tongue. She stirs and whimpers, so I grip her buttocks to hold her in place. This might be my only chance, so I'm about to do some serious damage here. First, I work my tongue into her, and the intensity increases when she realizes she can't touch me and can barely move. Her taste and her moans get a serious reaction from my dick. I then take my tip and follow that same path, teasing her by inserting myself only to the head.

Lori's body writhes, and I try to hold her in place as I pull away to start licking, sucking and tasting her. *God, I love to hear her moan!* I want to know this woman's most intimate secrets. If every inch of her is mine to please, I just need to reinforce it. I grab the chocolate syrup and make a trail from her breasts to her navel and the devil in me says, "Don't stop there," so I take that trail all the way down past her thighs. I put my lips at her center once again, and I gently lick away the chocolate until she's losing her mind! "Ray, *pleeeeeeeeeeease!*" she says in a voice an octave higher than normal.

She tries to lift up off the table, and I pull her buttocks to the edge as I seat myself comfortably in a chair. This is my morning meal, and I plan to be here for a while. I want her this way, dripping, writhing and totally out of control. I take my time and nibble on the outer lips and work my way back in. Then I move my tongue further out to the fleshy part of her thighs. Holding her buttocks off the table, I create a rhythm that she can focus on before she takes us both onto the floor. *I prefer to eat my meals at the table, thank you very much!*

I place an ice cube inside of her and work it with my tongue. I push it in as far as it can go, and she's so hot inside that it melts quickly. I'm there to catch all the wetness that comes out.

"Ray, please untie me," she pleads breathlessly.

"Why?" I ask.

"I want to hold you."

"Will you behave yourself?" I ask. Her expression says *behave? What's that?* I pause for a few more seconds and she still doesn't answer. I tell her, "Soon, baby, real soon."

I continue until she's trembling in the way that always tells me that she's about to release. I stand up and place the tip of my dick at the center of her lips and use it to tease her. I untie her hands and then circle my tongue around her nipples and breasts. She immediately wraps her arms around me. "Ray, don't tease me like this. *Put it in there!*" My dick is teasingly circling that area down there as I ask again. "What did you say you want, Lori?" Lori's breathing is ragged, but this time she demands, "Inside, Ray! I want you inside of me *right now!*"

"Well, Lori, I don't think you're ready for me yet," I say while teasing her just a little more. I kiss her breasts, her stomach and then suck her nipples a little more until they're standing strong. I can see that she's getting frantic, so I place my dick at her opening and just as she opens her mouth to ask again. I thrust into her and she cums and screams my name at the same time—*Raaaaaaaaaaaaaaay!* I watch her, and think to myself, *Now that's what I'm talking about!*

She tries to turn away from me, but I pull her to me and work her the way that she likes me to until she's able to stop shaking. From the corner of my eye I see Diane come out of the bedroom and stand at the door to watch. She walks toward me and asks softly, "Is everything alright now?"

She strokes Lori's face, and Lori can only nod. Lori is full right now, her hunger has been thoroughly fed. Diane holds my hand as I pull away to lead Lori to the sofa. I wrap a blanket around her and make sure that she's comfortable. I kneel by her side and stroke her forehead.

"Lori, I'd like your permission to taste you again." I don't get a response, but I know she can hear me. "Baby, you won't deny me the pleasure of your taste again, will you?" She still doesn't answer, but her breathing is hurried. I stroke her face and ask once again, "Lori?"

Her voice is barely a whisper. "No, Ray. I won't deny you."

She turns her body toward the inside of the sofa and closes her eyes. I stroke her hair for a few moments until her breathing returns to normal. The intimacy between us is just beginning....

I extend my hand to Diane and lead her to the other side of the kitchen table. I still have a bowl of ice nearby and another bottle of syrup—strawberry, Diane's favorite. I don't normally go in for second helpings when a meal has been very satisfying, but whoever said you can never have too much of a good thing, was telling the absolute truth!

DIANE

Ray's flight leaves in two hours. Surprisingly, we're all in good spirits. We went to Izola's to have a "traditional" breakfast and now we can barely move.

As we drive to the airport, I'm in deep thought. My mind goes over these eight days, and I realize it's very different when we're talking on the phone, but our experience during this time was beautiful and exciting. Ray came here with ulterior motives. Why else would he bring two kinds of Nestle's syrup? *The little devil!*

We've talked about so many things, and he didn't trip when he found out about our relationship. I didn't think I would feel this strongly about Ray. I never thought I could feel this way about any man again. I don't want him to leave, but I know that he has to. I'm very happy because our search is over. This is the man Lori needs, and I find that I need him too. While Lori and I lived well as a twosome, it will be even better when it's a trio. The beauty and fun from this point on is to maintain the trio in a way that keeps all of us growing. I can't wait until we're making progress on our business plans. That's going to take every bit of creativity from each of us. Speaking of creative, I've got so many wicked and fantastic things I want to try with Ray!

I look over at Lori and find she's sitting quietly. I know I must be strong for both of us. She's the emotional one. I remember a time when that wasn't a way to describe her. Lori is a fighter by nature and she fought about everything that she thought was a threat to her—even love. Now she only fights to protect herself or people that she loves if they have been slighted or hurt.

We've finally found someone that is exactly what we need, and he recognizes that he's on the the same level, mentally and spiritually, that we are. It's always been inside of him. He's so strong, intelligent and creative too. Ray is truly our mate in every way. I feel like a part of me is leaving with him.

I can't begin to measure the changes that will take place in our lives. For one, we'll have a daughter soon. I've never regretted not having children of my own, but I thank the Creator for the experience of helping to raise Brandon, and I feel Janese will be a wonderful addition to our family.

I forgot, maybe, I'm thinking out of turn. Lori hasn't made her decision yet. If she doesn't agree, it will all fall apart now. *Damn!* We've worked so hard to get to this point! I can't predict how Lori will decide, but I can tell that Ray is serious, and I have to respect him for that. I won't push Lori to make a decision no matter how badly I want this. She can't do this for me. She has to do this for herself. I know that saying yes means Ray has the assurance of our level of commitment, and if one of us says yes, then he has both of us because Lori and I are committed to each other too. I have to give it to him, he's a smart man. That's why I love him. He's not afraid to stand up for what he wants. He's also not afraid to admit when he's wrong, or when he doesn't know something. He's not too arrogant to take the advice of a woman. Those are the signs of a real man. There's so much we can learn from him too. He's intelligent and the more he realized that we respect his judgment, the more confident he became in dealing with sensitive issues between us.

I think back over our first "breakfast" this morning. From the kitchen table to the shower and then the bed. He's no slouch when it comes to *that* area. Damn that man's tongue is marketable! Maybe we can make a cast of his tongue and add a motor and battery pack to re-create his movements. Just think of the sales we could get with that one....

AT THE AIRPORT
RAY

We find a quiet corner in the airport, and I hold Diane in one arm and Lori in the other. I bring each of them to me for a kiss. Hopefully, finances will allow for me to visit more than twice a month until I'm here permanently—if it works out that way. I'm beginning to really dislike that word *if.*

I look at both of my women. I keep saying "my women" because I'm reinforcing in my mind what I want to happen. "Do you know that I'm leaving a part of my heart here with you? I appreciate everything that you've done for me, and would never be inconsiderate or unkind to either one of you. Your minds have always intrigued me and being with you is spectacular. I've never dealt with any women of your caliber, and I'm glad you are different from others. I have learned so much from both you. Once, again, I thank you for that. Trust me, this is a first time, all around.

"I want you to know that I love you and consider you both my wives. I'm sure we can find a way to share this with our friends and family. But for now it's in our hearts and minds. I reach in my pocket and pull out a small box. I've been carrying it all week, waiting for the right time. I open it for them to see. Their eyes open wide, and Diane takes in her breath. The look on her face is the same one the jeweler had when I made my request. I'm holding three matching platinum wedding bands. One for each of my future wives and one for me. The first one is placed on Diane's finger. This is symbolic between us because she has one more thing to do before she can totally be mine. But it is a promise of things to come. I kiss her hand, and I take out the second ring and hold it out to Lori and realize that we're going to have a problem.

Her face displays a look of absolute terror. She's silent, and she's shaking. Lori is a woman of her word and she knows our commitment is legal as well as spiritual. She looks at me and the conflicting emotions show on her face. I tell her, "Trust in us. Trust in the three of us." She breathes deeply. *This woman is so damn stubborn!* She won't let go. Damn! I'm going to have to accept defeat on this one.

No. Scratch that. I think to myself *I deserve everything good that comes to me.* I'm not ready to put this ring back in the box. Disappointment washes over me, and I'm trying to calm myself as I stand and wait. My flight leaves soon, and I hope that's not what she's waiting for. If necessary, I'll just catch the next plane. Maybe I shouldn't have made marriage an ultimatum. Lori doesn't take too kindly to those. None of us do. I didn't give myself a back-up plan for this because I truly expected her to say yes. I thought we had moved past all of her reservations.

Maybe I should stay an extra day so we can talk more about it. I told her I wanted an answer before I get on the plane. I'll just delay that option by getting on the plane tomorrow. Actually that won't work either because whether it's today or tomorrow, I've made my case with Lori, and there's no more that I can say. I lean in close to her ear and whisper, "I deserve everything good that comes to me. Say it with me, baby."

Lori looks at me, and we both say aloud, "I deserve everything good that comes to me." I ask, "Have I been good to you, Lori?" She continues to look at me, and I can see her thoughts going a mile a minute.

"Yes," she whispers.

"Have I been good for you?" I ask softly.

"Yes," she says as she lowers her eyes.

I lift her chin so her eyes can look into mine. "Lori, have I been good with you?"

"Yes," she answers.

I use all of my energy to focus into her eyes. I want her to believe in me—and believe in us. I hold her close as I say, "Then let me be even more than that. We'll work through it, baby. I promise you I'll be by your side through it all. I want you by my side through anything I may experience. I need us to work together like this. Always, Lori."

I look at her once again and realize that her mind is truly made up. She holds out her hand to me. I take her hand in mine, and it's shaking. It's not from fear this time. The tears course from her eyes unchecked. I don't think she's traditional, but I get down to one knee anyway. I ask, "Lori, will you be my wife, my love, my woman, my companion and my friend?

She answers, "Yes, until we can't love anymore. Yes, I will."

Thank God! Relief flows through me. I understand

what she means, and it's as good as it's going to get. *I'll take it!* I rise and bring her into my arms as I say, "My wife," and then I kiss her forehead. I look at her. "Say it, Lori." She looks puzzled for a moment and then realizes what I mean. "Say it, Lori." She looks up at me and says, "My husband." As I hold her she says it once more "My husband." I want her to know that I'm just as much hers as she is mine.

I bring Diane to me, and I switch to my other knee. "Diane, I want you to be free to make this same commitment to me because I will ask the same of you. And by all means do it quickly before my knee gives out on me." Diane smiles at me and chuckles. I hold her hand in mine as I say, "I want you to file for divorce, and I will stand with you. I will be in the courtroom by your side. He can't touch you when there are people who will be there to protect you. I know Lori feels the same way I do."

Diane just nods her head. I rise and hold her once again. I think I see tears in Diane's eyes. No, that couldn't be because Diane doesn't cry. I don't think she would let tears fall no matter how deeply she feels about me. I must accept that because it's her way. I pull back from her to kiss her forehead, her eyelids and the tip of her nose. This is the second time today that I've seen that look of total love and caring in her eyes.

This woman has been through a lot. They both have. Come to think of it, so have I. All of us are strong. But we can be so much stronger—together. I whisper to Diane. "I won't hurt you, and I won't hurt Lori either. Hurting either one of you is like hurting myself." Diane wraps her arms around my neck, and I bury my head into her softness. I say to her "my wife" and she replies by saying "my husband." I look at her and see that I was wrong. There's a single, solitary tear rolling down her cheek. Relief. She feels relief, and she believes me, and I hold on to her once again. I must show her that her belief is always well placed.

Diane removes the jewelry box from my pocket. She takes the last ring out of the box and Lori holds my hand. Lori and Diane place the ring on my finger and then kiss me. "I love you, Ray." For the first time since I've been here they say this at the same time. I say the words that I will be saying for a long time to come, "I love you too. Both of you. So very much." I hold them close, and my heart is lifted.

I hear the call for my flight. Diane pulls away and says, "Ray, you've got to get moving." I pick up my suitcase and garment bag and walk toward the boarding area. I see Diane reach for Lori's hand and hold it. As I turn to go back to them, I see Diane move closer to Lori, and I realize that she's sending me a message. *It's alright, go on now—we're in good hands.* I'd rather they were in my hands. I walk back to them and put down my bags and place a hand over each woman's heart. Lori smiles through her tears, and Diane looks me squarely in the eye. They've taught me the true meaning of this gesture. I use it as a seal to our agreement. They each place a hand over my heart and then over each other's hearts. This is a show of commitment to me and to each other. I don't know how other relationships like this one have worked, but ours is starting off in the best possible way.

As I board the plane, I feel a slight tightening in my chest. I haven't felt that since my father passed. I realize that I've never missed anyone quite as much as I miss him. At least, not until today. If home is where the heart is then I'm definitely leaving my heart right here in Chicago.

Author's Note

Thank you for taking this journey with Mykal and Maya. It was a healing time for me as well.

I hope that something in *She Touched My Soul* made you laugh, cry, and feel moments of peace, joy or triumph. If there is something within these pages that has started you on your own personal journey toward healing and peace, then my work here is done.

NALEIGHNA KAI

Naleighna is a Chicago native who plans to keep bringing out novels that will have eyebrows lifted all over the country. She is an alumni of Chicago Vocational School and College of Automation.

Naleighna lives with a family of writers and is currently working on her next novels: *My Time in the Sun* and *Mercury's Sunrise.*

Her second novel is *She Touched My Soul*

VEE DENISE KAI

Lives in Chicago and has started her own publishing company.

KEVIN KAI

Lives in New York and currently attends college, majoring in computer technology. He is also pursuing a career in music.

Contact the authors by e-mail: naleighnakai@infinitypub.com, veedenisekai@infinitypub.com, and kevinkai@infinitypub.com

Sponsors

Thank you for your support and for making this book possible.

Donny
Sandy
Renee
Brenda Williams
Covita Grey
PPF
Monica
Scott
Michael
Lady Avalon e'lan
J. House
L. Hawkins
Larry
Loren